STARBRAT

by JOHN MORRESSY

STARBRAT

by JOHN MORRESSY

WALKER AND COMPANY • New York

for
Harlan Ellison

First published in the United States of America in 1972 by the Walker Publishing Company, Inc.

Published simultaneously in Canada by Fitzhenry & Whiteside, Limited, Toronto.

ISBN: 0-8027-5549-6

Library of Congress Catalog Card Number: 78-188478

Printed in the United States of America.

BOOK I: THE EDUCATION AND LIBERATION OF DELIVERANCE-FROM-THE-VOID WHITBY

1. *The eve of decision; I learn a secret and make a resolution.*

I was a starbrat, born at a feathery 0.314 gravity in the grimy, overheated lazaret of a reeking, creaking, intersystem freighter chugging its terrified way at 6.8 lightspeeds from the outer edges of a Rinn battle formation. It took me the first sixteen years of my life to learn even half that much about myself, and that much is not much. It might have been enough, but once I was given the chance, I had to know more, and that took a lot of looking and some far traveling. The galaxy is a big place, and answers are hard to find. It takes a long time just to learn the right questions. Sometimes that's more than enough.

Until I was sixteen years old, my name was Deliverance-from-the-Void Whitby and I was the only child of a pious, god-fearing old farmer named Zealous

Endeavor Whitby and his wife Persistence-in-the-Ways-of-Righteousness. We lived in a small community on Gilead, a planet settled some four centuries back by the New Enlightened Rudstromites, a sect from Brittania on Old Earth. It was a quiet life, in many ways a good one, and if things had gone on uninterrupted I suppose I'd be living there still, wearing dark homespun clothing and thinking gloomy thoughts about eternity, married to the girl from the neighboring farmstead, growing my crops and feeding my little herd of *trettles,* and caring very little about the star-studded blackness overhead except in moments of curiosity about which one of those tiny points of brightness could have been my true home. But life did not go on uninterrupted.

I always knew that I was different from the other kids on Gilead, but it was not something I dwelt on. I didn't really know what I looked like—Rudstromites didn't hold with mirrors, which they considered tools of vanity and deception—but I knew I was smaller and a lot quicker than my hulking playmates, big ruddy healthy kids devoted to hard work and strenuous play. When I was only six, I could snatch *bzzits* right out of the air as they buzzed around the *trettle* pens, and as I grew older, I became the central figure in a popular local game. The other kids would line up in front of me and throw rocks, and I'd catch them as they came and send them back twice as fast. The game ended when someone was hit. It didn't matter how many of them played, I always won. My skill purchased their grudging acceptance, but our relationship never went much further. I didn't really like any of the other kids on Gilead except Cassie, and until I became seriously interested in her, I spent most of my free time at home, where, after a hard day's work, Zealous and Persistence instructed me by way of readings from *The Book of The Voyage.*

Every evening after third moonrise we'd sit before the fire, my parents at one side of the hearth, by the raised stand that held the book, me seated at the other, and they'd take turns reading aloud. It always went the same. Zealous did most of the reading. He had his favorite passages, and he'd keep coming back to them despite the repeated admonitions of Persistence, who felt that everything should be done in an orderly fashion and no chapter should be repeated out of turn, no matter how much one liked to hear it. I liked the prophetic chapters myself, with their haunting references to a man who walked on the winds and rode among the stars and bore the mark of Rudstrom on his wrist and the secrets of all worlds and all men in his heart, but Zealous preferred the "Chapter of Maledictions," and he read it with great relish and ferocity, his eyes blazing and his little tuft of gray-flecked beard wagging like a *trettle's* tail.

"Accursed be the planet of evil ways, and woe befall the inhabitants thereof!" he would thunder, and Persistence and I would respond, "Woe unto them!"

"Accursed be those who befoul the sweetness of the land and poison its wholesomeness with the waste of their evil endeavors, and woe befall them and their progeny!"

"Woe unto them!"

"Accursed be the planet where rise the works of pride, and woe befall the builders of high walls!"

"Woe unto them!"

"Accursed be those who bury the land beneath the stonework of their hands, who cover life with death, and woe befall the makers of stone dwellings!"

"Woe unto them!"

We'd go on like this until Zealous reached a certain malediction that always bothered me. Every time he recited it I asked him the same question, and he always gave the same answer.

"Accursed be the dwellers in great cities who commit all manner of abomination upon the innocent, and woe befall the foul procurers of pleasure!"

"Woe unto them! Father, what's an abomination?" I asked quickly, before he could get on to the next malediction.

"Not for thee to know, lad. All will be made clear at the time of decision."

"When will that be, Father?"

"Even now, the day and the hour fast approacheth," he'd say, and then go on. "Accursed be the makers of plans . . . !"

Since my parents wouldn't tell me what an abomination was or what the time of decision meant, I asked my only friend, Cassie. Her real name was Castle-of-Perseverance Hammersmith. She was the youngest daughter of our neighbors, and it was assumed by both the Hammersmiths and the Whitbys that Cassie and I would be married shortly after my time of decision. Until I was about fourteen, I had viewed the whole idea with loathing. By the time I reached sixteen and Cassie was fifteen, it didn't seem half bad. Cassie was a pretty little girl, a bit smaller in scale than the others and thus more suited to a little fellow like me. She was flaxen-haired and rosy-cheeked, quick to smile and full of an understanding far beyond her years of the troubles simmering within me. But she couldn't answer my questions. At the time, we were both unacquainted with abominations.

One evening, after dinner, I learned that my time of decision was at hand, and I learned a great deal more. I had gone up to my little room after the meal, and when I heard someone enter the house, I came down to greet the visitor, as was the Gilead custom. Just outside the door of the hearthroom I hesitated when I heard the voice of Contemplation-on-the-Eternal-Wisdom Scrooby, one of the Elders of Gilead. On a sudden impulse I drew aside and concealed myself. He had something to do with the time of decision, that much I knew, and I believed I'd learn more if my presence was unknown.

"Forbearance and brotherly love to all true believers, Brother Whitby," Scrooby said. "May thy way be ever smooth."

"Health to thee, and harmony to thy house and all who dwell therein," my father replied. "May their lives be uneventful."

After exchanging the same ritual greeting with my mother, Scrooby at once asked my father, "Brother Whitby, is the lad named Deliverance-from-the-Void in the house?"

"He is, Elder Scrooby. He is closeted in deep study of the Book. Shall I summon him?"

"In time, Brother Whitby. Before this, thee and I must speak of his future, for the time of decision is come for him."

I squeezed a little closer to the crack in the door. No more was said until my mother left the room, and then they passed a tormenting amount of time talking about crops and weather and the threatening *trettle* epidemic. At last Scrooby got down to business.

"Hast thou yet informed the lad of the truth of his origin and shown him the strange cradle from the heavens and the writings therein contained, Brother Whitby?" he asked, and I felt a sudden uneasiness that opened my mind to a flood of doubts. What did he mean by "the truth of his origin"? Could it be that Zealous and Persistence were not my real parents and Gilead was not my true home?

"I have not done so, Elder," Zealous said softly.

"His time of decision is at hand. He must be told all before the next moonrise."

"It shall be done."

"It must be done, Brother Whitby," Scrooby said sternly. "When thou and Sister Persistence took the foundling under thy care, these obligations were known to thee. Thou hast long enjoyed the lad as thine own son, and now that he is to become a man, thou must tell him of his strange arrival among us, that he may decide from full knowledge."

"I will tell him, Elder," Zealous said.

I slipped away quietly and returned to my room, where I threw myself down on my pallet and stared out at the darkening sky. If Scrooby told the truth—and an Elder of Gilead could not do otherwise—I had come from out there somewhere, in a strange cradle that held mysterious writings. Why hadn't they told me before? I thought, sitting bolt upright in a sudden rage at the adults who had conspired all these years to keep me ignorant. And what if they had? I thought then. What could I have done? What could I do now? Somewhere out there I had once lost a set of parents I never knew, and now I was losing a second set, the only ones I had ever known, people who loved me and cared for me. It was too much to lose all at once. I slumped back on the pallet and thought of Cassie. Maybe now we would not be permitted to marry. Maybe I'd have to go away, back where I came from, wherever that might be. To lose everyone I loved and be driven into exile among cold and hostile stars . . . to wander forever, homeless, loveless. I was so deep in my broodings I was not aware of the presence of Zealous in the doorway until he spoke.

"Up, lad. It is not good to lie abed before the time

for sleeping," he said gently. As I rose, he said, "Come, walk with me. I have somewhat to say to thee."

Outside, he led me back past the pens and stables toward a small shed at the far corner of his lands. It had always been locked, and whenever I inquired about it, Zealous and Persistence had avoided my eyes and quickly changed the subject.

"Thy name, lad: Deliverance-from-the-Void. Hast thou never pondered on the reason it was given thee?" Zealous asked as we walked.

"No, Father. It seems a good name to me. Has it some significance unknown to me?"

Zealous grunted in reply, and we continued walking in silence for a time. Further on, he asked, "Hast noticed, lad, thou art not in all ways like the other youth of Gilead?"

"I have noticed that."

"Hast noticed, too, that whereas the other youth all closely resemble their parents, thou art much unlike good Sister Persistence and me?"

"I have noticed that, too," I said.

"And yet thou has never questioned me."

I shook my head evasively. The locked shed was in sight ahead of us.

"The time has come to speak of these things," Zealous said. He hesitated, and his voice broke when he went on, "Forgive me that I have not told thee long since, lad. I was loath to lose thee as my son."

"I am thy son," I said, reaching out to him.

"Truly thou art, in all ways but one. Thou must now know that good Sister Persistence did not bear thee, nor did I beget thee. Thou camest to us as a child from the heavens."

A sudden absurd hope dawned in me, and I tried to

smile. "I know these tales of birth, Father, and I know the truth as well. Children do not come from the heavens."

Zealous stared at me, laughed once, then blinked his eyes hurriedly and wiped them on his sleeve. "No, lad, no, other children do not. But look within and see."

He took out a key, undid the lock on the shed, and threw the door wide. Inside, against one wall, stood a silver cylinder nearly as tall as I. He pointed to it. "Thou camest to us in this, landing on this very spot. The Elders took it as a sign and gave thee into our care until thy time of decision. Now the time is come."

I rushed inside and tore open the lid of the cylinder, revealing a tiny harness just big enough to hold an infant. The interior of the little craft was filled with complicated devices far beyond my understanding, but two things caught my eye. Inside the lid was a plate inscribed "Pendelton's Base, 106-22LC", and at the bottom of the craft was a scrap of paper. I snatched it up and read it eagerly: "Birth: 9/22-23/2607 GSC.°

° The Galactic Standard Calendar (abbreviated GSC) is a method of computing time introduced by the Old Earth pioneers in the earliest phase of space exploration. It is based on the Old Earth *day* of twenty-four equal *hours,* each divided into sixty equal *minutes,* which are further divided each into sixty *seconds.* The time of one complete revolution of Old Earth around its mother star equalled 365.25 of these *day* units, and was called a *year.*

The Galactic Standard Calendar was used by the pioneers to provide a standard method of dating events which occurred on planets with widely varying periods of rotation and revolution. Each planet, of necessity, had its own planetary calendar (PC), and it was the practice to assign a dual date to all planetary events and a single date, GSC, to any event occurring in space. For this reason, no planetary date is assigned to Del's birth.

Expedition intersystem freighter *Flanders,* L. S. 6.8, G. 0.314. Parents: Malellan"—the rest was illegible, covered with a dark stain that might have been blood.

"Now thou knowest all we know," Zealous said.

"But I know nothing!" I cried. "Words, numbers! What do these scribblings mean?"

"Thou knowest thou art not of Gilead. But if thou so choose at the time of decision, thou shalt be one of us forever, and no man can deny thee. This craft will be buried and forgotten. The Elders and Sister Persistence and I will never speak of it. Thou shalt marry Sister Cassie and live as my son on lands adjoining mine."

"But I will always know I am not of Gilead."

Zealous put his arm around my shoulder and led me away from the shed. "Thy body was not formed on Gilead, true, but thy mind and nature were. These are the true things about a man. At the first light, we will go to the Elders and announce thy readiness to commence the time of decision."

"Am I ready?"

"Yes. The Elders will answer all questions about our ways and our beliefs. They are sworn to speak truly and evade nothing. When thou hast satisfied thy mind, we will return. For one planting season, thou shalt keep apart and ponder all these things. Then thou must decide to stay among us or go away."

"I will stay," I said firmly.

Zealous shook his head. "The time for that decision lies in the future."

"I will stay and marry Cassie."

"It would be welcome to us."

"May I speak to her of these things?" I asked, gesturing to the shed.

"I do not advise it, but I cannot forbid thee. Thou hast reached the time of decision. Go to her now, lad, and do what thou thinkest best."

I embraced him, thanked him, and thrusting the scrap of paper with its cryptic message into my pocket, I was off across the fields to the Hammersmith farm. Cassie slipped out at my signal, and we went to a favorite spot to talk of our future and my newfound past. She was not as surprised as I thought she'd be.

"It was clear to me when I first saw thee. Dear Del, thou art so unlike the others," she said, smiling.

"It is true I am much smaller—"

"But quicker."

"And not as strong as Toiler-for-Glory Dimbleby—"

"But ten times as smart."

"I cannot herd *trettles* as well as—"

"Thou art finer looking than all of them. Oh, Del, dear Del, decide with us and stay and marry me!"

I took her in my arms and kissed her hard and nestled my face in her soft, sweet-smelling hair. Then and there, in my mind, I buried the silver cylinder and the strange writings and all the questions that had tormented me so grievously a short time ago, and I knew that my future was sealed that very night.

And so it was, in a way I never suspected.

2. *The Daltrescans come to Gilead; my parting from Cassie.*

We stood in the bright moonlight for a long time, tight in each other's arms, speaking no words because we needed none. And then, suddenly, I became uneasy. My hearing was good, and I heard faint sounds that troubled me.

"Cassie," I whispered, "there are people about."

"I hear no one."

"I do. Moving through the trees on two sides of us."

"I have heard that when the time of decision comes to a man, the boys of the settlement sometimes test his courage," she said, looking up at me apprehensively.

I liked her choice of "man" and "boys." I stooped down and gathered a handful of stones, then I took her hand. "There is no one on this side of us," I said in a low voice. "Walk with me to the turn of the path, then run home."

"I am loath to leave thee, Del."

"I cannot run, and I would not have thee hurt."

"But what of thee?" she asked.

"Have no fear for me. Thou hast seen me play the throwing game with the others. There is more danger for them than for me."

We reached the turn in the path. I could hear them clearly now, eight of them, perhaps more, moving clumsily through the underbrush. I kissed Cassie quickly and said, "Now, run, and do not stop!"

As Cassie sped off toward home I slipped into the shadows and waited for our pursuers to reveal themselves. I planned a surprise for them and had no doubt that I would leave them with bruises and empty hands. A loud crash off to my left was followed by a string of words I had seldom heard on Gilead. I began to wonder. Whoever was around me, they were not the boys of the settlement. I readied a stone for throwing.

Two figures broke out of the trees and stood in the moonlight, and I felt my heart jump in a sudden spasm of fear. They wore leather jerkins covered with iron plates and clumped along on heavy boots. They were brawny men, twice my size, with big shaggy heads and thick necks, and each one carried a long pointed prod. No pranksters these—they were Daltrescans, the slave traders of the galaxy. Once before in my lifetime, when I was very small, they had come to Gilead and carried off forty young men and women to sell to the practitioners of foul abomination on the other worlds. The word came back to me now, and I was filled with fear, but the fear hardened at once into determination. They would not get Cassie, if it cost me my life.

The two slavers conferred hurriedly, and a third soon joined them. The newcomer pointed down the path after Cassie, and the three of them set off after her at a run. I heard the others close behind them.

I took a short cut through the trees and waited beside the path. As the first slaver passed, I thrust a stick between his feet, and he toppled headlong. The second, at his heels, tripped over his fallen henchman and went sprawling in the gravel. The third one lunged for me, but I side-stepped and re-entered the woods. They picked themselves up and came after me.

Cassie, forgotten now, was safe, and I had only myself to worry about. I knew the woods well and was confident that I could elude them. They were big and clumsy and slow of foot, while I was small and quick and on my own home ground. Three of them went down before my hard-flung stones, but I could tell from the noise that there were many more than I had first suspected, and they were closing in on me, encircling me in a ring methodically growing smaller.

As they drew nearer, I crouched behind a fallen tree, and when a Daltrescan passed by me close enough to touch, I let him pass and then bolted for safety. But I was unaware of their tricks. Their encircling ring was a double one. I ran directly into a slaver. He seized me by the throat, and all my kicking and struggling was of no avail. My last stone was gone, and I was helpless.

He shook me violently and called to his companions. When they were all gathered around, he flung me to the ground. Before I could scramble to my feet, they all began to kick at me and beat my back and legs with the heavy prods they carried. My last thought before I passed out was of Cassie.

3. *My first battle, and the consequences of it.*

I awoke on a pile of stinking rags in a dark little chamber that reeked of grease and sweat. A Daltrescan was jabbing me in the back with his prod, shouting, "Get up, you little *bzzit!* You'll earn your way on this trip!"

I struggled to my feet, aching all over. I felt a tapestry of bruises from top to bottom and side to side, and was hurting clean through. One eye was puffed and tender, and my upper lip was swollen. My right hand was raw and scraped where a big Daltrescan boot had trod upon it.

"Water. Please, some water," I croaked. My throat was dry and the sickening taste of blood was in my mouth.

The slaver cuffed me on the side of the head, seized me by the shoulder, and thrust me out into a narrow, ill-lit passageway. He prodded me forward. "You'll work for your water, you slippery, rock-slinging Gilead scum! Because of you we lost a pretty little piece who'd fetch a fortune on Barbary. You'll make up for that."

So Cassie had escaped, and from something far worse than I had imagined. Barbary was a place seldom mentioned on Gilead, a pleasure-planet devoted to indescribable abominations. To have saved her from that was worth a beating to me, a beating and whatever else my captors could inflict. I felt that I could take anything, and I fortified my bruised and aching body with the words of Zealous: "All strength is in him who does battle with the minions of evil. Though he suffer, yet shall he triumph, and though he fall before the power of the wicked, yet shall he be raised over them, for great is the power of the righteous man." I had often heard Zealous intone those words, and now I would put them to the test. I didn't beg for water again, or for anything else.

I was made mess boy on the slaveship. It was a hard, dirty job, for the Daltrescans were gluttonous eaters, and when they left the mess area, the tables, walls, and floor were strewn with their slops and leavings. I had to scour everything clean for the next shift, and the ship's cook encouraged me by free use of boot and prod until my speed suited him.

I said nothing and listened to everything, for I had no idea where we were headed or how long it would take to get there. Wherever it might be, I was resolved to find my way home somehow, and it was this resolution that kept me going through those awful early days.

I did my work well, my bruises healed, and the cook left me more and more to myself. I learned the names of all the crew, and more important, I gradually came to sense the divisions and alliances among them. Most of the slavers were loyal to the ship's commander, a squat, grizzled brute named Gree, but there was a second faction, led by a foul-mouthed ogre, Agarix by name, who often spoke out against Gree in his absence, though he showed great respect when Gree's unblinking eyes were upon him. Gree was a silent, moody man, and I was never sure if he was aware of Agarix's talk and plotting. He gave no sign, but he kept a close watch on everything and everyone. It would not have broken my heart to see the whole crew of slavers fall on one another and butcher themselves to the last man, but even as I dreamed of this, I knew it would be worse for me if they did. The other prisoners on the ship—I fed them, too, as part of my duties—were mostly farmers like myself, *trettle* herdsmen, miners, or artisans, men no more at home in a driveship than I. Without the Daltrescans, we'd be at the mercy of space, marooned forever between unknown stars. They kept us alive for their profit; we needed them alive for our own survival.

In my ninth week of servitude, at a meal when Gree and Agarix, with seven others, were in the mess, the talk turned to our arrival and the captives on board who were to be offered for sale. I went about my work unobtrusively, scurrying back and forth with platters of *trettle* meat and beakers of *scoof* boiled thick and black, but I took in every word.

"The big miner and the herdsmen will fetch the best price on Tarquin VII," Gree said. "We'll save the other men for the Kepler system and the women for Barbary."

"No need to take all the women to Barbary," one of the Agarix faction said.

"Why not?"

"They use women in the arenas, too. We've got a few who wouldn't be worth hauling all the way across to Barbary. We can dump them on Tarquin and pick up fresh ones on the way."

Gree shook his head. "Barbary wants anything we can bring them. We'll get our price there."

I was passing behind Agarix as Gree spoke, and Agarix reached out, grabbed me by the neck, and dragged me to the table. "What about this little schemer? If it hadn't been for him, we'd have a pretty package to deliver on Barbary. She'd have paid for the whole voyage."

"What's done is done. We'll sell him on Kepler. They want them his size for their mines," Gree said.

"I say we save him for Barbary. Let him take the place of his tart. There's many an old merchant's wife would pay well for a turn with a pretty little fellow like this mincing Gilead scut."

"Many an old merchant might like the brat, too," said the slaver next to Agarix, and they all roared with laughter. All but Gree, who sat expressionless, his eyes fixed on his rival.

"He goes to Kepler," Gree said.

"His talents will be wasted in the mines," Agarix said, squeezing my neck painfully in his big hand. He turned to me and said, "Tell us some of your tricks, brat. What's your name, now—Deliverance-from-the-Void, is it? Come on, tell us, what did you deliver to those simpering, splay-footed, barnyard trollops on Gilead?"

"Nothing," I said. I was carrying a beaker of *scoof* and was close to spilling the hot, thick liquid all over me with the pain and pressure of Agarix's grip, but I tried not to show it.

"Nothing? Come on, now, brat, you're among real men. We saw you with your little tart the night we took you aboard. I bet we interrupted your plans for her, eh? Too bad she got away," he said, thrusting me aside and turning to his companions. "I would have enjoyed a ride on her myself. What do you say to that, you shifty-eyed—"

He turned to me, and I flung the hot *scoof* into his face. I knew at once that it was a mad and suicidal thing to do, but there was no reasoning involved. His words made me want to kill him, and the beaker of *scoof* was the only weapon at hand.

Agarix leaped to his feet, roaring in pain and rage, and took a savage swipe at me. It would have knocked my head off my shoulders if it had connected, but I ducked and slipped to one side. A slaver pinned my arms from behind, and as I stood helpless, Agarix drew his knife.

"No man has ever dared to raise his hand against Agarix, and no skipping, slithering, son-of-a-*trettle* from a holy-mouthed planet of gibbering weaklings is going to do what you did and live to brag about it. I'll carve you up like a haunch of *haxopod,* brat, and when—"

"Stop, Agarix," Gree interrupted, and Agarix, astonished, fell silent. "Release the brat," Gree said, and my arms were loosed.

"Don't interfere with me," Agarix said. "I have a right to my revenge."

"That you do, Agarix. And we have a right to our amusement," Gree said. He snatched the knife from the belt of the slaver at his side and tossed it at my feet. "Pick it up, brat. Show us whether you're a man."

Agarix laughed contemptuously and looked around at his companions, then suddenly launched himself at me, whipping his blade up in a slashing arc. I dove between his feet, grabbed the knife, and scrambled to my feet as he turned to face me. I had used a knife often enough before, but never in anger against another living thing. The Daltrescan fighting blades were bigger and heavier than anything I was accustomed to from the farmstead. They were superb weapons, perfectly balanced, and I found myself in tune with the feel and rhythm of the knife in my hands at once. I had to grip it in both hands, and Agarix mocked my lack of strength. What troubled me more was my lack of experience, which put me far on the bad end of any sensible odds; but the arena in which I fought my first battle was constructed so as to shorten the odds against me considerably. The mess hall was small and crowded. Agarix could not hope to stalk me down and overpower me with sheer mass and strength. I could circle the table, vault over it, or slip under it to avoid his sweeping slashes and wild thrusts, and as long as I could maneuver, I was safe. But I couldn't avoid him forever. Sooner or later we had to close, and then the advantage was all to him. I tried not to think of that moment, but I knew that if righteousness was going to give me strength, as Zealous had so often promised, it would have to hurry.

Still, I was armed and free to move. If I had to die, I could die fighting for my life, not like an animal slaughtered in a farmyard. And Agarix didn't have me yet.

We lunged and circled—Agarix doing the lunging, me doing all the ducking and dodging and circling—for what seemed an endless time, though in fact our bout lasted scarcely more than a minute. The spilt *scoof* I had flung to start it all was still steaming in a puddle on the table when it was all over.

Agarix drove me back against the table with a feint and a sweeping, neck-high slash. I ducked under and rolled to the far side, and he made his move, anticipating my emergence with a headlong lunge across the table to spit me on his blade as I popped up. But I hesitated, and he slid forward on his own momentum, his head and shoulders skidding on the wet surface to appear above me over the edge. I thrust upward, and the blade seemed to leap with a will of its own, sinking to the hilt in his hairy throat. He let out one choking, gurgling cry, his blood spurted over my hands, and then the blade fell from his hand and he lay still, his big head hanging reversed and open-eyed before me, his brawny arms hanging limp to brush the floor. The blood seeped over his face, into his gaping nostrils, and dripped in a slow trickle from his lank hair.

Agarix was dead. A few seconds earlier, he had been alive, and now he lay dead on a dirty table in a stinking outlaw ship, and his blood covered my hands. I knew he was a cruel, butchering Daltrescan slaver, the scum of the galaxy, a man who would have skinned me alive and used my pelt to dust his filthy boots, but he was a living being, and I had killed him. I slid out from under the table, feeling sick, and dropped the bloody blade at Gree's feet.

He picked it up, wiped it on his thigh, and tossed it to its owner. "Well done," he said. "You'll go to Tarquin VII. They'll teach you to be a real fighter. Now clean up the mess you made."

Two of the slavers dragged Agarix's body to the airlock. The others filed out without a glance at Gree or me. I got my pail and a rag and set to work.

4. *I am offered to Raphanus; Gree makes a wager.*

Three weeks later, the Daltrescan driveship put down on Tarquin VII and twelve of us, chained and heavily guarded, were led out to be sold. We were prodded along at as fast a pace as our manacled legs could manage, and as I hobbled, wincing under the prods, I marveled at the crowds and the splendid buildings all around me. This was my first sight of another planet, and it was a far cry from the simple farmsteads and small communities of Gilead. The streets were paved with smooth stone, and the buildings, some of them ten times the height of a man, were also of stone, gleaming white under a bright sun in an open, blue sky. People were everywhere. In my first few minutes on Tarquin VII, I saw more people than I had seen in my entire life on Gilead. I was a bit frightened by the noise and movement and crowds, the bright colors and strange vehicles, but my curiosity overcame my fear, and relief at finally getting off that ship overcame every other sensation. I noticed that on the whole, the Tarquinians were a smaller race than the Daltrescans, and they did not appear to be as dirty. I took those signs as promising.

We were led into a huge building and thrust into separate cages, with guards circulating to discourage communication between us. I was given food, and having eaten and tried unsuccessfully to gain some information from the guards, I stretched out on the floor of my cage and went to sleep. It was not a gesture of bravado. I was exhausted.

I was awakened in the manner that had become familiar over the past few months, a prod jabbed into my back, accompanied by a string of threats and oaths. I sprang up, and there outside the bars was Gree, with a group of Tarquinians. They were all smaller than Gree and quite different in appearance. The first thing that came to my mind was a line from the Chapter of Maledictions, and I could almost hear the voice of Zealous as he recited, "Accursed be those who scent and oil their bodies and cover their flesh with soft garments and shining vanities, and woe befall those who surrender their lives to the pursuit of luxury!" Involuntarily, I whispered the response, "Woe unto them!"

One of the Tarquinians, an older man, very distinguished-looking and better dressed than any of the others, stepped forward to inspect me more closely. When he had satisfied himself, he turned to Gree and said in a mild, weary voice, "He is a pleasing little fellow, Gree, for all his appalling filthiness. I will consider him, but you must know that I have no use for him here. He might be made a gift to the co-adjustor Auloedus, but first he requires a good scrubbing." He lifted a small, sweet-scented ball that dangled from one wrist by a slender chain, and sniffed it daintily. "I do wish you would make your offerings more presentable before bringing them here, Gree," he said with genteel distaste.

I could understand most of what he said. Like the Daltrescans, he spoke a language that was closely related to that of Gilead, with only an occasional word or phrase that was totally unfamiliar, and I could usually figure out the strange words from their context. I had little difficulty in following the conversation. Neither the Tarquinian nor Gree used the "thee" and "thou" forms that made every conversation on Gilead sound like a reading from *The Book of The Voyage,* and in general, their way of speaking sounded like a broken-down version of good Gilead speech, but at least I could understand them and learn what was happening to me.

"You can use this one for more than a gift," Gree said.

"Indeed?"

"He can go in the arena."

The Tarquinian raised an eyebrow, smiled politely, in the way an adult smiles at a child, and shook his head. "Like all Daltrescans, Gree, you have an absolutely primitive sense of humor. This grimy little waif would have no more chance in the arena than he would in a cage of *snargraxes.*"

"Do you remember Agarix?" Gree asked.

"That dreadful brute with the filthy mouth?" The Tarquinian made a grimace of distaste and raised the scented ball to his nostrils. "I'm so glad you kept him aboard this time. He disgusts me."

"Agarix is floating up there with his throat cut," Gree said, pointing upward and grinning with fierce relish.

"Well, the galaxy improves a little each day! Did you finally lose patience with him?"

"Yes. I gave this little *bzzit* a blade, and he cut Agarix down in fair fight."

The Tarquinian's expression changed. "No more jokes, Gree. Please."

"I make no joke, Raphanus. The boy was born for the arena. Think of the odds you'd get on him against a Skeggjatt or a Thorumbian! You could make a fortune on his first three matches."

"He'd be cut down in twenty seconds, Gree. I have a reputation to uphold, and I do not uphold it by sending little boys into the arena to battle grown men," Raphanus said loftily.

"Try him."

"Oh, Gree, stop this foolishness!"

Gree took a pouch from inside his tunic and drew out five gleaming cubes, each one worth an Armstrong. He held them out to Raphanus. "Here's what you paid for the herdsman. I'll wager it that this slave can beat your trainer two passes out of three. Even bet."

"Even cash bet, plus the slave," Raphanus said. "If he wins, I'll pay what I paid for the herdsman. If he loses, he's mine for nothing."

"Agreed."

"Very well, Gree. I'll do it just to teach you a lesson." Raphanus turned to his staff. "Get testing blades," he said to one, and to another, "Bring cushions and refreshments to the viewing box." To the two remaining he said, "Scrub him and oil him and give him a decent outfit. The match begins in one hour."

I was taken from the cage and led to a little room with a pool of warm water in the center. After all those weeks aboard the slaver, I couldn't get into that pool fast enough, and the two attendants had to haul me out bodily to get me dried and ready for the oiling.

"Where are you from, lad?" the older attendant asked as he dried me.

"My home is on Gilead."

"I've heard of Gilead. Some years ago, the slavers brought us a shipment from Gilead, I believe. Big, strapping fellows they were, but they turned out to be poor in the arena. They're a very religious people, are they not?"

"I guess so. More religious than the Daltrescans."

"Anyone is. What sort of warriors do you have on Gilead?"

"We don't have any. I'm not sure what a warrior is. I've heard the word, but no one ever explained it to me."

The second attendant, who had entered during our conversation, set down a jar of oil and turned to his associate. "I told you that when they first arrived, remember? I said 'These people have no warrior tradition to build on. Raphanus is wasting his money.' "

The first attendant shrugged his shoulders and said, "You heard what this lad did, didn't you?"

The other one looked at me hard and asked, "Did you really kill Agarix?"

"Yes."

"In fair fight?"

"Yes, in fair fight. I was . . . ." I started to say that I was lucky, but when I saw the expression of genuine awe on the faces of the attendants, I paused and corrected myself. "I was provoked. He insulted the name of a woman, and I punished him."

"Had you fought often on Gilead?"

"We do not do these things on Gilead."

"And yet you overcame Agarix," the first attendant said.

"Agarix was slow and clumsy. He fought carelessly," I said, with all the easy scorn of an old veteran.

"Well, soon you'll be fighting Loripes. He's not slow and clumsy, and he's never careless," the first attendant said as he began to rub oil into my back and shoulders. He made me move my arms around and roll my shoulders, and pointed out the development to his assistant. "You are well-muscled for one so young. You must work hard on Gilead," he said to me.

"We do."

"Loripes is also well-muscled, and experienced. He's been a trainer for three years. It will be a hard match for the lad," the other said. "What is your name?"

"Del," I said. My real name would have sounded out of place among the melodious, smooth Tarquinian names I had heard so far, so I gave them the short form.

"Remember this, Del. If you defeat Loripes, you will be marked for the arena. Lose, and you will be sent to the co-adjutor Auloedus. He is a wealthy man, and his slaves live a good life as long as he is pleased with them," the first attendant said.

"In time, he may give you a wife. You might live a long and easy life in the household of Auloedus," the other added.

"And in the arena, you might die in your first match."

"This one with Loripes?" I asked.

"Oh, no. This is a test of skill. You will use the testing blades. But in the arena, the weapons are real, and the combat is to the death."

"The arena sounds like a place to avoid," I observed.

"Oh, it is, it surely is." the first attendant said. He thought for a moment, then added, "Of course, in the arena, there is always the chance of gaining great wealth and even winning one's freedom."

"It happens very seldom," the other said.

"But it does happen," the first declared.

"How can I win my freedom in the arena?" I asked.

"Be the best. The people follow the combats closely, and they have their favorite companies and champions. On the great festivals, they sometimes demand freedom for a particular favorite. When they do, even as powerful a master as Raphanus bows to their will."

"Still, it rarely happens," the second attendant said. "Better a long life in the household of Auloedus than a bloody death in the arena."

"Better freedom than either," I said.

"Perhaps. The choice is yours, if you can defeat Loripes." He handed me a pair of skimpy breeches and low, soft boots. "I'll get a tunic when I remove your old garments. I'm going to burn them. Is there anything you want to keep?"

"Nothing," I said. Then I remembered the paper I had taken on the night of my capture. "No, wait—a scrap of paper in my pocket."

"This?" The attendant held up the paper.

"Yes. Keep it for me."

5. *My second battle: I surprise Loripes and acquire a new friend.*

I finished dressing, and my attendants took me down a cool, dark passageway to a barred gate that opened on a small, enclosed area. Two Tarquinians were waiting there. Above us, in a box with a clear view of all below them, Gree and Raphanus reclined at their ease.

I knew right away which one was Loripes. He was the taller and younger of the two, perhaps ten years older than I, and he was a very impressive figure. When he shrugged off his tunic, letting it fall carelessly from his shoulders for his assistant to catch as it dropped, he managed to make every muscle in his arms and chest ripple at once. I suspected that this match was going to be a lot more challenging than my bout with the hulking Agarix. I slipped off my own tunic, flexing as many muscles in the process as I could, not impressing Loripes or anyone else. The man with Loripes beckoned me closer.

"This is a fair fight, blades only, slash and thrust," he said mechanically. "The challenge is for two out of three. When I call "Mark!" you will separate for my inspection. Any questions?"

Loripes did not deign to answer, and I had no idea what to ask. The referee went on, carefully extending two odd-looking blades, one for each of us. They were ordinary blades, except that the edge and tip were of some soft, colored substance, black at the tip and green along the cutting edge. It dawned on me that these were the testing blades Raphanus had called for, special blades designed to leave a mark instead of a wound. I let out a great sigh of relief. Despite the attendant's assurance, I had expected worse.

"Anything wrong?" the referee asked.

"Everything's fine," I replied, grinning.

"Do you expect this to be amusing?" Loripes asked.

"I'm just glad to know it's not going to be fatal."

"Let's get on with it," Loripes said to the referee.

The referee separated us and stepped to one side. He raised his hand, held it up for a moment, then cried "Engage!"

Loripes was at me in a flash, slashing upward and sideways in a lightning double feint and following with a backhand as I dodged by. He missed me by no more than a hair. He spun on his heel and continued the attack, pressing me hard. There was no place to hide and nothing to duck behind in this arena, and I had to move fast, far faster than I had thought I could.

I kept moving, circling around Loripes, passing at him only hesitantly and with great caution to keep him from running the whole match his way, forcing him to think of his defense as well as his attack plan. As in the battle with Agarix, I felt myself functioning on several levels of action at once. My moves were automatic, instinctive, as if my body knew exactly what to do while my mind raced ahead to juggle complicated patterns of defense and attack, and all the while a portion of my consciousness remained aloof and detached, observing the struggle and judging each move with a cool, critical eye.

As Loripes closed on me in a difficult pattern of side slashes, I sensed his intention. I let him drive me back almost to the wall, then, as he feinted low and wheeled his blade up for a downward neck thrust, I slipped under him and caught him just below the breast bone.

"Mark!" the referee cried. We separated and he looked at the black smear on Loripes' chest. "First mark to the challenger. A fatal thrust. Do you dispute?" he asked Loripes.

"I accept."

"And you are satisfied?" he asked me.

"Yes," I told him, assuming that it was expected of me.

"One of three to the challenger," he called up to the observers. Gree gave a nasty laugh, and Raphanus inclined his head to him politely, sniffed his ball of scent, and motioned to the referee.

"Engage!" came once again, and this time Loripes moved in on me more cautiously. I did not attack, but forced him to take the offensive while I studied every move and developed a pattern of my own. When he moved into position for the same double feint he had tried at the very outset, I let him close in on me, then spun around his other side and thrust at his unprotected back, just under the ribs. As I touched, his own blade swept around in a backhand slash and left a long, green track across my belly.

"Mark!" cried the referee for the second time. He studied us both, then announced, "I accept both touches. An injury for Loripes, fatal thrust for the challenger. Do either of you dispute?"

"No," we replied.

He turned to the viewing box and announced, "The challenger takes the victory, two to one."

The referee took our blades. Loripes held out his hand, and I clasped it in the Gilead gesture of amity. He smiled at me, and there was no resentment in his manner.

"You are very good. You defeated me fairly and I praise your skill," he said warmly.

"Thank you."

"What is your experience? Were you a champion among your people?"

"This was my second match."

"Your second?" Loripes looked astonished. "Then all your skill comes to you naturally?"

"I guess it does. Nobody ever taught me."

"Incredible. In three years as a trainer, I have lost only two testing matches. The other was to a Skeggjatt who went on to become a Champion of the People."

"Did he win his freedom?" I asked.

"He was offered it and given the jeweled sword, but he chose to remain in the arena. He was slain in his very next match. He died magnificently."

I responded with a noncommittal grunt. Loripes seemed very pleased with his story, but I personally thought the Skeggjatt was crazy. Offered my freedom, I'd be on my way to Gilead before the cheering stopped. They could keep their jeweled sword.

We were dismissed from the arena, and as Loripes and I walked back to my new quarters, he said, "I will go to Raphanus and ask him to place you in my squad. Within two months I can have you ready for the arena."

"Can I start any sooner?"

Loripes laughed and slapped me on the shoulder. "You are very eager. Ordinarily, it takes six months of training to ready a man."

"You said I was good."

"You are, but there is much to learn. Ours was a fair match, man to man, blade against blade. You must learn to use other weapons and defend against them, and you must prepare yourself for multiple, unrestricted matches."

"What are they?" I asked. Loripes was beginning to worry me with all this talk.

"One man against two or three, no rules. Haakmat—the Skeggjatt I spoke of—could fight six men at once. He defeated six in one turn of the sandglass on the day he won his freedom."

I whistled. "How many did it take to beat him?"

"Only one. He was much like yourself, small and very quick. He came from a planet devastated by the Rinn, poor fellow."

Loripes grew thoughtful then, and we walked the rest of the way in silence. When we separated, he assured me once again that he would try to have me assigned to his squad for training.

6. *In training; reflections on Daltrescans, Tarquinians, and Otherworlders in general.*

Loripes was as good as his word. The next morning I was awakened early—by a soft bell, and not a prod in the kidneys—given the best meal I had eaten since leaving Gilead, and taken to an arena much like the one I had fought in the previous day. Loripes and nine other men were there, surrounded by a small army of stuffed dummies hung on ropes or mounted on pedestals and an array of weapons and armor the like of which had never been seen on Gilead.

The attendant left us, and Loripes introduced me to the others one by one. Each nodded as his name was called off, then looked away, as if my name was all he cared to know about me. They were silent men, not much given to friendship, and I soon learned that those destined for the arena did not form close ties with one another. They knew that sooner or later they might be matched, and friendship would only complicate their business relationship.

Every day for the next six weeks I was marched to the training arena in the morning. We exercised for the first hour, and the rest of the morning was given over to lectures and demonstrations. After a light midday meal, we spent the afternoon in practice. At the end of the day's training we were bathed, massaged, and rubbed with oil, and then we ate our main meal, a lengthy affair with many courses of exotic dishes and delicious beverages that I soon learned to drink only in moderation. As we dined, we were regaled with songs and stories of great combats and famous champions.

The attendants and entertainers conversed with us freely, but even at table, we did not talk much to one another. I regret this, for I might have learned much from my fellow warriors.

After dinner, we were sent to our chambers to study, for Raphanus believed that a good warrior must know not only everything that could be taught him about his trade, but other things as well. In the eyes of Raphanus, his warriors represented him outside the arena as significantly as they did on the field of combat, and he considered the social graces as important in our training as the martial skills. He often visited with us and engaged us in conversation, testing our wit and quickness. He seemed pleased with me, and I was flattered at the time, thinking myself quite the nobleman. Now I can see that he must have been amused by my naiveté.

I learned much about the Tarquinians during my early training. They were of pure Old Earth lineage, never having intermarried with other races, and they prided themselves on the fact. Raphanus carried his pride even farther than the others, boasting that he accepted as warriors only those of Old Earth descent. But he was willing to stretch his conditions in order to admit an exceptional man. He took even greater pride in winning than he did in purity of breed.

The Tarquinians had been among the first pioneers to leave Old Earth. The original settlers had encountered great hostility on the part of the native inhabitants of Tarquin VII, the only inhabitable planet in the system. After more than a century of bloody war, both sides sought a compromise that would allow them to survive. A tournament was arranged, the winners to retain the planet uncontested, the losers to go into exile. The newcomers prevailed and won the planet for themselves. Since that time, the tradition of the tournament had become the main feature of Tarquinian life, its very focal point. For half the year, tournaments were held almost daily, and a good warrior might appear in nearly a third of them. During the remainder of the year, when the promoters were recruiting new men and the warriors were recuperating and training for the next season, most of the talk was of old matches and the prospects for the following year. Although he was technically little more than a slave, a warrior was a highly respected figure on Tarquin. The outstanding ones were frequent guests at the homes of the great families; hence Raphanus' insistence on training in manners.

While I was in training, I wondered what the rest of the Tarquinians did to keep the planet operating. No one ever spoke of work, which had been the second most popular topic on Gilead, ranking just behind *The Book of the Voyage.* I was puzzled. I had now met two new races, and was soon to meet—though not often for social purposes—representatives of a hundred more, and the full extent and variety of life in the galaxy was beginning to dawn on me. Back home on Gilead, the existence of other worlds and other peoples was not denied—that was hardly possible—but it was mentioned only grudgingly and not dwelt upon. Otherworlders were not wanted on Gilead. They did not know our way of righteousness and were not at all troubled by their ignorance. At best, Otherworlders exhibited a kind of fumbling good will; at worst, the malevolent behavior to be expected of all slaves of vanity, deceit, and abomination.

I began to think that lumping all Otherworlders together in this fashion was too much of an oversimplification to be accurate. Both the Daltrescans and the Tarquinians were fond of their own style of abomination, to be sure, but they were as differ-

ent from one another as each was from the Rudstromites of Gilead. The Daltrescans were ugly and
brutal, with names that spat out like curses; the Tarquinians were smooth and well-mannered, melodious
of name and speech, more concerned with performance than with mere results. In the arena, they cheered
louder and longer for a man who fought well and
lost than for a clumsy victor, and the warrior who
accepted the death stroke gallantly and without
showing fear was sure to win a popular immortality
and have his name sung at feasts for years to come. To
the Daltrescans, on the other hand, a dead man was
just so much useless trash to be jettisoned at once and
promptly forgotten. His only memorial was the little
stock of personal belongings divided among the
survivors, a ritual that often occasioned further
disposal problems. Even their driveships differed. The
Daltrescans used great hulking leviathans that carried
a crew of thirty and a cargo of slaves numbering over a
hundred, plus supplies for a two-year voyage; the
Tarquinians favored light, needle-like, one-man craft
for all purposes except the long trans-galactic
expeditions they undertook every few years.

There were some things about the Tarquinians that I
never quite mastered. Their names, for instance. Like
many other Tarquinian practices, the naming-system
was based on that of the Old Earth Caesaro-Etruscan
civilization, which had flourished all over the
European states from the early days of Genghis Khan,
the great warrior-prophet of the East, to the decadent
times of the Napoleonic Revolutionary period, or, as it
was often called, the Middle Ages. All Tarquinians
were given a name at birth, usually something simple
and descriptive. At one year, their horoscopes were
cast, and a star-name was added. At maturity, the
names of both grandfathers were adopted (provided

that they were known and honored), and from time to time during a man's life he was permitted to add new names celebrating his achievements and triumphs. A man who lived an eventful life might carry enough names for a small town, and since every one of them was his rightful name, a conversation could become very confusing. I always stayed with the name of Del, even when my name had grown to Del Cometfire-by-Dawnstar Deletriculus Quickslash Nimblefoot Swift-thrust Threesmiter. Del was so much simpler.

7. *The tournament of Land-fall; I win a new name.*

For six weeks I trained and studied in the little arena. I was well-fed and got plenty of rest and exercise, and I could feel my strength increasing as I filled out and grew a bit taller. I was still the smallest of Raphanus' company of warriors, but I had learned that size had very little to do with performance. The others had been training for four months before my arrival, but I had caught up and surpassed them all. Though no one said so openly, I was the best man in Loripes' squad, and we all knew it.

After six weeks we moved from the little arena where we had trained as a squad and went into intensive final training with Raphanus' entire company of warriors, about two hundred in all. The lectures ended, and our days were spent entirely in exercise and mock combat. The meals served us were larger, but the food was simpler and the hours of dining shorter. The training was all important now. The atmosphere grew tense, and expectancy filled the air.

At last the morning of my first tournament arrived. We assembled in the large training area, dressed in magnificent new outfits bearing the red talon symbol of the company of Raphanus, and after our final close inspection, we were addressed by Raphanus himself.

He mounted a low platform, erected in the center of the field, and we formed a semicircle around him. On a lower level of the platform, arranged in order of rank, stood the trainers, medicos, and lesser attendants, all newly outfitted. Behind them, racks of weapons flashed in the morning light. I had never seen such splendor before, and I was overwhelmed by it all. I could feel my excitement growing from the moment I put on my new tunic.

Today, I learned, was the great feast of Landfall, the five-hundred-and-fourth anniversary of the arrival of the Old Earth pioneers on Tarquin VII and the opening day of the tournament season, which continued through the feasts of various early heroes, the days of appeasement, the commemorations, the triumphs, and finally came to a grand culmination in a ten-day tournament to mark the anniversary of the first great victory over the old inhabitants. "For this day," Raphanus said, "and for the days of blood and glory to come, you have all trained diligently. Now, as ever, the company of Raphanus is match and master of any foe, and I wish you the victories you deserve. The Landfall Tournament will last for three days. Each day, seven squads will take the field, and each man of you will have a chance to test himself in single combat. May you all return victorious to the feast I will provide on the third day of Landfall!"

Everyone cheered and shouted Raphanus' name. I felt myself filled to bursting with eagerness to meet my first foeman and win glory for myself, my squad, and my benefactor and patron the noble Raphanus. I

shouted myself hoarse, and almost exploded with pride
when I learned that the squad of Loripes, with me at
the head, right beside our trainer and just behind the
carriage of Raphanus himself, would lead the march to
the arena.

We swung out proudly to the blare of trumpets and
passed down broad avenues ablaze with flags and
banners, the walkways lined with cheering spectators.
I was dazzled by the sheer weight of magnificence, the
crowds, the waves of sound pouring over me, and by
the time we reached the arena, I was ready for any
foeman on any terms. I would have fought an army of
giants. It was not until much later in my career as a
warrior that I discovered that my courage had all been
induced by a scent that impregnated my brand-new
tunic. The Tarquinians had mastered the uses of
various scents, and the one that aroused courage and
ferocity was in common use among the warrior
companies. As a newcomer, I was given a heavy dose,
and it worked extremely well. At the time, I was
unaware of this. I simply felt braver than I ever had
before.

The noise was muffled as we passed through the
long archway leading into the grand arena, then it
burst out redoubled, with flourishes of brass slashing
through the roar of fifty thousand voices. Raphanus
presented his company to the co-adjutor who presided
over the tournament and then read off the names of
the first squad of combatants. Mine led all the rest. We
stepped forward, returned the co-adjutor's salute, and
then went to the benches behind the wooden barrier to
await the summons to battle.

The ceremonies finally drew to a close, the noise of
the assembled crowd fell to a murmur, then hushed as
the co-adjutor's herald rose to announce the first
match of the tournament. "For the company of

Raphanus Darkstar Teleus Calendricus Red-Talon Father-of-Warriors, from the squad of the trainer Loripes Moonlustre Loripes Rustus Swiftslasher, the first combatant, Del of Gilead!" A roar went up, and I stripped off my tunic, drew my blade, and walked proudly to the center of the arena. My opponent was announced, but I paid no heed to his company or origin. I studied his walk and his every move, for my life now depended on it. He was a man about my height, but twice my bulk, a typical squat chunky Quespodon, hairless, with mottled skin. His eyes were bright but narrow, and I watched as he studied me closely, then slowly shook his head and sheathed his blade. I realized suddenly that the herald was still reading off his name, and that all his victory-titles had something to do with bone crushing. Raphanus had decided to start me off at the top, against the best the opposing company had to offer. I felt a rush of fierce pride—all scent-induced, but nevertheless quite real—and a desire to justify Raphanus' choice and Loripes' faith in my skill. I sheathed my own knife, and a great shout of approbation went up all around me.

We fought a long and grueling match. I ran circles around the Quespodon, keeping always just a tantalizing hairbreadth beyond his deadly grasp, until I forced him, in a rage of frustration, to draw his blade. I kept mine sheathed while he attacked me in six intricate passes, and the noise of the crowd grew deafening, exciting me to a silent promise that when I drew my own blade, it would be for a single thrust. And so it was.

I walked stiffly and proudly to the barrier, stepped out twice to acknowledge the ovation of the crowd, and re-entered just as my knees buckled and I doubled over, retching helplessly. The effects of the scent had worn off, and for a moment I was just a frightened boy with bloody hands, belatedly aware of his close brush with death. An attendant quickly threw my tunic over my shoulders, and I regained control of myself. I sat beside Loripes, who was exultant over my victory. Raphanus came to offer his personal congratulations, and I was scrupulously polite to him.

The next three matches were businesslike affairs, quickly over. The fifth and sixth were spectacular, in my eyes, but Loripes assured me that my performance had surpassed them. I found it hard to believe, but now I was free from the first intense impact of the fighting scent and unaware of the full effect it had had on my emotions and reflexes. The six remaining matches went quickly, and when the first fighting sequence was over, Loripes' squad was still intact. Two of the men were badly injured, but even they had won their combats, although one of them, Stap, a big mute from Rebolushchka III, would never be able to fight again.

After the third fighting sequence, there came an interlude of acrobatics and dancing by children of the noble families of Tarquin VII, and then the matches resumed. Raphanus' company did well in the second series, and we ended the day with fifty-four victories out of seventy matches, a good record.

On the second day, I attended as a spectator. The crowd for the third and final day of the Landfall Tournament was larger than that for either of the previous days. After the sixth match came a second interlude of entertainment, and I asked Loripes if anything special was planned for the conclusion. I recalled Raphanus' mention of seven squads for each day, and I knew that our company numbered only twenty squads. He winked slyly and motioned to me to be patient. Patience was the virtue I was least inclined

to, for my tunic that day had again been steeped in
fighting scent, and I was a vicarious participant in
every match.

The trumpets blared and the crowd fell silent. The
herald rose to announce the contestants in the final
match, ten men chosen by popular vote from each
company. My name was the first for Raphanus'
company. Loripes grinned and slapped me on the
back. Even my fellow squadsmen, customarily
reserved, wished me luck.

For the second time, I fought well. I was carried
back to the school of Raphanus on the shoulders of
cheering spectators, bearing two trophies: a bronze
amulet awarded by the co-adjutor and a new name
conferred by the men of my own company. I was now
Deletriculus; in the old Caesaro-Etruscan tongue that
was the official language of Tarquin VII, "Little
Destroyer."

8. *Raphanus rewards me;*
Loripes reassures me.

We feasted long and loudly that night, and drank
freely of the tangy, blood-red beverage of Tarquin.
When at last I rose to walk unsteadily to my chamber,
Raphanus took me aside, smiling, and said, "Today
you proved yourself a man in the arena, and you
deserve a reward. Tonight you can prove yourself a
man in your chamber." I thanked him and took my
leave, wondering in a befuddled way what kind of a
reward awaited me.

When I entered the chamber, a girl was sitting on
my bed, combing long dark hair that shone with
highlights in the soft illumination from above. She

looked up at me, smiled, and held out her arms.

"Come to me, Del. I have been waiting."

"Who are you?"

"I am your woman for tonight, your victory prize. I sought out Raphanus and asked to be given to you," she said.

"To me?"

"I saw both your combats. You are very brave. Come, Del," she said, beckoning me to her arms.

I took a step toward her and then stopped as I thought of Cassie. I could not betray her like this. "I have a woman. She waits for me on Gilead," I said.

"Gilead is far away."

"Someday I will win my freedom and return to her."

"And until then will you live apart from all women, like the Guardians? You are too young for that, Del."

"But I . . . I love her," I said confusedly.

She rose gracefully and walked to me. Placing one hand on my shoulder, she stroked my hair with the other. The strong, sweet scent of the ball on her wrist filled my nostrils. "Am I so displeasing, Del? Can we not talk?"

"No. Yes. No, you are not displeasing, you are very . . . you are lovely. If I were . . . . If there were no . . . ." I could not think. The sweet aroma flowed into me and coiled around my mind and will, drawing them to the dark-haired girl who stood before me, growing more beautiful and desirable with each beat of my pulse. I looked down into the dark eyes that shone with a hunger I shared, and my thoughts of Cassie were buried under a wave of desire that made me shudder with its intensity and pull the soft body of my prize to me.

She left my chamber in the first light. When I awoke again, my head was clear and I felt crushed under a

burden of shame, for I had betrayed Cassie. I blamed
my own weakness, inflamed by the strong Tarquinian
wine. I was not yet aware of the powerful love-scent
used by the courtesans of Tarquin VII, and knew only
that I had broken my firm resolve to give my love to no
woman but Cassie, my promised bride.

The deaths I had caused were as nothing to this
betrayal, for now I had broken a promise to myself,
and to a man of Gilead on the verge of his time of
decision, this was the ultimate fall from the way of
righteousness. I had given myself into the hands of the
slaves of the abomination. Up to this time, I had not
felt any real qualms about my actions, but I had given
them much consideration in the silent moments before
sleep.

The New Enlightened Rudstromites of Gilead were
believed, throughout the galaxy, to be a grim and
righteous race, but since they kept strictly to
themselves, their true code was little understood by
Otherworlders, who held the dour folk of Gilead in a
kind of amused contempt. Their predecessors, known
as the Rudstromites, had suffered much on Old Earth,
and during the Bloody Centuries just before the
Wroblewski Drive opened the stars to mankind, their
homeland in the principality of Pennsylvania, a final
refuge after many persecutions, was destroyed and
they fled to new homes in the states of Europe. One
branch settled in Brittania, a large western island, and
lived there in peaceful isolation until the exodus to the
outer worlds. This group, from which my people were
descended, had in their long exile developed a strongly
personal ethical code with a minimum of general
precepts. They subscribed to the belief that killing was
not a good thing, but they made no laws forbidding it.
They simply did not kill anyone or talk of killing as if
it were an acceptable means of settling differences. If

a man chose to act against the common practice, he did
so at his own risk, in the light of his own decision. In
my lifetime on Gilead I had never heard of anyone
doing so, in the matter of killing or of anything else;
but this was the result of free choice. Nevertheless,
such unanimity was persuasive to a youth. I grew up
believing that to kill was an evil deed, but in my
months away from home, my belief wavered and I
began to reconsider my position. One sign of a
righteous man was the smooth path of his life and the
complete uneventfulness of all his days. I had avoided
bloodshed for all my sixteen years, and yet I ended up
on a Daltrescan slaver, beginning a very eventful life.
When I killed a man, my lot improved. Now that I had
slain two more, it had improved further, and I knew
that if I went on killing, I would win honor and
eventually freedom to return to Gilead and claim my
place there and my bride. It seemed clear to me that in
my present situation, my life would find its smooth
path only if I shed the blood of others, and so it was
right for me to do so. Once reunited with Cassie and
restored to Gilead, I would have no reason to kill
again, and I would not. So I decided to do my best as a
warrior.

I learned later that this reasoning process was called
Rationalism and was the most widespread philosophy
on Old Earth.

But I had also decided to be true to Cassie no matter
how long we were apart and to give my love to no
other woman, and I had acted against that decision.
That was a great evil. I brooded on it all that day and
could find no excuse for myself. Loripes noticed my
mood and questioned me about the cause.

"The woman was given to you as a lawful prize, and
you accepted her. Where's the evil in that?" he said,
when I had unburdened myself.

"The evil is not in the woman, Loripes, it is in me. I denied my own free decision."

"You could not refuse the reward. Raphanus would have been insulted."

"No, but I could have . . . I could have done something else."

"What else?" he asked.

"I don't know. I never thought it would happen."

"Then how can you blame yourself? When you made your decision you had no idea what would come in the future. Things change, Del, and sometimes our firm decisions must change in the face of facts."

I shook my head. "That is not the way on Gilead."

"And Tarquin VII is not Gilead. Each planet has its own ways, and we have a saying, 'When on Tarquin, do as the Tarquinians do.' Do you understand?"

"I think so."

"Think of this, Del. There are thousands of inhabited planets, and each planet has its own ways. Most races believe that their ways are the right ways. If a man disagrees, he can go to a planet that suits him better. If he is not free to leave—as you and I are not—then he saves himself much suffering by accepting the ways of the planet. I myself spent some years on the planet Pranchalahandri, where the people spend their days in meditation on the 11,111 True Utterances of the All-Knowing Mind. I thought them foolish, but I joined in the meditation."

"Why do they do that?" I asked.

"They believe it makes them moral."

"Does it?"

He shrugged. "I really can't say, Del. It had little effect on me, except to keep me too busy to devote much time to being immoral. There were evil men and evil ways on Pranchalahandri, just as everywhere else."

"Then you believe that it makes no difference what a man believes to be right and wrong?" I asked. I had never yet met anyone who subscribed to such a belief and declared it openly, and I wanted to know more.

"It makes no difference to *me*," Loripes said carelessly.

"Please, Loripes. You're my only real friend here. I'm very confused, and I can't joke about my feelings. How can you say that a man's beliefs about right and wrong make no difference?"

"I said they make no difference to *me*. They may make a great deal of difference to *him*."

"But is that all?" I asked him desperately. "Is there only my opinion, and your opinion, and everyone else's opinion? Surely there must be something beyond all that."

"I used to think so, but I no longer do."

I grew quite anxious. Loripes was saying the sort of things Zealous and all the Elders of Gilead warned against, and I could not refute him. Worse still, I found myself wanting to know more. His beliefs sounded as if they were much less troubling to a man than mine.

"Do you think there is only us? Is there no one who sees all, and knows, and cares what we do?"

Loripes shrugged his shoulders helplessly. "How can I know this, Del? When I look at the stars, and I think of all that surrounds me, I believe that there is someone—something—who sees it all. Perhaps a race of great men, or a machine, or something I cannot even imagine. But then I tell myself that a being so wise would not care very much if Loripes laughs at the True Utterances, or Deletriculus sleeps with a courtesan. This is how I feel."

He left me then, and I thought long on his words. The code of Loripes was not as firm or as clear as the code I had lived by on Gilead, but it seemed to satisfy him. The path of his life was smooth; smoother than mine so far, certainly. The more I thought of it, the more attractive his code became, for there was no place in it for guilt. I decided that I would try it until I could prove it false.

At the time, I thought Loripes to be immensely wise. He was my trainer, and he knew everything about the world of the arena—which to me, then, was the only world I had to deal with—so I followed his way. I can see now that he was not so very wise after all. He had lived with his uncertainty and confusion long enough to feel comfortable with them and had learned to present them articulately and persuasively, so that his ideas sounded like wisdom to a naive and troubled young man. But he knew no more than I did.

9. *The life of a warrior; disillusionment and new hope.*

I fought many more times during that tournament season, and I always won, even on the few occasions when I was wounded. In the final Tournament of Tournaments, I was matched against two opponents in unrestricted combat, and I emerged victor after a display that had the crowd in the great arena on their feet, chanting my name. I ended the season with many honors and new names, and I was rewarded many times.

A second and a third season came and went, and with each one my fame increased. I learned new techniques and mastered new weapons, among them the longsword, javelin, and pistol; but no matter how

well I fought with them, the crowd always demanded
that I return to the short knife, and Raphanus
eventually restricted me to this weapon. Nevertheless,
I remained in practice with everything in the armory.
It was a safety measure. No warrior could ever be
quite certain what awaited him in the arena or in the
mock combats presented at noble homes for a private
audience.

The men of Raphanus' company were often invited
to perform at the homes of prominent Tarquinians.
Raphanus considered his warriors too valuable to be
squandered for the pleasure of a few, regardless of
their rank or distinction, but he willingly staged
elaborate mock combats of all sorts for the after-
dinner amusement of the well-born. By the time I
became part of his establishment, he had a wide
reputation and his warriors were in great demand. We
were considered good entertainers.

In the first interseason I fought at several homes and
was well received each time. By the end of the third
season my reputation was such that I was invited to
perform alone, competing against time and my own
skills, in a variety of exhibitions carefully worked out
by Raphanus himself. When my performance was
completed, I was usually asked to take a place among
the nobles, join them in conversation, and comment
(from my expert vantage point) on the lesser
performers who filled out the evening's program. This
was heady stuff for a boy from Gilead, and it's no
wonder that by the time I reached twenty—well
before that, to be quite honest—I was filled to bursting
with my own importance. I never let it make me
careless in the arena, but I couldn't prevent it from
making me a very pompous young man. Still a boy,
really; an ignorant boy who had mastered a talent that
was marketable only in a corrupt and corrupting,

decadent society like that of Tarquin. In a sane world, a clean world, I'd have been seen as the destroyer I was and shunned by all who came near me. Any planetary government worthy of the name would have told me to leave at once. But on Tarquin VII, I was a celebrity, a man of enviable accomplishments, in great demand, richly rewarded, courted by the powerful and well-born. It was crazy.

The nobles indulged me, since they were a pompous, arrogant lot themselves and considered my behavior normal. Perhaps "normal" is a poor choice of words here, since it suggests standards that the noble Tarquinians did not apply. "Normal" and "abnormal" were not used in their circle; their standards of judgment were "pleasing" and "displeasing," and these, as I learned, were relative terms. At the time, they found me pleasing. Since I was quite pleased with myself and pleased to be found pleasing by great men, we got on well together.

The tournaments and combats pleased them most of all, and I was surprised to find that the less likely a man was to make his appearance in the arena, the more bravely he talked and the more he found to praise in the tradition of the tournament. We who fought for our lives and our living were not at all like that. When we had to fight, we found a reason to think well of it; when we did not, we thought about other things. But the nobles, as they grew older, fatter, weaker, and more enfeebled, talked braver and braver. The oldest and weakest were the bravest of all, at the dining platform.

One night, between my third and fourth seasons, I was a guest of Auloedus, the co-adjutor, a man of high rank, noble blood, and considerable influence in high Tarquinian circles. I respected Auloedus for his accomplishments but did not like him at all, and I imagine he felt much the same toward me. I think he was put out by the knowledge that he might have had me for his own household if only I had lost that match with Loripes. But I was a fashionable amusement, and so I was summoned to his home to perform. Afterwards, I was seated with three distinguished nobles who were eager to meet me and discuss the true glory of the arena with one who might be expected to echo their views.

"How fortunate for you, Deletriculus, for us, for the people and the history of Tarquin that you were brought to us and not buried in the mines on Kepler," said Favonius, a mellow-voiced, white-haired man who had preceded our host as co-adjutor of tournaments. "In a mere three seasons, you have breathed a new spirit into the life of the arena."

"Indeed he has. Indeed he has," said Notus, his brother, a massive globe of a man whose life for the past fifty years had been one continuous meal. He stuffed a sweet into his mouth, raised his cup to me, and drank. After a delicate belch, he announced, "Splendid example to the people. Deletriculus does them more good than the Guardians, with all their incense and their chanting."

"I try my best," I said, smugly humble.

"Therein lies the difference between you and the mob. You try your best, but they do not. It makes your role on Tarquin the more important, Deletriculus, when you realize this. You, more than any of the others, provide an example for the mob, as my brother points out. You show them what courage and stamina mean. This is the purpose of the tournament."

"Surely not the sole purpose, Favonius," the third diner pointed out. He was Caurus, founder of one of the great weapons houses of Tarquin. Most of the tournaments were fought with weapons of his design and manufacture.

"Of course not. But the providing of an example is the primary purpose of the tournaments."

Caurus frowned and made a careless little gesture of doubt. "If I were asked for the primary purpose of the arena, the chief benefit of the tournaments, I would say . . . I would consider it to be the healthful purgation of emotion by the sight of skills bravely exercised and suffering bravely endured."

"Dedecoro's definition," Favonius murmured, smiling politely.

"Slightly altered," Caurus replied, returning the smile. "Dedecoro spoke of the mimic theatre, and made no reference to bravery."

"A very slight alteration," Favonius said.

"But of great significance."

Notus belched. They turned to him and nodded indulgently, and Caurus continued, "I speak of 'healthful purgation' in a double significance, referring to the health of the citizens and the health of the state."

"Ah! I see," Favonius said appreciatively.

"If the citizen has no innocent outlet for his tensions, no opportunity for vicarious aggression, he might turn, in his desperation, to . . . . Do you see, Favonius?"

"I do, indeed, Caurus."

"So long as there's a tournament, there'll never be a revolution," Notus said solemnly.

The others looked at him quickly, then turned their attention to me, Favonius saying, "But my dear Caurus, we have overlooked the single great justification of the arena: to give a warrior of the magnificence and skill of our Deletriculus the opportunity to display his valor and thereby win approval, honor, and prizes. Surely, this is the primary purpose of the arena."

"It could not be otherwise. Do you agree,
Deletriculus?"

I gave an answer that was a masterpiece of sheer
fatuous pomposity, and they received it with a great
show of deference and respect. Apparently they found
it pleasing. Anyone else would have laughed aloud,
but Tarquinian nobles seldom did such a thing. I'm not
sure whether this was because they were too well-
bred, lacked a sense of humor, or simply didn't
consider most things funny. But whether they showed
it by laughing or not, I'm sure they had many an hour
of genteel amusement at my expense.

Though I was feted by night, my days were still a
continuous round of study and training, and the
regimen became less and less bearable as I grew
progressively more spoiled. After the fourth season,
when the crowd proclaimed me one of their Ten
Champions of the People, I realized that though
Raphanus furnished me with the best trainers,
attendants, and weapons, quartered me in the roomiest
chambers, matched me with the most honored
opponents, and rewarded me with the most desirable
women, someone else made all my choices for me. I
wanted to start making my own decisions. I craved
freedom, and found flattery a poor substitute for it.

I spoke of my growing dissatisfaction to no one, but
my outward attitude changed visibly. I became moody
and sullen during training hours, surly toward
everyone around me, more reckless than ever in the
arena. At the close of the fifth tournament season,
when I was once again named a Champion of the
People, Raphanus summoned me to his private
quarters. We dined and were lavishly entertained, and
when the feasting and ceremony were done and we
were left alone, Raphanus spoke to me as to an equal.

But as always, he was indirect.

"Loripes is a close friend to you, Deletriculus. He knows you well," Raphanus said.

"He is my only good friend."

Raphanus raised an eyebrow, sniffed his ball of scent, and said in a wounded voice, "Indeed? I always thought myself your good friend."

"A warrior cannot be friends with the master of his company, Raphanus. You've done a lot for me, but how can I be a friend to a man who owns me?"

Raphanus nodded his head, as though he had just verified a suspicion in his mind. "I should have foreseen this. You wish your freedom."

"Today I heard the people calling for it. You heard them, but you ignored the demand."

"The people, the people," Raphanus said wearily. "Tell me, what have the people given you, Del, that they have the right to determine your future? What would you do if you left my company?"

"Return to Gilead," I said without hesitation.

"Where you would die of boredom within a month. You can never be happy on Gilead, Del. You are an artist in the arena. Like all true artists, you must practice your art or cease to be a man. Herding *trettles* in a muddy farmyard is not for you."

"There's a woman I love on Gilead."

"No. There was a girl you once loved, long ago. Now you love a memory. This makes for a very pleasant romance, provided you never see the girl again and have your sweet dreams shattered. Think of how much you have changed in your years on Tarquin VII, Del," he said, silencing my reply with a wave of his hand, "since the day I saved you from the mines of Kepler, or a worse servitude on Barbary. You came here as a boy, and now you are a man and a warrior. A great warrior. Can you really believe that this girl has

not changed as much as you? You were not of Gilead
to begin with—"

"How do you know that?" I broke in. This was
something I had never spoken of to anyone.

"Simply by looking at you. No man of Gilead has
your coloring or features and certainly not your
agility. They're a slow-moving, earnest breed. Utterly
unfit for the arena. Surely you must have realized
that."

"I always knew I was different. On the day I was
seized by the slavers I learned that I had come to
Gilead in a small driveship. I was a foundling."

Raphanus' attention picked up. "And what of your
origin? Do you know anything of that?"

I drew the scrap of paper from an amulet around my
neck, where I always carried it, and passed it to him.
He studied it, handed it back, and said, "Malellan. Of
course."

"Do you know anything about Malellans,
Raphanus? Are any of my people on Tarquin?"

"I've only seen one true Malellan in my life. He
defeated one of my great champions, Haakmat."

A vague memory stirred within me. I had heard that
name before, long ago. I pressed Raphanus for more
information, and as he spoke I remembered the
incident related by Loripes on the day of my arrival.

"What happened to this Malellan? Can I meet
him?"

Raphanus shook his head. "He won his freedom
during that tournament season and left to seek his
home. He's not been seen since."

"How far is his home?"

"Quite far. No one is really certain, Del. It lies in a
part of the galaxy that has never been explored, and
the charts are poor. The whole area is infested with
Rinn. I suppose they got him."

"They won't get me."

Raphanus laughed softly. "Have you forgotten your little girl on Gilead so quickly?"

"No. I'll go back for her, and then we'll find my own people."

"And how will you do this? Forgive my curiosity, but I wonder how you'll purchase a driveship, staff it, and equip it for a voyage that may last a lifetime."

"I have my winnings," I said.

"Barely enough to buy passage to Gilead, if you should find a ship bound there."

"I'll win more."

"I'm sure you will, if you stay with my company. If you leave . . . ." Raphanus spread his hands helplessly and shook his head. "There's not much a warrior can do when he leaves the arena, Del."

"The noble families think well of me."

"Of course they do. You're a celebrity. When you come to their tables, your fame comes with you. But they have very little to offer you beyond a good dinner, some flattery, and a few trinkets. Ever since the abolition of politics on Tarquin VII, the nobles have had no need for bodyguards or bullies."

"What are politics, Raphanus? I've seen the word and heard it used, but the meaning has never been clear to me."

Raphanus, with an expression of disgust, raised the ball of scent to his nostrils. "Politics," he said carefully, as if reciting, "is an Old Earth aberration which causes people to complicate the simplest things in life to such a degree that—"

"Raphanus, this is the sort of thing I read in the books. I want to know what a politic is."

He laughed softly, and composed himself for an answer. "Very well. I'll give you an example." He took two forks from the table, impaled a piece of fruit with one, and laid them down end to end. "Now, imagine that this empty fork is you, the one bearing the fruit is another person."

"Who?"

"It makes absolutely no difference, Del. What matters is that the other person has something and wants to keep it. You have nothing and want what the other person has."

"Then I'll demand it, and if he doesn't give it to me, we'll fight, and I'll take it. Is that politics?" I felt a bit let down.

"No, no, no," Raphanus said impatiently. "*This* is politics." He picked up a third fork, transferred the fruit to it, and ate the morsel with exaggerated relish. Wiping his lips, he said, "The one who has something loses it, and the one who has nothing gains nothing, even though they fight and perhaps die in the struggle. It is the third man, the one who does no fighting at all, who takes the prize. That is politics, Del. And this is a politician," he said, dangling the third fork. "And we still have them among us, though now they go by other names."

"Politics is very stupid, unless one is a politician," I said, and Raphanus laughed aloud. "Well, isn't it?" I demanded.

"What the people of Old Earth never learned, and the men of Tarquin accepted grudgingly only after two centuries of unrest, you grasp in seconds. Del, I've made you a famous warrior, and now I've turned you into a philosopher. What more can you ask of me?"

"Freedom," I said quickly.

"Oh, dear. We're back to that," he said, and his face fell. "It will come soon, I promise you that, but you simply aren't ready for it now, Del. Your earnings would enable you to live decently here on Tarquin VII, and you could always make something extra as a trainer—you're welcome to stay here in that capacity, it goes without saying—but intersystem flight is extraordinarily expensive. If you're serious about returning to Gilead and then setting out to seek Malella, you'll need a hundred times what you have now."

I felt as if a prize had been snatched away from my very fingertips. It had taken me five tournament seasons to build my winnings to their present amount, and here was Raphanus telling me I'd need a hundred times as much. Five hundred tournament seasons. I was lucky to have lasted five, and if no human or humanoid opponent stopped me, time would force me out after twenty. I slumped forward and buried my face in my hands.

"What's wrong, Del?" Raphanus asked gently.

I looked up. "How can you ask that? You've just told me that I'll always be a prisoner. I may get back to Gilead, but I'll never be able to learn who I am or where I came from. I'll always be wondering . . . and so will Cassie."

"I had no intention of disappointing you. You need a great deal, true, but you can acquire it."

"How?"

"There are many ways. Have some more wine, Del," he said, reaching for the decanter. "This is really an excellent—"

"Raphanus, how can I make enough to go home?"

He sipped his wine and leaned back. "Now that the tournament season is ended on Tarquin, I am at liberty to consider challenges from Otherworlders. They come infrequently, because few care to face trained Tarquinians, and fewer still would challenge the company of Raphanus. And, as I mentioned, the cost of transporting an entire fighting squad, with their equipment, trainers, and so forth, is staggering.

Nevertheless, for various reasons, the other—"

"Raphanus, have we been challenged?" I cried.

"I'm coming to that, Del." He sipped his wine once more, set it aside, and withdrew a message from his tunic. "I've heard from the thanes of the Skeggjatt system. They seem to be arranging a festival on one of their planets, and it calls for days of battle between their champions and others. They have asked me to send a group of my best men. They offer a good price, and the participants can win large amounts. Enough, perhaps, to meet your needs."

"Send me."

"Don't be hasty, Del. The tournament will be with sword and shield only, and the sword is not your best weapon. You'd need intensive training."

"I'll train. Send me, Raphanus."

He agreed to consider me for the Skeggjatt squad, and that night I slept well and dreamed often of Gilead and Cassie and the unknown planet of my forebears. I still had a lot of fighting before me, but now my goal was clearer than ever, and my freedom to pursue it was in sight.

10. *The Skeggjatt tournament; dismemberment and death.*

For a month, I practiced with sword and shield every day and late into the night, and when the squad was picked for the Skeggjatt tournament, I was named among them. We left early one morning in a lean, trim, high-drive intersystem cruiser, one of the Third Stage models. The accommodations were austere and the ship crowded, but it made the long voyage in a scant three weeks.

The festival planet was a rocky, windswept place with long nights and short days of pale, chill light, a far cry from Tarquin VII. As if to compensate for their grim surroundings, the Skeggjatts feasted continuously in their halls, large wooden buildings brightly painted and fantastically carved, with a roaring fire in the center sending out heat in welcome waves and striking gleams of light from the arms that hung on all the walls. For a week we trained by day and feasted by night, and during the feasts a harpist regaled us with ancient tales of the Skeggjatt races of Old Earth: of warriors and warrior maidens, of ettins and dragons and firedrakes and giants, of one-eyed gods who fought with thunderbolts, of armored virgins on winged, white steeds who carried fallen heroes to a place of eternal feasting by night and battle by day, of the great tree that supports the universe and the frost wolf that gnaws at its roots, of evil things that dwell in sunken caves and burrow among encrusted mounds of ancient treasure buried by forgotten races from the dawn of time. I found it hard to think of those days among the Skeggjatts without falling into something like their battle-speech, a long-winded boasting system that turned every simple utterance into a recitation.

It didn't take much to get them started. One night in the drinking hall one of our squad asked Hnaggr, a hulking, squint-eyed brute with a twisted scar down one side of his face, where he had obtained his sword. I'm sure he was only making polite conversation, but Hnaggr was off on a boast: "Know it well, Otherworlder, that this is the very sword forged by the three-armed swordsmith of the giants of eld, Tok the Firethief, with living flame snatched from the heart of a dying star. With this same blade did Skorri

Singleslash, tamer of ettins and sole guardian of the dark gate, slay the gray host in the Three Battles of the Hill of Broken Bones, when Xandashal Rune-Reader led an army of gibbering ghosts against the stronghold of the sleeping gods. In the mighty hand of Ruri, son of Skorri Singleslash, did this sword vanquish the firedrakes of Gaz, and with one stroke hew down the pillar upholding the Bridge of Shadow. And now this blade, true battle-friend, hangs by the side of Hnaggr, awaiting its time to flash in blood and glory in the thick of battle, creating legends for the sons of Hnaggr to sing in feasts to come."

A respectful silence followed, then another Skeggjatt rose and said, "Glorious indeed is the legend of Hnaggr's blade, but hear now of the bright bloodletter that I, Elgi, bear at my right hand to cleave a battle-path through all who stand before me. For this is the blade of Laef, the Seven-Lived, chosen champion of the realm of the Blue God, wielded in furious battle . . . ." And so on.

I didn't hear the rest of Elgi's speech, because I turned to Sagro, one of the Tarquinians, and asked, "What are they talking about, Sagro?"

"Sword legends. It's a big thing with the Skeggjatts at tournament time. That's how they build up their confidence, I suppose," he said, his voice faintly suggesting contempt.

"Is it true?"

"Of course not. They buy their swords in lots from Iboki III."

"Then why all this boasting?"

"I told you. It builds their confidence. Personally, I prefer our way."

I didn't understand what he meant by that and assumed that he was contrasting Skeggjatt boasting unfavorably with the taciturnity of our warriors. This sort of talk was never heard on Tarquin. We all knew that if a man was good in the arena, he didn't have to talk about it, and if he wasn't no amount of talk would help. But the Skeggjatts loved it.

In spite of the surrounding bluster, I thrilled to these tales, so different from the sunny legends of ancient Tarquin and the grim parables of Gilead, and was pleased to learn that our forthcoming festival was a re-enactment of the old legends. By means of complicated instruments which I did not understand and my hosts did not bother to explain, the people of Urdur, Verdandi, and Skuld, the three inhabited planets of the Skeggjatt system, would participate visually in all the events here on Vigrid, the battle planet, where the great events of their legend were brought to life in festival years. It amazed me to learn that a man on one planet could watch the events on another, and completely overwhelmed me to be told that men could also speak from planet to planet. I had heard of none of these miracles on Gilead, and the few machines I had seen on Tarquin were used for straightforward practical tasks, such as digging up the ground, cleaning the arena, and transporting nobles to and from the tournaments. I had no real grasp of the complexity of a driveship and looked upon it simply as a bigger and faster version of the simple land vehicles common on Tarquin. It became clear to me that Raphanus had held back many things in the process of educating me, and I resolved to broaden the scope of my studies once I returned. It unsettled me to learn that I, who knew so much about the arts of the arena, knew so little about any but the most trivial things outside it.

Our week passed, and the day of battle came. As we armed and gathered, a strange feeling—more accurately, an absence of accustomed feeling—came

over me, and I looked upon the coming battle as I had
never looked on a battle before. I felt no eagerness to
face my opponent, no desire to maneuver our match to
a peak of perfection before ending it with a single
swift slash or a precise thrust; I wanted only to cast
aside my arms and armor and flee from the deadly
challenge. Pride and shame combined to keep me
steady, but inwardly I was in turmoil. This was the
greatest opportunity of my fighting career, and I was
afraid for the first time in my life. I was so concerned
with my own disturbed state that although I did not
notice it at once, I soon grew aware of an unrest among
the other members of our squad. These men, ordinarily
so silent and solitary in the last hours before combat,
were clustering together like children, talking
excitedly, gesturing wildly and extravagantly in a way
to match their loud speeches. Sagro, the leader of our
band, was sitting apart from the others, sharpening his
sword and staring into the fire. I approached him, and
he paid me no notice when I sat down beside him.

"Sagro, what's wrong with us?" I asked him. "I see
it in the others, and I feel it in myself. Something is
different."

He did not look at me, but sighted along his blade,
turning it in the firelight. "We've been betrayed, Del.
That's what's different."

"How? I . . . . I don't . . . ."

"Raphanus sent us here to die."

"He'd never do that, Sagro. We're his best men."

"Right. And he was offered a good price to send his
best fighters here without fighting-scent, so the
Skeggjatt champions could look like heroes to their
people by cutting us to pieces."

I shook my head in confusion. "Wait. I don't
understand, Sagro. What's fighting-scent?"

He looked at me, and I saw genuine sympathy and

sorrow in those pale eyes that gleamed out of his flat, scarred face. "You poor kid. Didn't Loripes ever tell you?" I looked at him blankly, and he went on. "Every time we marched to the arena, we wore tunics steeped in fighting-scent. I don't know what it is or where it comes from, but it works. It soaks into a man and for a time, it changes him. His reflexes are quicker. He's less aware of pain, and he doesn't know fear. All the companies use it, but Raphanus always had the best stuff. That's why we always did so well."

"Then . . . ," and I paused to swallow before asking, "I'm not really a great warrior?"

"Maybe none of us are, Del. I don't know. We'll soon find out."

I was shattered. Five years of pride and victory crumbled in an instant at Sagro's revelation and left me with nothing but a residue of fear and the humiliation of having been an incredible fool. I did not hate Raphanus for his treachery or Loripes for his silent deception. I gave them no thought at all. The only thing in my mind was the bleak certainty that despite the shield and helmet I wore and the bright blade that hung at my side, I was going into battle unarmed, stripped of my strongest weapon, my confidence. I had come so close to freedom . . .. and now it was all over.

But not a man of Sagro's squad broke. We marched off to battle without a sign of weakness or fear, and there on the wind-scoured, rain-pelted highlands of Vigrid I saw my companions fall one by one under the swords and axes of the great, roaring Skeggjatts. I still had my speed and my agility, and I eluded a hundred blows that would have split me from crown to crotch, but the Skeggjatts were too many for me. One glancing blow carried off my helmet. My shield was hacked away, and I was left with only the boss to cover my

knuckles. I flung it into one snarling face, set my back
to a rock, and waited for them to close in and end it. It
was over quickly. One blow severed my sword hand at
the wrist, and as I clutched at the stump, a second
blow on the head sent me sprawling in the bloody mud
at the feet of my enemies.

I lay on my back. After a time I opened my eyes and
looked up at the black sky, torn by violent streaks of
lightning. I felt nothing, and wondered if I was still
alive. Far above, in the sudden glare of the lightning, I
saw faint, white specks moving over the battlefield. I
closed my eyes, and when I opened them again the
white specks had grown to horses, great, winged
steeds each bearing a figure in armor. They circled
low over the wreck of battle, those great, white wings
rising and falling in a slow rhythm of awesome
majesty. One of the figures in armor pointed to me and
sounded a note of inexpressible beauty on a horn
raised to her lips. It was the warrior maidens, the
choosers of the slain, and they had come for me. I was
indeed dead. I closed my eyes and plunged into
blackness.

11. *Dr. Hjalti furthers my education; the prospect of my return to Gilead.*

I opened my eyes to a cool, blue world. All around
me was blue, walls and ceiling and the firm but
comfortable bed on which I lay propped in a half-
sitting position. My sword arm was wrapped from
elbow to wrist in a blue bandage, and below that
bandage was my hand, my own hand, the very same
hand I had seen struck from my arm just before I died.

I made a tight fist. I shot my fingers out, flexed them, wriggled them, and knew beyond all doubt that my hand was restored to me as good as ever. I raised it high and let out a wild shout of joy, and my head nearly split open with a sudden jolt of pain. So I was alive. Only the living could feel a pain like that.

I lay back, gasping, eyes closed. Then I heard a soft rustling noise at my side and felt a cold touch on my forehead. I pictured the beautiful warrior maiden standing over me, looking down with silent admiration at her chosen hero, and I smiled and sighed. A flat, metallic voice said, "If you experience discomfort, please describe."

I opened my eyes and shut them again at once. No warrior maiden stood by my bed. I looked once more and saw a square, gleaming object with a blue band painted around it just about where a human would have a chest. But this was not like any human I had ever seen. It had four projecting eyes that moved independently of one another. Two of them were looking at me. It had altogether too many arms, bristling out of the front, top, and both sides. One was still on my forehead, two were smoothing the bedclothes, two were inspecting my bandaged arm, and the rest were up to some obscure business of their own. It looked like nothing I had ever seen, or even imagined, but it acted quite solicitously. It spoke again.

"Repeat: if you experience discomfort, please describe."

"My head hurts," I said.

Two more arms joined the one on my forehead. I felt the bandage loosen, then a pleasing cool sensation spread over my scalp and all pain vanished.

"Discomfort removed. Please verify," the thing said.

"It doesn't hurt any more. Thank you," I said.

"Gratitude unnecessary. Please enumerate remaining discomforts."

"Who are you? Where am I?"

The little object clicked several times, buzzed, and said, "Repeat: please enumerate remaining discomforts."

"I'm thirsty, if that's what you want to know."

He clicked a few more times, hummed softly, gurgled somewhere inside, and one of the arms emerged from his belly holding a cup of pinkish liquid, which he extended to me. I pushed it aside.

"I don't want to drink your blood," I said.

He went through an elaborate sequence of clicks, hums, buzzes, and clatters, was silent for a moment, then said, "Misunderstanding. Surgical EXU does not contain blood."

"Oh, no? What's that?" I asked, pointing at the cup.

"High-nutritional analgesic solution, formula 3673."

"It's not blood?"

"Surgical EXU does not contain blood. Only supplementary and emergency units contain blood."

"Is that your name, Surgical EXU?"

"Affirm."

"Why don't you contain blood? Everybody contains blood."

After a bit of noise, he said, "*Everybody* refers to life forms, usually human or humanoid. Surgical EXU is not a life form, therefore terminology is inappropriate. Please drink."

"You're not human," I said. Somehow, I found the knowledge reassuring.

"No, of course he's not human," said a genuine human voice, and a tall, light-haired man dressed in blue appeared beside the square object. "Report," he said to it, and the thing clicked and whirred and spat

out a long tongue of some thin material with marks on
it. The man took it, studied it for a moment, and said,
"Dismissed. Remain in readiness." Surgical EXU
wheeled noiselessly out the door.

"Your wounds are healing very well," the man said
to me, after an inspection of my hand and head. "We
found you just in time. You lost a great deal of blood,
you know."

"I lost my *hand*."

"Oh, that's no problem. We've had plenty of
experience in limb replacement."

"Those women on the white horses—did they bring
me here?" I asked.

He checked a tag on my wrist. "You were brought in
by Field Unit 6. Yes, that's one of the flying units."

"I thought they only took fallen heroes to the place
of eternal feasting and battle."

He looked at me strangely, then laughed. "I'm glad
to see you haven't lost your sense of humor. For a
moment, I thought you were serious."

I had, of course, been deadly serious; but not
wanting to look foolish, I laughed along with him. He
went on. "It's not very practical, but the directors of
the games insist that we do it that way. They claim
that it would destroy the effect if the audience should
see ordinary ambulance units swooping down on the
battlefield. I suppose they're right. They charge the
people to see the old myths, so they have to keep
things as authentic as possible. In any event, we've
modified the units to fit inside a craft shaped like a
horse and dressed the attendants like valkyries. The
poor fellows are always being teased about it."

The doctor, whose name was Hjalti, was a pleasant
and talkative young man. After that first meeting, he
came to visit me nearly every day, often bringing other
doctors with him to study the results of the hand graft

performed by Surgical EXU under his direction. He
was very proud of it. One day he entered in the
company of a very tall, very thin man, white-haired
and solemn of expression, whom he announced as
Master of Surgeons Ingjald-Kolsson. Hjalti seemed
awed by the older man and spoke very little in his
presence. He stayed a few steps behind him as they
entered and hovered off to one side during their entire
visit.

Ingjald-Kolsson said nothing to me during his
examination, treating me as if I were no more than an
interesting piece of meat made available for his
inspection or a curious example of craftsmanship
worth looking over. He listened to my heartbeat,
studied my charts, then lifted my arm and examined
the scar of the graft closely, uttering occasional low
sounds of approval. Finished, he dropped my arm and
looked at Hjalti and then at me with ferocious,
challenging eyes. He began to speak, but not to us; he
seemed to be speaking over our heads, to some
invisible audience.

"The Otherworlders label us barbarians because we
continue the tournaments, but this is proof of their
small minds and lack of vision. Only because of the
tournaments have we reached our present heights of
civilization. In the past seven years, working
exclusively with training casualties, our staff has
perfected eight new limb-graft techniques. If not for
the tournaments, this young man's life and his hand
could never have been saved," he said.

"The Otherworlders speak only of the men who
die," Hjalti said. "They condemn the tournament for
this reason."

"And how absurd of them to do so. True, men die in
the tournaments, but they die gloriously, in the ritual
of an ancient tradition. They do not age and weaken

and rot away by slow degrees like a dying oak, to end their lives in decay; they blaze brightly and glow ferociously for a moment of magnificence, and if they die, their deaths serve others." Ingjald-Kolsson lowered his gaze and fixed his blazing eyes on mine. He pointed a gaunt finger at me, and I involuntarily shrank down into the bed. "You, young warrior! When you hear us called barbarians, show the foolish accusers your hand! Tell them what I say. Tell them how civilized the Skeggjatts are!"

He turned and strode off on long legs and left me thinking how fortunate I was to be in the care of a man like Hjalti and a robot like Surgical EXU. I tried to learn something about the Master of Surgeons from Hjalti, but he would say nothing. I think he was terrified of the old man, and I could understand his feelings perfectly. I shared them.

Whenever Hjalti was free, he came to my room, and we talked for hours on end about all manner of things. I preferred to have him do most of the talking, because he knew so much that I didn't, and I wanted to learn. But since he seemed as interested in my story as I was in his knowledge, I spent about as much time talking as I did listening, and my stay passed quickly. On the eve of my discharge, Hjalti asked me what I planned to do.

"I guess I'll go back to Tarquin VII," I said.

"Why? Do you like the warrior life so much?"

"No, not any more, not since I've had time to think about it. But until Raphanus gives me my freedom, I have no choice."

"But you're free now, Del. Hasn't anyone told you?"

"Free!?"

"Of course. Freedom for all survivors is the first law of the festival. I thought you knew that," Hjalti said.

"No, I knew nothing. I never expected . . . . Can I go anywhere I want?"

"You'll have to stop at the festival administration center to collect your prize, but after that, you're free to go where you choose."

"How could I win prize money? I lost, Hjalti. I was cut down. Dismembered."

"You were the last of your band to fall, and you fought well. The watchers voted you an award."

"Then I can go back to Gilead!" I shouted exultantly.

Hjalti's expression clouded. "You're free to try, Del, but don't get your hopes too high. There's seldom any traffic out that way. You said yourself that the only driveships you ever saw on Gilead were your own little craft and the Daltrescan slaver. There's no trade out there, and it's too close to the Rinn for most people. You may be a long time getting there."

"At least now I'm free to try. I'll find a way. Thank you for everything, Hjalti. I've learned a lot."

"It was a pleasure meeting you, Del. Most of the men I work on are hardened cutthroats. They can't wait to recover so they can get back to fighting. It seems to be the only thing men care about in the galaxy these days," Hjalti said sadly.

"Not on Gilead," I corrected him. "I never saw a fight on Gilead or heard an angry word spoken."

He placed a firm hand on my shoulder. "All the more reason to return to Gilead, then, and never leave. The galaxy's a filthy place, Del. Half the driveships in space are run by slavers or pirates, and half the systems are devoted to tournaments like the ones on Tarquin VII or festivals like ours. Sometimes it seems as though the Bloody Centuries have traveled from Old Earth with us. Five centuries of progress, and most of us are still wallowing in barbarity. Even my own people, Del. We have the best hospitals of all the neighboring systems, the best schools, beautiful cities . . . and yet we have our decennial festival of the old gods, when we gather to watch men cut one another to pieces. And then we put a dozen of the survivors back together and boast about how civilized we are. Maybe we're all mad, Del. If you can find sanity on Gilead or anywhere else, never give it up."

"I won't, Hjalti," I assured him.

We shook hands firmly, and I left. I've often wondered if Hjalti ever became Master of Surgeons. I hope he did.

12. *I sign on the 'Antap.'*

I was treated well at the festival administration center, a baffling complex of tall, five-sided buildings on Verdandi, the largest and most distant planet of the Skeggjatt system. For all their numerous differences from the Tarquinians, the Skeggjatts shared their attitude toward a good loser, and this made things much easier for me. Without the cooperation I was given, I could never have found my way from bureau to bureau in that maze of busy buildings, much less have coped with the dozens of forms thrust at me. The Skeggjatts were a conscientious people. They did not hand a man his reward and then forget him. I was outfitted, fed, and closely questioned about my plans for the future. One high official tried very hard to sign me up as a trainer in his brother's combat academy—they had them on Verdandi, too, and the work was considerably easier, since their festivals occurred only at ten-year intervals—but I had had enough of that. I kept telling them that all I wanted to do was get back to Gilead, and they kept telling me that no driveship had gone to Gilead within the memory of anyone on Verdandi. I went through this routine every day for many days, and it grew quite depressing. But I wasn't going to give up.

One day I was summoned to the Office of Reassignments at an unusually early hour. I entered and greeted the assistant, an old friend of mine by this time, and he returned my greeting with a broad smile. Thrain was not a man for smiling without good cause, so I knew he had encouraging news.

"I think I've got something for you, Del," he said, ushering me to a small meeting-room. "There's a pilgrim ship going out to the Beckley system, and they need guards. Beckley's in the right direction, and on a pilgrim planet you may meet people who want to go on to Gilead."

"How close is the Beckley system to Gilead?" I asked.

"Well, it's a lot closer than you are now. Maybe a quarter of the way there. It looks to me as though this is what you've been waiting for."

"Maybe. What does a driveship guard do, Thrain?"

He made a casual gesture and said, "Most of the time he does nothing. If the ship is attacked, he fights. The pay is good."

"Who's going to attack a driveship?"

"Slavers, pirates, outlaws . . . maybe the Rinn, although they haven't been active in recent years. Nothing you couldn't handle, Del."

That was sheer flattery, but I let it pass. I knew how anxious Thrain was to find a ship for me and get me off his hands. Still, this sounded good. It certainly beat waiting here on Verdandi with nothing to do, and it was a job I was qualified for. I had promised myself that no matter how bad things got, I'd never again go into combat for the vicarious pleasure of others, and since I was trained for nothing else, my possibilities for employment were limited. Here was work for which I was suited, and honest work, too. I'd be protecting good people and at the same time be moving closer to Gilead and Cassie.

We entered the meeting-room, and Thrain introduced me to the commander of the driveship *Antap*. His appearance was not one to fill a man with confidence. He looked to me more like one of the villainous brigands I was being hired to protect against than a man who'd be a father to his crew and a shepherd of pilgrims. But as we talked, I grew to like him. He was blunt and honest, and he hid nothing.

"My name's Voit," he said, extending a strong, stubby-fingered hand. "Are you the one wants to be a guard on the *Antap*?"

"I am."

"Your records are good. I thought I'd be seeing a man twice your size," he said gruffly.

"I'm still growing. I was big enough for the arena."

"He was twice proclaimed a Champion of the People on Tarquin VII, you know," Thrain pointed out.

"I saw his records. I'll be straight with you," Voit said to me, leaning forward over the table, as if about to reveal great confidences. "It will be a rotten trip. We're packing two hundred pilgrims, Scarabees, every one of them as crazy as a *streefrit*. They're on their way to some galactic convention of fanatics. Going to sing and holler and carry on and try to convince each other that the truth is their own private property and there's no hope for the poor fool who sees things another way from theirs. It's a big show, that convention, organized by swindlers and patronized by lunatics. I hate to dirty a good ship with the likes of them, and most guards would rather sign on for a four-year cruise with the Daltrescans than set foot on a pilgrim ship, but it's good business. The lunatics and swindlers make up half the galaxy, and they have plenty to spend. I'm offering double wages." He glared at Thrain for verification. "That's right, isn't it? Tell him."

"It's true, Del. Double wages."

"There's another thing," Voit said. "The *Antap*'s a good ship, but she's no high-drive, intersystem cruiser. It'll be a long trip to Beckley, and if anyone attacks us, there's no hope of outrunning them. We'll have to fight, and the Scarabees will be no help to us."

"I understand," I said.

"We may meet Rinn out there, you know."

"If we do, we do. I want to get to Gilead, and Beckley is on the way. If I have to fight Rinn to get there, I'll fight them."

Voit studied me for a moment, nodded once, and said to Thrain, "He'll do. Sign him on, Thrain." He rose and went to the door, where he turned to me. "We leave in three days. Be at the port tomorrow, Berth 71, to help with loading."

"Right," I said.

"And from now on, call me 'Commander Voit,' you hear?" he roared.

"Yes, sir, Commander Voit," I said.

I signed on the *Antap* under my old name, Del Whitby. It felt good to shed all those mouthfilling Tarquinian titles I had been dragging around with me. I was becoming myself again.

13. *I meet Grax and learn a new skill; Poeites and Lovecrafters.*

The loading was routine, and when the pilgrims

began to board I looked them over and steeled myself for a boring voyage. They were Scarabees of the Poe Rite, with a few Lovecrafters; a pale and timid lot who walked softly, with downcast eyes, spoke infrequently, in low voices, to one another and not at all to the crew. We might have been invisible for all the notice they paid to us. It didn't matter to me. Some of the crew members and other guards were looking over the women, but I was only interested in getting under way and coming a step closer to Cassie. Most of the Scarabee women were homely, anyway.

We left on schedule, and once beyond the Skeggjatt system we went into drive. It was a queer sensation, that transition from sub-lightspeed into the silent, dimensionless, drive range, and I never did grow accustomed to it. I always had the feeling that for those split seconds of the changeover I simply ceased to be and could never convince myself that I'd come out of it intact and in the right dimension.

I bunked and shared my watch with a fellow named Grax, a lean, rangy, windburned gunner from one of the inner systems. He was only a few years older than I, but he had traveled far and had a stock of tall tales that filled the quiet hours of our watch. One night, as we strapped on our pistols to go on duty, I caught him studying me covertly.

"What's the matter, Grax?" I asked.

"Nothing," he said, waving off my question.

Later on, after we had eaten and reported to our stations, I found out what was on his mind. Grax couldn't hold his questions back for long.

"Del, I just got to ask you something," he said awkwardly. "Now, don't you answer if you don't want to, but this is bothering me."

"Sure. What is it?"

"Who ever taught you to wear your pistols like

that?" he asked, pointing to the pistols that swung, loosely holstered, from my belt.

"My trainer, back on Tarquin VII."

He shook his head in disbelief. "You mean you went into the arena to fight like *that?*"

"Oh, no. We carried our weapons in our hands."

"I never heard of that style. How'd you fight?"

"They'd send us into a tracking maze. The spectators could see the warriors, but we couldn't see each other. We'd each have one bullet, unless it was a two-on-one or a three-on-one. Then the solo would have one bullet for each opponent, and they'd each have one. The trick was to make the other man waste his shot. You had to be accurate."

Grax nodded appreciatively. "That's pretty good, but it won't help you much if we run into trouble. If we're boarded, it's all a matter of speed. You don't know how much firepower the other man's carrying, and it don't pay to wait around and find out. You got to be accurate, but you got to be fast, too. Here, let me show you something. First unload."

We emptied our pistols, and Grax had me stand facing him about arm's length apart. We folded our arms, and he told me to call the signal to draw.

"Draw!" I cried, and before my fingers closed on the pistol butts both of Grax's barrels were pointing at my chest. We tried it again and still again, and he beat me every time. The pistols seemed almost to leap into his hands as he reached down. I confessed my amazement. I had always considered myself—and been so considered by others—to be fast and agile, but Grax made me feel like an old *bromblugg* stuck belly-deep in a swamp.

"It's just practice, Del," he said. "I've been doing this since I was five years old. You just got to work at it. And before you start, make sure you got your pistols on properly."

"Where'd you learn this, Grax?"

"My Uncle George taught me. He knew all about Old Earth. He told me that during the Bloody Centuries, everybody carried a gun, and they were good with them, too. They had to be."

He showed me how to lower my holsters to comfortable reach and tie them tight to my legs for steadiness. We tried once again, and I did better. From then on, I spent most of my time in practice.

I really would have preferred to do some studying and learn about all the things Dr. Hjalti had brought to my attention during our long conversations. After all, I had been away from Gilead now for nearly five years and had seen more of the galaxy than anyone on that entire planet, and yet I was returning with very little knowledge beyond the arts of the arena, which were not going to get me very far once I arrived home. During his time at the hospital, patching up the survivors of the festivals and the training casualties, Hjalti had met men from hundreds of systems, and he spoke casually to me of sights and wonders that had my imagination spinning. I wanted to know more, to learn everything I could about the busy galaxy of which my home world was such a tiny, isolated part. But there wasn't much to study aboard the *Antap* except the pilgrims, and they were a chilling lot to talk to. So I practiced my draw, and became almost as fast as Grax in a short time.

I did try to talk with the pilgrims once in a while, but it was not very rewarding. They were Neo-Hoffmanite Reformed Galactic Scarabees of the Poe Rite, with a few Poe-Lovecrafters mixed in. All I had to do was ask them one simple question and they were off on a long recitation from the Revelations of Poe, a mystic who flourished in the East American city-state

of Baltimore-Maryland in the early years of the
Bloody Centuries. They'd go on about maelstroms and
pendulums and ravens for the better part of a watch
and still never make clear just what they were trying
to say. The Lovecrafters were worse. They recited
from Poe and then went on to quote the commentaries
of his disciple, Lovecraft of Arkham, and half of what
they said was in no language I had ever heard but it
still made me uncomfortable. Every time I listened to
one of those Lovecrafters I dreamt of ghouls and
demons and tentacled fiends covered with ichor. They
never explained what ichor is, and I'm just as glad. It
sounds nasty. Those Lovecrafters ruined my sleep.

Being in such close contact with the Scarabees got
me to wondering all over again about right and wrong
and what to believe. I had settled down into living by
the Gilead code, more or less, and I had absorbed
enough from Loripes to accept the fact that what the
other fellow believed was none of my affair unless he
happened to be one of the ritual blood-drinkers from
Taluma IV, or a Thanist strangler, or someone like
that. If the Scarabees were happy believing that the
universe was a great whirlpool, I had no objection, but
it didn't seem to make them any better or worse than
anyone else. They had their thieves and their liars, and
while they did no killing aboard the *Antap*, more than
once a Poeite came to blows with a Lovecrafter over a
fine point of interpretation.

14. *An alarm, a mystery, and a wild idea.*

We were about halfway to Beckley when I was
awakened from sleep by the unmistakable sensation of

transition down to sub-lightspeed. I was just drifting off to sleep again when the guard alarm went off.

Grax was tying his holsters down by the time my feet hit the floor. "Hurry up, Del," he said. "This probably means trouble."

It meant trouble, as we soon learned, but not the kind that Grax or I could cope with. The *Antap* had stayed on drive too long without relief, and one of the drive coils had blown.

The rest periods in the sub-lightspeed range were the most dangerous part of any intersystem voyage. At those times a ship was most vulnerable to detection and attack, and fair prey for any cruising pirate, outlaw, or stray Rinn raider.

I never did come to understand all the mechanics involved—not many people did, and even the drive crew and commanders had to stick close to the old manuals and do a lot of guessing, because no one had actually built a new driveship for over a century, and a lot of information was lost. But I knew that, for some reason, a ship on drive couldn't be detected. As far as scanning equipment could tell, it just didn't exist. They couldn't use outside communication, either, and if an emergency came up, a ship had to drop to sub-lightspeed to call for help and take the chance that whoever answered would be friendly. Once a ship was in the sub-lightspeed range, though, it showed up on every scanner in the area, and so the pirates and outlaws cruised the intersystem lanes at just under drive speed, with all scanners operating, and waited for a likely victim to pop into view while they rested their drive coils or sent a message. Then they struck.

Commander Voit explained the situation. We were stuck for at least one full day, while the old drive coil was replaced, and if any complications arose, we might be drifting a good bit longer. All scanners were activated and the guards went on emergency shifts. If an attack came, it would come fast. The usual tactic was for a raider to get a fix on his quarry, jump to lightspeed, and drop back into view as close as possible to the victim. Warning time was usually well under a minute.

Grax and I stood our first long watch, then a second, and then a third, and nothing happened. Commander Voit kept reassuring the Scarabees that we'd be going back to lightspeed any time now, but he didn't say anything like that to the crew. The truth was that he was feeling his way through the repairs and not doing very well, and he knew that every minute we remained here at this speed our danger increased.

On the fourth watch, a ship registered on the scanner. Grax set off the alarms, the guards raced to their defense stations, and we waited for the faint dot to wink out and then reappear seconds later in boarding range.

But the dot remained in sight. It had come up from behind us on a course almost parallel to ours, and it was maintaining a steady speed, closing in slowly. Voit studied the readings, cursed in bewilderment, and threw up his chunky arms.

"That's impossible!" he roared. "It's a driveship. It's got to be hostile, but it's crawling along at a rate that will take it four hours to close with us. No pirate ship does that!"

"Maybe it's not a pirate," I suggested.

"It has to be. The last authorized driveship in this sector completed its run two months ago, and the next one isn't scheduled for nearly a year."

"Could it possibly be a meteoroid, Sir?" a crewman asked.

Voit snorted and pointed to the scanner readings. "No meteoroid ever gave those readings. It's a driveship. It can't be friendly and it doesn't act like a hostile, so what *is* it?"

No one cared to offer any more suggestions. We resumed our watch on the scanner, the other guards remained at defense stations, and we waited. The little point of light grew, and when it came within magnification range we had our first clear look at it.

Grax whistled softly. "That is one old ship, Del. I'll tell you that much. One real old ship."

"How old?"

He studied the screen, frowning in intense concentration. "It looks to me like early Second Stage. See the ports up front? They stopped using ports about midway through the Second Stage. My Uncle George told me all about them. This thing's got to be three hundred years old."

Voit stepped up to the scanner, studied the image, and nodded. "A derelict. That's what she is. Well, she'll be no trouble to us. That's a relief."

He recalled the guards and announced the status of our neighbor. We were sent back to our scanner watch, and as Voit left to resume his repair work, I had a sudden wild idea. I called after him.

"What do you want, Whitby? Make it fast," he said.

"I want to volunteer to board the derelict, Sir."

"You're space-happy. We're not on a souvenir hunt, we're trying to get the drive coil fixed and get ourselves onto Beckley in one piece. Those old hulks are bad luck, anyway. Forget it."

"But the derelict may have something we need—tools or manuals or maybe even a replacement coil."

Voit raised a stubby finger, pointed it at me, wrinkled his brow in hard thought, then poked me in the shoulder and laughed aloud. "That's good thinking. The odds are against it, but there's a chance.

The drive principle is the same, so the parts will fit, if they haven't all been used up centuries ago. And if they have the tools . . . . All right, Whitby, prepare to board. I'll send you and two techs over as soon as she's in range."

"How about Grax, Commander?"

"Can't spare him. Go on, get ready."

15. *I board the 'Phoenix' XXVII and acquire a crew.*

An hour later, when the derelict was within range, I left the *Antap*. I was hoping to find the right equipment to make repairs, as I had told Voit, but I also wanted to see what I could learn aboard the derelict. Here was a chance few men had ever received. I was going to walk into a ship that had been drifting in space for over three centuries, a storehouse of all the old knowledge lost when men began to spread out in the last phase of galactic colonization and scatter themselves so widely among the stars that all the old ties were broken and the old ways forgotten (although I probably didn't think of it quite so clearly at the time). I had another idea in the back of my mind, too, but I wasn't mentioning it to anyone. I was trying not to think of it myself, because it was too crazy. But it stayed there.

The silent trip across the great gulf between the *Antap* and the derelict, *Phoenix XXVII*, was a queasy experience, but nothing like that first step through the atmosphere lock and into the belly of a dead driveship on its way from nowhere to oblivion with a cargo of dry dust. All those tales of the Poeites and Lovecrafters had me properly spooked anyway, and when I entered the control cabin and saw those skeleton hands still on the controls, I almost gave it up right then and there. But I kept reminding myself that this could be *my* ship, my own private transportation through the spaces between here and Gilead, and that gave me all the courage I needed.

The techs went directly to the propulsion room, and I joined them there after checking out the control room for charts and navigation equipment. On the way, I looked in on the stores, and found that there was enough for a long trip, all in good condition. Everything was working out.

The techs were poking around, looking for the spare drive coils that all these old ships carried—the *Antap* would have carried them, too, if Voit hadn't sold the storage space to pilgrims—and not having much luck. They wanted to find what they needed and get out. I stuck close to them and asked questions, and all the answers were encouraging. The internal machinery was still functioning; only the drive mechanism was out. Repairs were needed, and it would take time and a lot of hard work, but this derelict could make drivespeed again. The manuals and the repair equipment were all there. When I heard that, I made up my mind.

One of the techs pulled open a door and let out a yell of delight. Inside a little locker were four spare drive coils, Second Stage standard design, that would fit the *Antap*. They wrestled one out and started back for the atmosphere lock, and as soon as they were safely on their way, I bolted it shut from the inside. When that last bar slid home, I became Commander Whitby of the *Phoenix XXVII*. I was sole owner and operator. And the entire crew. And all the passengers. For just an instant, when I thought of all the lonely months in

space ahead of me, I almost reached out to open the
lock and shoot out after the techs. But then I thought
of Gilead and Cassie, and I knew I had to stay.

I could guess pretty well what Voit was saying about
me back on the *Antap*, but I knew he'd never order me
to return. He was visible enough out there without
sending messages to advertise his whereabouts. He
might curse me out in every language in the galaxy,
but he wasn't going to send me the message. I was
written off for good. I didn't feel bad about leaving
him. The *Antap* would make it to Beckley in one hop
now, with the fresh coil, so I wasn't needed. And I
hadn't collected a single Sput of my wages. We were
even.

I got right to work. The atmosphere in the *Phoenix*
was still secure after all that time, so I stripped off my
suit and went to the propulsion room. My first job was
to get this ship back to drivespeed condition. After that
I'd learn how to aim it. Since I had to learn everything,
one step at a time was plenty.

Those old manuals were so clear and simple that
even I understood what I was doing in a very short
time. I guess they had to be that way, in case an
accident wiped out the crew and the passengers had to
take over on their own. I checked the drive unit from
end to end, spotted the trouble, and dug out the tools
and parts I needed. It would be a long, hard job for
one man, but it could be managed. I felt like singing. I
did sing, for a little while, but the sound of singing
didn't feel right in that old dead ship, and I stopped.

When I was too tired to work any more, I got myself
a meal and stretched out in the commander's berth to
sleep. It wasn't so easy getting to sleep, but I finally
drifted off. When I woke up, the *Antap* was still out
there, a faint silver speck in the distance. I ate a light
meal and got back to work. She was still there when I

looked again, and this time, as I watched, she disappeared. The drive was fixed, and she was on her way. Now I was truly alone.

I didn't think the sight would affect me the way it did. I stood at that port for a long time, cursing myself out for a thousand kinds of fool. It burst upon me with a clarity that nearly tore me open—I'd never be able to repair a driveship if the original crew hadn't been able to do it. And if I did, how could I find my way to Gilead? And what if a pirate or an outlaw ship came along and decided to see if this old crate still carried anything worth stealing? Or suppose a Rinn raider turned up? I had done the craziest, most suicidal thing a man could do: willingly cast myself adrift alone in space. Something horrible was sure to happen to me, and I richly deserved it.

And then, far out where the *Antap* had been, I saw a tiny speck that hadn't been there before. I watched it grow as it approached, and soon I could see that it was one man in a propulsion suit. I waved frantically through the port, ran to unbolt the atmosphere lock, and raced back to the port in time to see my visitor clamp on to the outer door of the lock. When Grax stepped aboard my ship, I don't believe I was ever as glad to see anyone in my life as I was to see him then.

"I figured you might need some help, Del," he said as he climbed out of his suit. "I slipped off the *Antap* just before she went into drive."

"I got myself a ship, Grax. Want to sign on?"

"Can you get her going again?"

"I think so."

"Got enough food?"

"Plenty."

Grax nodded thoughtfully. Under the circumstances, he didn't have much of a choice, but he wasn't one for hasty decisions. At last he said, "Well, I guess I'll stick with you, Del. Let's look her over."

I declared a holiday, then and there, and Grax and I began to explore the *Phoenix* from end to end. We were like a pair of kids with a brand-new surprise plaything, and even the little heaps of dust and bone we found in most of the cabins couldn't keep our spirits down for long. We never did learn what killed the crew and passengers of the *Phoenix,* but it looked to us as though it had been fast and unexpected. We did our best not to think about it.

16. *I begin to learn history; a course for Tricaps; Wroblewski's last message.*

Grax knew something about drive repair, and even a little bit was so much more than I knew that I left the work to him, lending a hand only when he needed it and keeping out of his way the rest of the time. I took to spending most of my waking hours in the control room, learning all I could about the handling of a driveship and the principles of intersystem navigation. When I wasn't studying that, I read everything else I could find, and I learned a lot, far more than I could fit into ten books the size of this one.

The very first book I looked into was the log of the *Phoenix.* I opened it to a page dated 7/21/2373 and read, "A rain of blood falls eternally throughout the galaxy, shed by the barbarous hand of man." That was too close to some of the bad dreams I had had back in the hospital on Vigrid. I put the log aside and turned to other works.

The ship had a good store of sound tapes and visual prisms, and I tried them all, but I concentrated on the books, real Old Earth books, printed on paper, something rare in the galaxy these days. I hadn't seen anything like them since *The Book of The Voyage* on Gilead, and that was centuries old. I learned a lot about life on Old Earth during the Bloody Centuries and the first centuries of galactic travel, but much of what I read was confusing. Politics seemed to be the favorite subject of Old Earth writers, and the books were full of it. The more I read about Old Earth politics, the more I appreciated the definition Raphanus had given me. He said it all, and very simply.

It wasn't only on their definition of politics that the books were vague. They just couldn't seem to agree on the facts. The writers disagreed on the causes of the Sino-African Wars and the Second Holocaust. They all wrote of the Death Fog that wiped out the population of the Atlantic coastal cities in the late Twentieth Century, but some of them called it an industrial accident, while others branded it sabotage or an act of aggression; and those who called it sabotage or aggression couldn't agree on who had planned it, or why. They couldn't even get together on the right name of the man who had changed history and closed down Old Earth forever. That was Wroblewski, and no two historians gave him the same first name.

Sometime in the late Twenty-First Century, Wroblewski invented the stardrive and opened the way to the galaxy. Wroblewski was a Pole, native of a place called Poland on Old Earth. Some books said it was a scientific city somewhere in the United Republics of Russo-China, others identified it as part of the People's Democracy of New Europe, and the rest didn't even try to locate it. As I mentioned, the history of Old Earth, especially during the Bloody Centuries, just isn't very clear. Even three hundred years ago, there wasn't much material left. Old Earth didn't seem to mean much any more, except to historians and scholars, and even they seemed content with hypotheses and guesswork. Nowadays, no one cares at all. It's almost as though the human race is trying to forget its early history, except for the parts that different planets try to recreate in their own societies, each of them labeling their way the true Old Earth tradition and calling all the others fraudulent. But I don't see much point in going into that.

The Wroblewski Drive sent men into galactic space before they had a chance to learn much about their own solar system. There had been a score of Martian expeditions, a disastrous Venus landing, and a few attempts at the other planets, but space exploration was continually being interrupted by war, and after the wars ended the survivors had to start from the beginning again. Old Earth must have been a discouraging place to live. Then the drive was invented, and people lost interest in the planets of their system. With a hundred thousand lightyears of space waiting, a few unexplored planets don't rate much attention. They weren't very inviting, anyway.

There were planets enough for everyone beyond the home system, and they were up for grabs. Men moved faster than laws, and anyone who could scrape together the price of a driveship—or steal one from his government, as Wroblewski did—could hunt out a world of his own and do as he pleased on it. The finding wasn't always easy. All the unmanned space probe projects dissolved when faced with the reality of the drive. Once they could actually go out into space, no one wanted to waste time waiting for the approval of an instrument package. They wanted to go, and risks be damned. The risks were plentiful. There were no reliable charts at all in those days—space looks and acts a lot differently when you're actually out here, and the old charts were usually worse than nothing at all—so navigation was mainly a matter of dead reckoning and good luck. It worked about forty percent of the time. A lot of those early pioneers were drawn into suns or smashed flat on heavy planets that plucked them right out of space and dragged them down to death. Some, like the *Phoenix XXVII*, never touched down at all.

Even now, three centuries later, the charts are skimpy. People have learned that if you can't find them, you can't hit them. At first, they clustered together, like kids taking their time to find their way around a big new house. But after a century they began to feel crowded again, and a second flight began. Some of the settlers stayed put, but the young ones headed out as far and as fast as they could. The Second Stage models could make up to ten lightspeeds, almost four times the speed of the first Wroblewskis. This time the voyagers left no maps behind, no charts, no forwarding addresses, and when they finally touched down they sent back no invitations.

Travel around the galaxy dropped off sharply after that. The driveship industry dwindled, since those who might have used them were already gone. The space academy closed for lack of applicants. The *Phoenix XXVII* must have been one of the last Second Stage ships built and also one of the last to leave on the final exodus.

The more I read, the more I had to think about and the more I wanted to know. I was learning so much all at once that my head felt stuffed to the bursting point, and some of the things were absolutely staggering. For one thing, I had never really grasped the enormous speeds and distances involved in galactic travel. When I actually worked out the distance involved in a casual reference to ten lightspeeds over a six-year trip, I looked at the resulting row of figures goggle-eyed for a full minute, then went through all my calculations again, three more times, until I knew that three-hundred-fifty million million miles, and then some, was correct. The galaxy was unbelievably big. And here was Del Whitby, farmer turned warrior turned driveship guard turned mechanic-navigator-commander of a centuries-old Second Stage relic, looking for a planet unnamed on any of the *Phoenix* charts so I could claim my bride and start searching for an even lesser known pinpoint in infinity. I decided I was absolutely, hopelessly crazy. And having settled that, I went on with my studies. I couldn't help being crazy, but I could do something about being ignorant.

One of the interesting things I learned was that Poe, the great prophet of the Scarabees, wasn't a prophet at all. He was just a writer, something like the bards who bum their way from system to system, earning their passage and their keep by reciting old legends and histories and improvising songs and poems for any occasion. The big difference was that Poe wrote his legends down, and centuries after he was dead, someone took his book and turned it into mystical prophecy. That didn't seem any crazier than what I was doing. It made me feel better.

It was funny, and sometimes a little sad, to read what man used to imagine about the facts of intra-galactic travel when it still seemed a long way off, and even in the early days of the driveships. They all assumed that by the time men could reach the stars they'd be a tidy, disciplined corps of clear-eyed experts, all wearing clean uniforms and saying "sir" to everyone on board, making every move by a book yet to be written in those times but certain to be precise and omniscient in its contents. Things were going to be neat and orderly. So they imagined.

It didn't work out that way at all. Nobody ever got around to writing that handbook of galactic etiquette. There just wasn't time. For a few years after its discovery, the Wroblewski drive was kept secret by the government that ruled Poland. The Old Earth governments used to do things like that and worse, if half the accounts are true. But just before he hijacked a driveship and lit out for the stars, Wroblewski sent his formula to scientists in every nation of Old Earth. Within a year, everyone was building driveships and heading for the big emptiness outside, and within a decade, Old Earth was nothing but a run-down slum of a planet, left to the too-old, too-tired, too-scared, and too-suspicious whose eternal destiny it is to cling to rotting worlds like a fungus. There wasn't much to keep the men of Old Earth at home. For the two centuries before Wroblewski, they had been choking the planet with their own filth, warring over it like rats on a garbage heap, and then covering the ruins with an ugly building, filling the building with people, and starting all over again. Wroblewski opened a door for the men of Old Earth, and they practically trampled one another to get out before some crazy government could slam it shut.

Not that the stars were put into their back pockets. It was still a dangerous venture, as I've said, and a long ride. But at least it was possible for a ship to set out for the far side of the galaxy and get there in less than a lifetime, and that was good enough. Once the lightspeed barrier was broken, there was no stopping them.

But they stopped themselves. That was another false assumption, the idea that once man got his feet off the earth he'd want to do nothing but spend the rest of eternity in star-hopping. They didn't know then what a boring experience an intersystem trip can be—in the moments when it isn't terrifying—and that most people would be sufficiently subdued by their months of alternating boredom and terror to settle down on the first tolerable planet they came to and stay there. What traffic there is now in the galaxy—and there isn't much—is mainly business, at least half of it illegal, with an occasional show of muscle by the professional warmakers of the Expedition for the purpose of impressing any possible Rinn observers. The truth is, most pioneers were looking for peaceful homes, not a lifetime of adventure. When they found what they wanted, they settled down, leaving space travel for those who still had something to hunt for.

For a long time, the pioneers found no company out here in space, and when they finally did, they were a bit disappointed. The other races in the galaxy were pretty much like the men of Old Earth. Whoever put the universe together—the portion of it that holds our galaxy, anyway—seems to have decided that where intelligent beings are concerned, it's best to work out one basic model and stick to it, with minor modifications to suit particular local needs. The only exception I ever encountered was the Crevnites. The pioneers found no overgrown amoebae, no thinking clouds of energy or philosophical vegetables; only a thousand versions of the warm-blooded, viviparous, upright, quadrupedal mammal called man. He came in a variety of sizes, from gangling, spidery Lixians three meters tall, who could scratch their knees without bending over, to scurrying, knee-high Quiplids. One race might have a handy set of tentacles sprouting from their shoulders, or a prehensile tail, or an extra set of thumbs, or webbed feet, but all in all, the races of the galaxy were a homogeneous bunch. In fact, as some venturesome early traveler learned, they were homogeneous enough to interbreed successfully, and did so.

Some of our latter-day philosophers like to think that

it was this final undeniable proof of universal kinship
that put an end to man's age-old habit of warfare, and
maybe they're right, but I have some ideas of my own on
that subject. I'm no philosopher, but I've seen a good bit
of the galaxy and met a lot of different people, and it
seems to me that men have gotten no better, no wiser,
no more loving or forgiving than they ever were.
They're just afraid of being alone. Pasquale Galileo, °
one of the great geniuses of Old Earth, said, "The
eternal silence of these infinite spaces frightens me,"
and it's as true now as it was back in the Renaissance, as
they called the Nineteenth Century on Old Earth. Men
feel the brotherhood of blood more deeply now that it's
thinly spread. They've realized that if they kill too many
of their fellow humans, they might wind up all alone in a
big, unfriendly galaxy, and the thought of that terrifies
them. And the Rinn terrify them even more.

No one knows who or what the Rinn are, but it has
been conclusively established that they don't like
humans, humanoids, or anyone who sides with humans.
That includes the Malellans, my own people, of whom
very little seems to be known or knowable. Perhaps it's
this lack of Malellan history that gave me the initial
impetus to study Old Earth history. Since the *Phoenix*,
I've found other reasons to interest myself in the subject,
but that may have been what started it.

In any event, the Rinn remain a great mystery. The
only humans to penetrate beyond the rim systems (it's
believed that "Rinn" is a corruption of "rim people")
found things out there that they couldn't explain, and

° Scientist and dynamist of the later Caesaro-Etruscan
Empire, inventor of the telescope and author of a book of
maxims entitled *Pasquale's Pen Says*, or *Pasquale's Pansies*,
dealing with the philosophical and theological implications of
an infinite universe.

didn't want to study. The corridors on Clotho and the inscribed wall on Skix are enough to split a human mind wide open. Those planets are quarantined and no one lands on them, not even pirates and outlaw ships. The general opinion is that these planets were Rinn outposts or warning stations, because it was shortly after the first human landings that the Rinn raids began and led to the confrontation of the Great Rinn War. That was about ten years ago, GSC. Things have been quiet since then, with no major engagements, but no one really knows where the Rinn have gone or what they're planning, and all uneasily suspect that the day may come when every human hand will be needed if we're going to save our galaxy.

Whatever the reason, we've stopped killing one another in groups, although we still do it regularly on a small scale, for purposes of popular amusement, as on Tarquin, or racial pride, as on Vigrid. Space is a frontier, and all too often the only law out here is a man with a gun, just as it was in the Bloody Centuries on Old Earth. It's hard to enforce laws on a galactic scale, and no one really tries. The galaxy is too big, too spread-out, too full of places to hide. Communication is skimpy, and the people on one planet don't care all that much about what goes on elsewhere, so long as the Rinn aren't involved. That makes things easier for slavers, pirates, and outlaws, and a lot more dangerous for legitimate space travelers. A man has to carry his own law, and most of us, for some unfathomable reason that might be a lot closer to nostalgia than we care to admit, wear a six-gun on our hip. I carry two, myself, and I'm good with them.

The custom started in the early days of the driveships, when it was discovered, through spectacular experience, that the hand lasers commonly used as a sidearm in the Twenty-First Century caused a reaction in the drive coils that turned a driveship into a tiny supernova. The men of Old Earth could not conceive of taking a voyage unarmed, and the knife, sword, bow, and mace seemed out of place on a driveship, so for a time they were very unhappy. Then some history-minded armorer resurrected the six-gun, and it soon became standard equipment in space and on the ground as well. So there's a purely practical excuse at hand for those who prefer it. But I still think nostalgia has a lot to do with the popularity of the six-gun.

With all my studying and Grax's work, the weeks passed quickly on the *Phoenix XXVII*. By the time Grax was ready for the final adjustments of the drive mechanism, I had mastered enough navigation to chart us a course for Tricaps, a trading outpost where we could sell this relic for the price of a high-drive Stage Three cruiser from the Rinn Expedition. We made the jump to drivespeed without complications and were on our way in earnest. I was heading home, with Grax as my guest.

I've never forgotten the book I read just before we began landing procedure. It was an early space history, and it contained the last recorded words of Wroblewski, received from somewhere in space two years after his departure. Two messages came, about five minutes apart. The first was, "I have given you the key. Use it, or to hell with you all." After a silence, his final words arrived: "To hell with you all anyway."

At the time, I thought it was very funny.

BOOK II: THE VOYAGES OF 'THE RENEGADE'

1. *I meet an unfortunate traveler.*

The arrival of the *Phoenix XXVII* on Tricaps had to be one of the great events of the century on that busy little planet, if only because of the total confusion we caused among the people. They recovered quickly and resumed business as usual, but for a brief time we had them in quite a state.

The root of the trouble was the Tricapet speech pattern. It was very rapid, and while their dialect contained few unfamiliar words or constructions, having been developed for ease of commerce, it was spoken so much faster than anything Grax or I were accustomed to that a communications problem arose. The Tricapets got the impression that we were the descendants of the original crew of the *Phoenix XXVII;* and as soon as this story spread, we were surrounded by space lawyers, a large and powerful class on Tricaps, all offering their services to help us establish our claim to whatever was due us. When we tried to explain the situation, we somehow gave them the impression that we were not the descendants of the crew after all, but their survivors, or perhaps their ghosts. It took a while to get everything settled, but eventually we picked one brisk, skipping, little man to attend to the filing of the necessary papers and arrange the sale of the *Phoenix*. That done, we settled down to our hunt for a new ship.

I guess our appearance caused as much confusion among the Tricapets as our speech did. Both Grax and I wore spectacular old dress uniforms we had found in the lockers of the *Phoenix*. I had discovered a beautiful matched set of presentation pistols, given to Commander Adamson on the day of departure; I had them at my side when I stepped out of the port. We must have looked as if we were stepping out of the past, as well. Our hair was long, and mine was plaited in the Skeggjatt style. We both wore full beards. They were very messy beards, too. The neat little Tricapets never got used to us, though they were unfailingly polite in their quick, impersonal way.

All in all, despite their movement and busyness, the Tricapets were an unexciting bunch to be with, and I was happy to find a trim little Third Stage scoutship with a fifty lightspeed maximum being offered at a price somewhat lower than the amount we expected to get for the *Phoenix*. The craft was made to carry eight—twelve in an emergency—but all it required for operation was one man. Grax wanted to inspect the drive mechanism before making an offer, so he went to work and I spent two days wandering around Commerce City, the capital and business center of Tricaps. Two days was more than enough.

The Tricapets had no concept of enjoyment divorced

from work. Since I didn't understand much about business and wasn't interested in learning, I had very little to do. The big dissipation of these people was *scoof*, which they drank by the mug, black and scalding hot, conducting business between sips. I drank endless mugs of *scoof* in the little shops, soon growing inured to that initial moment of astonished silence caused by my entrance among the sombre-clad Tricapet businessmen but never quite able to relax when, having inspected me and decided that my resplendent uniform and shaggy appearance promised no opportunity for profit, the *scoof*-drinkers resumed their rapid-fire conversations all around me as if I were invisible. I walked the crowded streets and found nothing to divert me. Tarquin and Vigrid had cities crowded with exciting sights, sounds, and colors, but Commerce City was nothing like them. Everything, even the people, seemed gray, and it was all the same, everywhere I went. No street shows or quick-merchants, no pleasure-stalls, no brawling, no off-worlders, nothing but scurrying crowds of identically-dressed Tricapets rushing from one identical building to another, all wearing the identical Tricapet expression of worried intensity.

My feet were sore from aimless walking and my belly was awash with *scoof* when I came upon an apparition. He popped from an outway and stood before me wide-eyed, a ragged old spacebum in a uniform that looked and smelled as if he had put it on for the Rinn Expedition and never taken it off since. His long, black hair was streaked with gray, and his pale face was lined and scarred, but to me, at that time, he was a welcome sight. I seemed no less welcome to his eyes. He hurried up to me and began to talk all at once. His dialect was close to Tarquinian, and I had no difficulty under-standing him.

"By the stars, it's good to see another spaceman! I've

been in this *bzzit's* nest two months, surrounded by these poor, dull space-swindlers, and I'm slowly dying of boredom. Who are you, stranger, and where are you from and where bound?" he rattled off.

"My name's Del Whitby. I just came from the Skeggjatt system, bound for Gilead," I said.

"Gilead?" He looked perplexed and shook his head. "I'm afraid that's one place I've never been. Where is it?"

"I'm hoping to find out."

He thought about that for a time, then burst into laughter. Several passing Tricapets, startled by the unfamiliar sound, glanced at us nervously and stepped aside to avoid us. "So you know where you're going, but you don't know where it is. I like your spirit, Del. I was that way once myself, long ago. I wanted to see it all, go everywhere, experience everything . . . and I have. Believe me, I have." He fell silent, then he looked at me intently and asked, "Are you in a hurry, Del? Have you got time to buy an old spacebum a meal and listen to his stories?"

"I've got time," I said, "and I'm hungry, too. Let's find a good place."

It took a bit of searching, but at last we found a place where we could eat a decent meal without being deafened by the chatter of Tricapets conducting business. My new friend, whose name was Gariv, stowed away a meal that would have fed four hungry men and then, over a bottle of wine, told me the story of his travels—some of it, anyway. The rest came later.

2. Gariv's story, and something more of my own.

Gariv had spent most of his early years in space. His

father was a powerful warlord in the Skorat system, and
Gariv had gone with him on a series of early missions
against the Rinn. At twenty-three, Gariv was married to
Nikkolope, daughter of another powerful warlord, and
for the next few years he spent most of his time at home,
managing affairs for his father and his father-in-law
while they were off in space. In his twenty-sixth year,
word reached him that both men had been killed in a
skirmish with the Rinn, and he was now one of the great
warlords of Skorat VI. For a time Gariv remained at
home, consolidating his power, but the thought of those
unavenged deaths nagged at him, and when he learned
of the Great Rinn Expedition ° that was forming in the

°   The Expedition is the name applied to an autonomous
intersystem military force originally organized to defend the
Old Earth pioneer systems and their allies against the Rinn,
and later redirected to the total destruction of Rinn civilization. The official activities of the Expedition are divided
into three phases, known as the First, Second, and Third
Expeditions.

The First Expedition was commissioned 4/19/2608 GSC
and disbanded shortly after the near-total destruction of the
Rinn Armada in the Battle of the Three Systems, 7/6-28/2617
GSC. This battle is sometimes referred to as The Great Rinn
War, but that term is more accurately applied to the entire
series of campaigns that culminated in the confrontation in
the Three Systems. Veterans of the First Expedition
immediately re-formed into an irregular force which they
named the Second Expedition. Its self-proclaimed mandate
was to seek out, pursue, and destroy all survivors of the Battle
of the Three Systems and to carry the war to the Rinn's home
sector.

Expedition Command was reluctant to recognize the
Second Expedition and did so grudgingly only after two
successful assaults on Rinn survivors; official commissioning
took place 3/3/2619 GSC. Within two years, reports began to
reach Expedition Command of atrocities committed upon

central cluster, a mighty striking force to seek out and
destroy the Rinn raiders forever, he decided to join it.
Leaving the rule of Skorat VI in the hands of his wife,
the faithful Nikkolope, he bid farewell to his son Lemak
and left with a small fleet of battle cruisers to join the
Expedition.

He fought well and distinguished himself in the great
final battle between the two fleets. But when the Rinn
were vanquished and his ships made ready for the long
voyage back to Skorat, his troubles began.

"It wasn't the war that did me in, Del, it was the
homecoming," he said, draining his glass, eyeing the
empty bottle, and looking at me thirstily. I ordered a
fresh bottle. He refilled his glass and went on. "We
smashed the greatest fleet ever assembled in space and
ended the power of the Rinn for all time. I came out of
that last battle a hero, and look at me now—a beggar,
selling his sad past for a meal and a bottle. For ten years
I've been wandering all over the galaxy, trying to get
back home and never making it. I've lost all my ships, all
my men, everything. Once I was only a day out of
Skorat—*one day*, Del!—when we stopped to rest the
drive coils and were boarded by slavers. They dragged
me off to the far side of the galaxy and sold me to the
pyramid builders. I escaped, but it's taken me four years

---

innocent systems by small forces under Second Expedition
field orders, as punitive, retaliatory, or preventive measures.
When conclusive proof of the destruction of Toqal V was
brought to Expedition Command, orders to disband were
issued, effective 6/4/2623 GSC. Little more than half the
field commanders acknowledged the orders, and many of
them replied in an openly defiant manner. Expedition
Command declared these commanders and their crews
outlaws.

The Third Expedition was organized in 2651. It never
engaged the Rinn.

to come back even this close, and sometimes I wonder if I'll ever make it. Maybe I should have gone with the Seekers when I had the chance and tried to find the Entry Point."

"What do you mean?" I asked.

"You know. The Seekers. The Entry Point. The Omphalos."

"No, I don't know any of that. What are they?"

"The Seekers are from Old Earth, I think. Nobody is really sure, but that's what most people think. They've been in space for centuries, in a ship the size of a small planet. They live in their own little world, just like Expedition Command. The Seekers are searching for a point in the galaxy where all things meet, the Entry Point, where everything is everywhere and nowhere at once. There's no time and no distance at the Entry Point. It's the place of eternal total ubiquity." He sipped his wine and stared thoughtfully past me. "If I had found the Entry Point, I could have taken one step and been back in my own palace. I laughed at them when they asked me to come, but maybe I was the fool, not the Seekers."

Gariv's story was getting to me. I knew how it felt to be torn loose from home and loved ones, and I sympathized with the poor old guy. "How far is Skorat from here?" I asked.

"A long way, Del," he said gloomily. "It's out near Watson's Planet, where the great machine rules. A ship leaves here for Watson every few years, but the Tricapets are a hard-hearted lot. If I can't talk my way on as a crewman, they'll demand full passage, and I'll never be able to make it. I guess I'm at the end of a long, hard road."

"Well, look, Gariv," I said, "I can't make any promises, but there's a possibility my partner and I might be able to use another hand. We may not go anywhere near Skorat, but we might be able to take you somewhere—"

"You mean you'd take me on?" he cried.

"If my partner doesn't object, and if we need a third man, I don't see any reason why we can't. We won't be able to pay much, but—"

"You've paid me already, just by making the offer," Gariv said, clasping my arm with a firm grip. "You've given me hope, Del, and that's the rarest thing in the galaxy."

"I wish I could promise you more. I know how you feel, Gariv. I was taken off Gilead by slavers when I was sixteen. I've been trying to get back for five years."

I told him my story, and when I was done, he looked at me curiously and was silent for a long time. Then he asked me for the scrap of paper I had taken from the lifeship. I gave it to him, and he studied it closely.

"The ship you came in was from Pendelton's Base, you said?" he asked me.

"That's what the plate inside said. Why?"

"I'm hesitant to mention this, Del. Raising false hopes is a cruel way to repay your generosity."

"Go ahead. If you can tell me anything, I want to hear it."

"It's too much of a coincidence . . . . And if you're pure Malellan, then I'm wrong. Here, Del, take it back," he said, handing me the paper.

"Listen, Gariv. You're the first man I've spoken to who knows anything about Pendelton's Base. Tell me what you know. If I get my hopes up, that's my problem."

"All right, Del. But I'm afraid I spoke without thinking."

"It's too late to stop now."

"So it is." Gariv sighed and hunched forward over the table. "There was a man on the Rinn Expedition, an

Attack Force Commander, the best I've ever seen. His name was Corey. Is the name familiar?"

I shook my head.

Gariv went on. "Corey was in command of my fleet and three others. We made up the Seventh Attack Force. He brought us into some of the tightest spots I've ever been in, and he brought us out again, and not a single Rinn was left after we finished with them. Corey drove himself harder than I've ever seen anyone driven, and he fought like a madman. One night after a briefing I asked him why he hated the Rinn so much, and he told me the Rinn had killed his wife and infant son in the Pendelton's Base raid. Corey was Old Earth stock, but his wife was a Malellan. I guess you know what the Rinn did to Malella."

"No. I don't know anything about Malella."

"I thought everyone did. The Rinn destroyed every planet in the system. There were six inhabited planets, all of them peaceful, bothering no one, and the Rinn picked them for a show of force. Now there are only a few score Malellans left, scattered around the galaxy. I'm sorry, Del, but you wanted to know."

"Yes. Go on."

"That's all there is. I don't know what became of Corey after the Expedition broke up. I heard that he was trying to form a fleet of his own within the Second Expedition to track the Rinn to their home system and finish them for good, but I don't know what came of it."

"You think this Corey might be my father?" I asked.

"It's possible. Someone could have shoved an infant into an escape craft and gotten it off Pendelton before the Rinn struck. You've got Malellan features, Del, and you move like a Malellan, but you're much too big. You're built more like someone of the Old Earth bloodline, not a Malellan. Now, if your mother was Malellan and your father was Corey, it would figure."

I thrust the paper in front of him. "It says here, 'Parents: Malellan.' So Corey can't be my father."

Gariv pointed to the paper and shook his head. "Look at that blot, Del. Maybe it conceals something more."

I had never thought of this before, but what Gariv suggested was at least possible. "Where can I find out more?" I asked.

Gariv thought for a time. "It's ten years since the First Expedition. Everyone's scattered. Maybe the machine would know."

"What machine?"

"The machine on Watson's Planet. The accounts of the Rinn campaigns were all relayed to Watson's Planet and placed in the memory banks. They might have kept track of the men involved. It's worth a try."

"It certainly is," I said. My mind was made up. Much as I wanted to get back to Gilead, I preferred to return with full knowledge of my true identity. If that required a trip to Watson's Planet, so be it.

3. *Gariv's story, continued.*

Grax was willing to take on a third hand. He was so enthused over the little cruiser that he would have agreed to anything. We settled the sale of the *Phoenix XXVII*, bought the cruiser and christened her *Renegade* because we liked the sound of the word, provisioned her fully, and still had a small profit left over. Two days after my meeting with Gariv, we were on our way to Watson's Planet, by way of Skorat.

The ship was almost completely automated, and we found ourselves with ample time to listen to Gariv's stories of his wanderings around the galaxy and how he, alone, unarmed, often injured, frequently in chains, always hungry and on the run, had managed to outwit a long roster of adversaries. He had been everywhere, even to Old Earth. We were especially curious to learn about this planet, which so many people thought of as home and so few had ever seen, but on this one subject Gariv was reluctant to talk. We kept prodding him, but he always evaded our questions. He related his adventures on Lennerman's Planet, the private preserve of a wealthy eccentric, where huge creatures extinct in the galaxy for millions of years roamed free and protected and the only prey was man; he described the water planet, where the people lived on city-sized rafts and traveled on cutters drawn by teams of trained surface fish; he told us of the cruelty of the pyramid builders, who used the very blood and bone of worn-out slaves as mortar for their monstrous constructions, and how he had crawled half-dead across a thousand miles of desert to escape them and make his way back to Skorat; he described his rescuers, the Gafaal, a green-skinned, golden-eyed nomadic race with two slender tentacles rooted in their shoulder blades, and spoke fondly of Santrahaar, the Gafaal princess who had nursed him back to health and wept bitterly at his departure; he told us about the Windwalkers of Triffit II, the furry, knee-high Quiplids of Farr's System, the planet of the Serpent, Gamesplanet, the fiery seas of Yll, the enshrouded dancers of the silent city of Hovonor, and a hundred other strange and fascinating things, but he never spoke of Old Earth.

Finally, one mealtime when we were drawing close to Skorat, Grax made one last effort to pin him down. "Gariv, you've told us stories about half the planets in the galaxy, but you'll never say a word about Old Earth. Why not?" he asked.

"There's nothing to say, Grax. It's a dead planet."

"But even the ruins must be something great! That's where it all began, Gariv, where the pioneers came from!"

Gariv shook his head and made a sour gesture of dismissal. "The ruins of Old Earth are nothing but a heap of dirty rubble. If you want to see magnificent ruins, go to Anom II. The towers are so high that you have to strain your neck to see the tops when you're still a day's travel from the city walls. When the wind blows in from the desert, it sings in those towers with a note that would bring tears from a stone. I landed there—"

"Gariv, tell us about Old Earth," I broke in.

"How can I tell you about nothingness? Silence, decay, emptiness, death everywhere—is that what you want to hear? There's nothing glorious or magnificent or inspiring about Old Earth. It's been a dead planet for centuries, a graveyard where nothing grows. *Nothing!* The seas are thick and choked with poison, the sky is a dirty brown mist, the land is rusty steel and crumbling stone and corpses, and the whole planet is haunted by dead dreams. I spent a week there with a survey team. We were supposed to stay for one full year, to check the accuracy of the Galactic Standard Calendar. I hoped I might find an abandoned ship there and be able to set out for Skorat on my own, but there was no need. Four of the crew killed themselves in that first week, and the Commander decided to abandon the project and return at once. That's what Old Earth is like. That's what it does to men."

Gariv left us to take his watch on the instruments. Grax turned in, and I picked up one of the books I had taken from the *Phoenix*. It was a book of long poems about the glory of Old Earth by the great Nendring poet Jaxper. I read about five pages, and then I had to put it aside. Gariv's words, and even more, the expression in his eyes when he spoke of those awful ruins, kept intruding between me and the thundering lines of Jaxper.

As we drew closer to Skorat, Gariv's talk turned more and more to home, and to his wife, the faithful

Nikkolope. "She'll be waiting for me," he said at every mealtime. "You'll see. She'll know me the minute she lays eyes on me."

At times he would grow bitter. "I may have a fight on my hands to claim my kingdom, once I return. Those young nobles don't know what loyalty is. I bet Nikkolope's surrounded by suitors even now, all of them telling her she's a fool to waste twenty years waiting for a ghost. They all want to get their hands on my kingdom. But Nikkolope's no fool. She knows I'm coming back, and she'll wait. They won't talk her into anything. If they've tried to force her into accepting one of the young warlords, they'll soon regret it, I tell you that."

At other times, when he wasn't mooning over his faithful Nikkolope, he was practically in tears about the women who had offered him aid and comfort during his wanderings. There had been quite a few. Terrible as his luck had been in all other respects, Gariv had certainly developed a knack for finding beautiful women to rescue him, care for him, love him, and see him on his way with tears and heartbreak. It reminded Grax of an old saying of his Uncle George's: "Nobody loses all the time."

Gariv always ended his reminiscences with Santrahaar. "The women of the Gafaal are the best in the galaxy, take my word for it. It's an odd feeling to have a woman's arms clasped around your neck and then feel a feather-soft tentacle stroking your face. I stayed with Santrahaar for a year, and I never did get used to it. There was a woman for you. Of all the others, only Trannamee, on the water planet, made me think of settling down and staying with her for good. But Santrahaar was the best of them all. I could have been her prince." Sometimes, the way he said this left me convinced that he was suffering from a severe attack of second thoughts; but I guess it was nerves, because just before we touched down on Skorat, he asked Grax and me to land with him and stay nearby in case there was trouble. We agreed. We had come this far, and by now we felt almost responsible for poor Gariv.

He guided us to a landing area known only to him, a kind of natural amphitheatre in the rock out of sight of the city. We left the ship in readiness for a fast departure, just in case things went bad, and started for the capital city on foot. From a short distance away, the *Renegade* was invisible among the rocks.

Grax and I had changed into outfits which Gariv assured us would blend inconspicuously with customary Skorat attire. Our pistols were strapped on, ready for use, concealed under loose-fitting jackets just long enough to cover the holsters. We made our way into the city together, then split up, agreeing to meet at the ship that evening.

4. *A royal wedding celebration, with an unexpected guest.*

For a major planetary city, residence of a great warlord and capital of his empire, Thak was unimpressive. I expected at least an attempt at splendor but soon found myself stumbling over loose cobblestones in a city that looked as though it had been thrown together in the dark, hastily, by the first settlers, and patched up, carelessly and reluctantly, with whatever materials came to hand over the course of the centuries. It was a very old city, with some very old refuse cluttering its streets. The ravenous appetite I had brought through the gates with me disappeared within minutes as I inhaled the musky reek of *trettle* droppings, sweat, open drains, and heaps of decaying food. Grax and I found a small inn, strategically located upwind from the center of town, and ordered a light meal. The innkeeper, a gross, hairy man in a dirty apron, was helpfully talkative.

"The food'll be here in a wink, gents. You're smart to get here early. Another hour, and you won't be able to squeeze in that door. You're not from Thak, are you?" We shook our heads, and he went on, "I thought not. It's a big city, but I recognize everyone. I can spot a stranger right off. A lot of strangers here now, too, for the celebration. Do you have a place to stay?"

"We'll be staying with a friend," I said.

"Ah, you're the lucky ones. Not a spare bed in the city, from what I hear. People here from clear across Skorat, traveled for days, so they did, and they'll be sleeping in the streets and happy to find a space to stretch out in, at that. Well, I don't feel sorry for them. They'll see something to tell their grandchildren about."

"The celebration?" Grax asked.

The innkeeper nodded. "They've been waiting for our good Queen Nikkolope, may she reign in triumph, to pick a husband for twenty years, ever since the old king went off to fight the Rinn in the Great Expedition and never returned."

"Is he dead?" I asked.

"He must be, by this time."

"Was that Gariv?" Grax asked offhandedly.

The innkeeper frowned thoughtfully for a moment, then said, "I think that was his name. It's close enough, anyway. He'd dead these long years, whatever his name was, and so is his poor son Lemak, cut off in his boyhood when his boat overturned. It's time Queen Nikkolope chose one of the Princes Consort to take Gariv's place. The marriage celebration will take place tomorrow, and the feasting will go on for a month. It's a good thing the harvest's in, I'll tell you that. There'll be no work done on Skorat for a good long time."

When the innkeeper had passed out of hearing, Grax observed, "We got here just in time. I like it better this way. No waiting around."

"Right. If Gariv doesn't need us tomorrow, he won't need us at all," I said.

We spent the rest of the day wandering through Thak, looking as much like gawking Otherworlders as we could, picking up information from peddlers, innkeepers, and workmen, and learning our way around the city. We kept a sharp eye out for the fastest escape routes. It was good to be prepared.

That evening, back at the ship, Gariv compared notes with us and outlined his plan. It was bold, but simple. An old tradition required the Queen to invite threescore townspeople to dine in the castle itself as representatives of all her loyal subjects and well-wishers. Gariv had learned where Nikkolope was going to choose these guests, and arranged for us to be in the waiting crowd, at the forefront, where we could scarcely escape being chosen. Once inside the castle, Gariv planned to reveal his identity, challenge the chosen consort, and reclaim his throne and his queen. If all went well, he would require no help from Grax and me; but if the consort's men attempted to silence Gariv, or attacked him, we would be needed to protect him.

I had considered my fighting days over when I left my position as guard on the *Antap*, but here I was, faced once again with the prospect of a battle. I pondered over my decision that night and came to the conclusion that it would be all right for me to back Gariv. After all, I wasn't going to be killing people for the amusement of spectators, I was going to help a solitary brave man, who had suffered much, to reclaim his rightful place and his wife. I'd expect any decent man to do as much for me. And besides, having brought Gariv here, I felt obliged to see him through any troubles that might arise.

Grax, of course, needed no convincing. After all the time he had spent in space over the past few months, he craved action.

We joined the crowd at the Gate of the Nine Kings early next morning, and soon after we arrived, the place went wild with excitement. Gariv's informant had been correct: Queen Nikkolope and her chosen consort and husband-to-be, Prince Sounitan, were heading this way in a royal procession to choose the wedding guests from among the people. In minutes, the crowd increased tenfold as citizens poured in from all the nearby streets and alleys. Gariv, Grax, and I pushed our way forward, careful to stay out of reach of the freely swinging clubs of the royal guardsmen who were conscientiously keeping the way clear for the royal couple's passage. Amid the deafening uproar of screams, shouts, curses, and cries of homage, I heard a rising cry of "There! There they are!" I followed the gaze of the crowd and saw, in an open carriage drawn by twelve brawny men in bright uniforms, heading directly toward me, a magnificent, beautiful woman and a tall, muscular man, both of them richly robed, the woman crowned. They reclined on cushions, smiling and waving to the crowd, acknowledging the cries of "May you reign forever!" and "May your years be many and full of triumph!" with pleased nods and gracious gestures.

The carriage came to a halt before us, and as Queen Nikkolope rose to speak, I studied her closely and appreciatively. She was a stunning woman, and when I thought of what she must have been like twenty years earlier, a young girl no more than twenty, I damned Gariv for a fool for ever having left her and pitied him for his long separation. It must have been awful for him, remembering her as he lay in chains halfway across the galaxy. I, at least, could not blame myself for my long absence from Cassie; I had been dragged from Gilead against my will. But Gariv had left his young queen willingly, in search of vengeance and glory. I thought him mad.

Nikkolope raised braceleted arms and the crowd fell silent. Sounitan, still reclining, looked smugly down on the people who would soon be his subjects. I didn't like the looks of him at all. There was a kind of lazy cruelty in his expression, a vacancy in his eyes, that I had seen in the nobles of Tarquin as they sat in the arena and watched men destroy one another for their amusement. I wished Gariv well and hoped he had not underestimated his rival. Sounitan did not look like a man who would lose with good grace. He looked to me, in fact, like a man who has already won and knows it.

"Beloved people of Thak," Nikkolope called out in a throaty voice that reached the far corners of the assembled crowd and brought them to attentive silence at once, "I come before you today to observe an honored custom of the royal families of Skorat. Today I wed Prince Sounitan, my chosen consort—" and here she was interrupted by loud cheers and wishes of long life, triumph, and so on "—and I have come to invite representatives of the people of Thak to join in the wedding feast at the palace. I will pass among you now and choose my guests."

Amid wild cheering, Nikkolope stepped gracefully down from the lowered carriage and surrounded by a cordon of burly guards, made her way through the crowd, looking everyone over with an appraising eye. From time to time she stopped before some man or woman to inspect them more closely before deciding. When she came to Grax and me, she paused to study us.

"You are not men of Thak. Where do you come

from?" she asked.

"I come from Tarquin VII, my friend from Carson's system. We have traveled to Skorat to see the royal wedding," I answered.

"You shall see it as my guests. Join the others and follow us."

She passed on into the crowd. One of the guards gave us medallions to wear around our necks as proof of the queen's invitation and pointed out a growing crowd behind the royal carriage. The guests were assembling, and we were to join them.

The long, drawn-out ceremonials I had been forced to endure on Tarquin had led me to anticipate endless hours of waiting under the sun while fanfares and speeches followed one upon another interminably; but the Skorats were not ones for ceremonials; once the guests were picked, we were on our way to the palace, and once inside, Nikkolope and Sounitan wasted no time in talk. They called forth the musicians and bid the festivities begin.

I had not been able to spot Gariv in our group as we marched to the palace, but now I saw him. He had a seat in the center of the hall, directly before the twin thrones, facing Nikkolope and Sounitan. I was off to his side near one wall, and Grax was at the other. We waited for Gariv to make his move, and while waiting, we enjoyed the food, the wines, the music, the dancers and chanters and bards, and the dazzling servant girls who hovered about us like benevolent angels. I was halfway through the second meat course, a perfectly-cooked breast of dawnhawk in a delicate sweet sauce, and hoping that Gariv would restrain himself until the meal was over, when I heard his voice ring out above the music and the murmur of conversation.

"Let there be silence!" he cried. "I have news of great interest for our beloved queen."

Guards bearing short javelins moved to converge on Gariv as he rose, but Nikkolope stopped them with a quick gesture.

"You are free to speak, stranger," she said calmly. "Tell us your news."

"The true king of Skorat lives!" Gariv said in a roaring voice, raising his arms high. "Gariv has returned from the dead to claim his throne, his kingdom, and his queen!"

A great collective uproar arose from the crowd. Nikkolope remained unmoved, her poise intact. Sounitan motioned to a guard, whispered to him, and the guard moved off quickly and disappeared behind the thrones. I could sense trouble, and I slipped from my place at the long table and moved to the wall, beside an archway. Across the hall, Grax did the same.

"If Gariv has returned, let him speak for himself. Where is he?" Nikkolope asked.

"Here! I am Gariv!"

Sounitan sprang to his feet and pointed at Gariv. "You lie! Imposter!" he cried.

"Usurper!" Gariv replied, shaking his fist.

"Guards, take this beggar to the gates and impale him!" Sounitan ordered.

Nikkolope made no move to interfere. Two guards closed in on Gariv, and he went for them, clubbing one with a heavy pitcher and seizing his javelin. He jabbed the other in the belly with the butt end, sprang to the table, and shouting "Death to the usurper! Gariv has returned!" he hurled the javelin at Sounitan. With a smooth grace that I had not expected of him, the prince consort glided from the throne, plucked the javelin out of the air, and sent it back at Gariv. It entered under the breastbone with such force that the point came out a forearm's length behind. Gariv froze, then toppled backward to the floor.

It was over so quickly that I stood by the archway, numb with the suddenness of it, until a guard nudged me courteously and said, "It's all right now, sir. You may return to your place." I nodded and resumed my seat, and the excited babble died around me as Nikkolope rose and addressed her guests.

"Nobles, honored guests, people of Thak," she began. "I, your queen, apologize to you for this disruption of our celebration. As we all know, Gariv is dead. He died a hero's death, giving his life to save Skorat and her people from the Rinn. I regret the unpleasantness this poor, crazed man has caused you, and I ask you to forgive him and wipe the event from your memories. Let this be a day for celebration."

At her bidding, everyone dutifully applied themselves to eating, drinking, and festivity. I didn't even see them drag out the body.

5. *A stowaway on 'The Renegade.'*

Grax and I slipped out of the palace late that night and made our way to the *Renegade*. We were a bit unsteady on our feet from a long day of celebration, and we spoke few words to one another. We managed to lift off Skorat, and as we shifted into highdrive and the stars winked out, Grax looked into the blankness of the viewplate and said, "What do you think, Del?"

"About what?"

"You know what. Was he Gariv or wasn't he?"

"Whether he was or not, now he's dead. Does it matter?"

"I guess not."

"Maybe the machine on Watson's Planet can tell us. It's supposed to know everything," I said.

"One thing it won't tell us, Del: what went on in Nikkolope's head when old Gariv stood up and started shouting."

"That's something nobody will ever know. I'm not even going to try to guess. I need some sleep."

"Good idea," Grax said.

I didn't move right away. I was occupied with troubled thoughts occasioned by my new suspicions about Gariv. If he were only an imposter, then everything he told us could have been lies. We were heading for Watson solely on the strength of his account of Commander Corey, and if it was all fiction, I really didn't want to be told so by a machine. Until meeting Gariv, I had all but forgotten my curiosity about my true identity, but he had rekindled it stronger than ever with his hints about Corey and Pendelton's Base and my possible mixed parentage. Even if he were an imposter, though, he could have been on the Rinn Expedition. That much could be true.

Anything could be true. That was the inevitable and unpleasant conclusion. All we could do was head for Watson and find out for ourselves.

As I sat moodily facing Grax, who rested his head on folded arms on the mess table, the sound of someone clearing his throat came from behind me. In an instant we were on our feet, guns drawn, facing an oddly dressed man who stood in the entry to the cabin.

The intruder was about my height, slim, with a reddish-blond beard streaked here and there with white. His face was lined and weathered, but his long slender hands were not the hands of a workingman. They were made for stroking the nineteen strings of the *linlovar* that was slung over his shoulder on a gaudy, woven strap. He was dressed in tight, brightly-striped trousers and soft boots, and he wore a short crimson jacket. He was trying very hard to look calm and unruffled, but not quite making it. It's not easy to look calm when two hairy, villainous-looking spacers are pointing guns at your midsection. Considering the circumstances, his self-control was impressive.

"Gentlemen, I offer my profound apologies for bursting in on you like this," he said, extending his hands, palms out, in a placating gesture. "I'm very sorry if I startled you. Actually, I find myself in a most awkward position. I slipped aboard your craft thinking it would be empty for the duration of the festivities, and now we're in space. Quite awkward, really."

"A stowaway," Grax said.

"Please, sir, you do me wrong," the stranger said, looking hurt. "I came to Thak for the wedding and the celebration, and could find no place to stay. By sheer chance, I stumbled upon your ship. It was so well concealed that I assumed at once it would be here for a long time. I climbed aboard to rest, intending to return to Thak early in the morning and try my luck again. I had no desire to leave with you."

"Well, you've done just that. What'll we do with him, Del?" Grax asked.

"We can't very well bring him back."

"Gentlemen, please. I wouldn't dream of asking you to return me to Skorat. It's too great an imposition on your kindness. No, not a word more on this subject," the newcomer said, raising his hand as if to silence us, though neither of us attempted to speak. "I've caused you trouble enough. If you'll let me off at the first planetfall, I'll find my way back. Just where are you headed, if I may ask?"

"Watson," I said.

His face fell. "Oh, dear. I'm afraid there'll be small welcome for me on Watson."

"Are you in trouble on Watson?"

"Not at all. It's Watson that's in trouble. Watson is a

planet without a soul. The only music on Watson's Planet is the clatter of machines, the only poetry the invisible markings on a nearly invisible wire spinning through the entrails of a great soulless brain. It's a tidy, orderly little world. No room on it for a spacebard."

"You're a spacebard, then."

He bowed to us and announced, "I am a spacebard, sirs. I am the greatest of living spacebards, word-weaver and song-spinner of a hundred grateful worlds. Alladale Anthem-maker is my name. No doubt you've heard it often."

"Not even once," Grax said.

"You've been in the wrong systems. And you, my friend?" he said, turning to me. "Surely you know the name of Alladale."

"I've heard it mentioned once or twice," I lied, just to be hospitable. Grax glared at me, but he said nothing.

"Truly a gentleman of wide experience and discerning taste. I could tell as soon as I laid eyes on you, sir. It is indeed a great pleasure . . . ." His voice trailed off weakly, and he covered his eyes and staggered back against the bulkhead where he rested, shaking his head as if to clear it.

"Are you all right?" I asked.

"Oh, yes, yes. Perfectly fine. Just a momentary weakness. It will pass. In all the rushing about on Skorat I had no opportunity to take nourishment. It's been quite some time . . . ."

"Come on, sit down," Grax said resignedly. "We'll get you something to eat."

Alladale was seated in a matter of seconds, protesting all the while about how he couldn't dream of depriving us of precious rations and couldn't think of imposing on our hospitality, generosity, and kindness. He managed, between disclaimers, to finish two hearty meals. When he was through, he leaned back, sighed, belched melodiously, and gave us an expansive smile. It was pleasant to see someone looking so full and comfortable and contented, but as I looked at Alladale rubbing his newly filled belly, I began to wonder if perhaps I was not turning into a soft touch for every panhandler in the galaxy. Gariv first, now Alladale . . . who next? But then I thought, why not? I hoped people would do as much for me, if I were down on my luck.

"Marvelous. Delicious," Alladale said softly. "I can think of only one way to repay such goodness—a song. What will it be, my goodly hosts? From the look of you, I'd say a Skeggjatt battle-song would stir your blood."

"No, thanks," I said.

"Something lighter, then? A drinking song?"

"We just finished a full day of drinking songs," Grax said. "I'd prefer not to hear any more for a long time."

"A love song? A laughing song? Something melancholy, perhaps?"

"Yes. Something melancholy would be just right for us now," I said, remembering Gariv and my growing doubts.

"I have just the thing. Short, simple, but exquisitely poignant. I sang this on Trulba, at the Court of the Father and Benefactor of All Worlds and Peoples Known and Unknown and Universal Protector of the Races. °

° A notorious despot. The Trulbans are a squat, hairy breed of Old Earth descent, offensive to the sensibilities of the civilized races of the galaxy. They are known for their arrogance, cruelty, ignorance, and cowardice, and figure in many vulgar and denigrating expressions in the Low Lixian tongue. The ruler here referred to is Krankl, sixth and worst of the Sdrat'sa Bizan kings who ruled over Trulba in her decline. His full title was Father and Benefactor of All Worlds and Peoples Known and Unknown; Master of All Stars, Planets, and Satellites, of all Celestial Bodies and the Spaces

The entire court wept. The Princess of All Worlds and Most Beautiful of Creatures was practically inconsolable."

"Don't expect us to burst into tears," Grax said.

"Well, it's true the Universal Protector *ordered* the court to weep, under the threat of flogging," Alladale admitted. "Nevertheless, it's a very touching piece. I call it 'Song of Old Earth.' "

He unslung his *linlovar,* plucked the strings, and made a few slight adjustments. Then he rose and began to sing, accompanying himself with soft chords.

"Here were tall trees, standing strong,
Deep roots knotted in the mother ground,
Green heads tossing,
Laughing in the blue sky.
Now no more,
Never again,
Never no more.

---

between the Stars; Supreme Pilot and Navigator of All Driveships; Paragon of Kindness and Generosity to His Loyal Followers; Unwavering Beacon of Enlightenment; Inspiration of All Seekers of Truth, Beauty, and the Ways of Faultless Living; Builder of the Impenetrable Defenses of the Most Beautiful of Cities on the Central Planet of the Universe; Mighty Arm Wielding the Sword of Domination; Conqueror of All Armies, Ever in the Forefront of the Battle; First Light of the Universe; Eternal Friend of the Friends of Trulba and Relentless Destroyer of Her Foes; and Universal Protector of All Races and Vicar of the Unnamable Powers Who Govern All Things.

Krankl died a curious death. While drunk, he choked on a *bzzit* that had fallen into his goblet. When his son Fegg came to the throne, his first act as king was to add the figure of a *bzzit* to his crest.

"Here were tall buildings, thrusting high,
Silver they were, and gold, and white,
Flashing a day-sky of winking eyes
Under the arcing sun.
Now no more,
Never again,
Never no more.

"Here were tall men, reaching far,
Treading the ground with bold feet
While their souls soared far beyond
Into the black spaces.
Now no more,
Never again,
Never no more."

Alladale ended on a long, drawn-out minor chord, and we sat silent for a time. Then Grax rose and muttered, "Turning in," and left us.

"No more melancholy songs, Alladale. Not tonight," I said.

I checked the course and then turned in myself. Alladale was asleep when I returned from the navigation post. He was slumped forward on the table, his head cushioned on folded arms, a peaceful expression on his face. I left him there to sleep.

6. *The songs of Alladale Anthem-maker*

The voyage to Watson was uneventful, and before we had covered half the distance, Grax and I were grateful for the presence of our stowaway. Alladale made the trip bearable; even, at times, enjoyable. He had as many stories to tell as Gariv, and his were a lot more entertaining. I didn't believe a tenth of what he told us, but I enjoyed every bit of it. For all his sense of fun, though, and despite all the laughter he evoked with his wild tales, Alladale preferred melancholy. He knew funny songs from every system in the galaxy, but his own compositions, every one of them, would have had a bunch of Daltrescan slavers crying their eyes out before they had heard three full verses. He sang us one song he had written about a planet where the sun shines only once in every generation. I don't know if there really is such a place or if Alladale just made it up so he'd have an excuse for his song. He called it "Day of Light."

"It is rising, it is rising!
The long dark now grows small!
It stands under!
It vanishes!
It is climbing, it is climbing!
We look up, and it is bright before us,
Bright behind us,
Brightness all around!
We look away,
And the colors dance in our eyes!
We are dazzled!
It is falling, it is falling!
The brightness fades now,
And the shadows clutch with long, dark fingers.
We sway, weeping.
We fear.
It is gone!"

Alladale really liked those sad songs. Grax didn't, and neither did I, particularly. I would have preferred to hear something cheerful once in a while. After he finished "Day of Light" I came out and asked him for a song that would make us feel good.

"This one will cheer you up," Alladale said
confidently. "This is about creation. It's 'The Song of
Abtai, The Wind-Shaper.' They sing it in the mountains
of Toxxo."

"How about a funny one?" Grax asked.

"I'll sing a funny song another time."

Grax turned to me and threw up his hands. "He's
paying his passage with these songs, and he won't even
let us pick the ones we want to hear!"

"An artist is the best judge of his own repertoire,
Grax," Alladale said huffily.

"But who cares about a creation myth from some
bunch of mountain people on Toxxo?"

"A great many people care. 'The Song of Abtai'
happens to be one of the most interesting creation myths
on Toxxo, or anywhere else, for that matter," Alladale
said, sounding just like an old schoolmaster talking
about his favorite subject, annoyed because other people
really don't care about something that he thinks is so
great. "The lowlanders have several myths, but they're
very crude."

"Go ahead, Alladale, sing it," I said.

He tightened a string on his *linlovar*, getting a bit
showy about the process, then he cleared his throat and
began.

"First was the wind, only the wind
Blowing silent through the emptiness,
Through the place of Abtai's long sleep,
The great no-place filled with no-things.

"Then the wind began to howl,
It was time for the wind to howl.

"The howling of the wind awoke Abtai from his
        long sleep.

And he knew that it was time to rise and begin
　　his work.
It was time for things to begin to be.

"Abtai rose up tall in the emptiness, amid the
　　no-things.
He stretched out his twenty-fingered hand and
　　seized a passing wind.
Abtai seized the wind and whirled it around his
　　head,
Whirled it faster and faster, for too long a time
　　to tell.
The wind grew hot. It began to glow.
Brighter and brighter it glowed.
Abtai flung it far from him, and it made a place
　　overhead.
The place is the sky.
The burning wind hung in the sky, giving light
　　and heat.
That is the sun.

"Abtai thought long about the sun he had made,
Then he rose, and again stretched out his
　　twenty-fingered hand.
He seized another wind and he squeezed it hard.
With his hands he squeezed it.
He squeezed the wind, and the wind wept
While the sun circled Abtai's head more times
　　than I can tell.
The waters wept by the wind gathered around
　　the feet of Abtai in a great pool.
That is the sea.

"Abtai thought long about the sun and the sea,
Then he rose, and stretched out his twenty-
　　fingered hand,

And again he seized a wind, a loud wind,
    fiercely blowing,
And he squeezed it harder than before,
Squeezed it until it wept no more,
Squeezed it into a ball,
And he held the ball up to the sun, for hardness.
That is the land.

"Then Abtai took the waters of the sea,
And he poured them over the land.
The sun warmed the waters and the land,
And the things of the land began to grow.
Abtai thought long about the sun and the sea and
    the land,
He thought long about the things growing on the
    land,
And he waited.

"The serpent came riding on a dry wind
And called 'Abtai! Abtai!
Why do you make things to be in the place of
    no-things?'
Abtai fought with the serpent for longer than I
    can tell,
And Abtai's blood fell in drops upon the
    mountains,
And the serpent's blood and venom fell in the
    valleys.
Where the blood of Abtai fell,
There arose the children of Abtai, the
    mountain people.
Where the blood and venom of the serpent fell,
There the others came to life, the evil ones,
    the children of the serpent, who dwell in
    low places.

"Abtai broke the back of the serpent and flung
    it from him,
And a dry and silent wind carried it away.
Then Abtai lay down and thought about his
    children,
For the serpent's fangs were in his breast, and
    the sleep was upon him.
'Who will guide and teach my children?
Who will protect them from the children of the
    serpent?
Who but Abtai?'
He plucked the serpent's fang from his breast,
And on it he wrote his teachings.
When he had written all, he thrust the serpent's
    fang into the peak of the highest mountain,
Then Abtai slept."

Alladale ended there, and when the notes of the
linlovar died, he smiled at us. "After this comes four
thousand lines of laws. I didn't think you'd want to hear
them."

"You were absolutely right," I said.

Grax reluctantly admitted that "The Song of Abtai,
The Wind-Shaper" really wasn't so bad, and Alladale's
ruffled feelings were smoothed. The rest of our voyage
was peaceful.

7. First dealings with the Watsonians.

The Watson landing procedure was elaborate and
damnably time-consuming. We spent six hours filling
out forms that contained some of the silliest questions I
had ever had put to me in my life, and when we finished
that part of the ordeal, we had to go through an

interrogation that lasted four hours more. We had rehearsed our story carefully, so there was no difficulty. Grax and I told them everything exactly as it happened, with one small alteration: Alladale was not an accidental stowaway from Skorat, but my personal trainer-servant from Tarquin VII. He had been there, and he knew enough of the tournament language and ritual to be convincing in his role. It was a nuisance, but since spacebards were classed as undesirables on Watson, and we didn't want Alladale to languish in a cell while we went about our business, we agreed on this story for the spaceport authorities.

The interrogation was an uncomfortable experience for me, as were my first few contacts with Watsonians. By law, all employees of the machine complex were required to wear white plastic masks bearing stylized human features during all business transactions. The masks were identical, and so were the blue uniforms the people wore. The idea was to preserve perfect objectivity in their dealings. I didn't understand that, since it wouldn't work unless the clients, too, wore masks and uniforms, which they didn't. But it was their planet, and I honored their right to live by whatever foolish rules they chose as long as no one tried to impose them on me. The Watsonians were able to distinguish individuals—although they rarely did so—but I could never tell one from another. For all I knew, I spoke to only a handful of men during our stay. It was a very unpleasant sensation.

We were assigned quarters, a neat and orderly three-man room, sparsely furnished, in a huge dormitory building within sight of Machine Central. As soon as we entered the room Alladale—whose name was now Scaevius—put his fingers to his lips for silence. He prowled about the room, looking behind, under and into the few furnishings and fixtures, and at last motioned us to a large tri-dimensional motion painting on the wall. It was a miniature of Watson's system, the six planets and their thirty-one satellites slowly revolving at scaled speed. Pointing to one of the second planet's moons, he mouthed the words, "listening device." We nodded. Our conversation that evening was guarded.

I left Grax and Scaevius the next morning for my transaction interview with a Machine Representative in the Inquiries Prelim Section of Machine Central. It was the same question-and-answer routine all over again, with a few new twists. Watsonians, I soon learned, were as interested in acquiring information as they were in selling it.

I showed my appointment disc to a white-masked attendant who consulted an elaborate chart and then took me to a small booth, one of hundreds, perhaps thousands, that honeycombed the Inquiries Building. The first attendant left me, and minutes later a second—for all I knew, it could have been the original one—entered by another door and without a word of greeting, seated himself opposite me at the small table and held out his hand. I was pleasantly surprised at what I took to be the first friendly gesture of my stay on Watson, but I had misinterpreted the gesture.

"Your disc, please," the attendant said. I turned it over to him. He checked it against a slightly less elaborate chart of his own, and said, "You are Deliverance Whitby, origin Gilead, co-owner and commander of driveship *Renegade,* bound from Skorat with three passengers, including yourself."

"I am."

"You have come to Watson to request the services of the Machine in acquiring information."

"That's right."

"Please describe fully the information you seek."

"I've already done that. Four times."

"Please restate for purposes of verification."

"Why?" I asked.

"Established inquiry procedure requires restatement of objectives to an authorized representative of Inquiries Prelim. I am Smith MR 371-64, accredited to function in the required capacity under Standard 84C, Section IV of the Manual. Please proceed."

All this was delivered in a voice as flat and mechanical as the words it spoke. I wondered if I were speaking to a robot, but discounted the idea when I remembered Surgical EXU, back on Vigrid. Smith MR 371-64 couldn't be a robot; he was too mechanical. I complied.

"All right. I want two things: a navigation chart to Gilead and complete information on Commander Corey of the Seventh Attack Force of the Rinn Expedition."

"Why do you desire this information?"

"For personal reasons."

"Please elucidate," Smith droned.

"I want to return to Gilead because my foster parents and my fiancee are there. I want the information on Corey because I have reason to believe that he knows something about my real parents."

"That is satisfactory. Please wait."

Smith slid back a portion of the desk top, revealing a screen and several rows of keys. He began tapping the keys at a good speed and continued to do so for several minutes. After a short interval, a message began to flow across the screen. I tried to read it, but the words moved too fast for upside-down recognition. When the screen went blank, Smith looked up at me out of that equally blank mask.

"We have the information you seek, and it is unclassified. It will be made available to you six minutes after payment is verified. The charge is two Patchiks, six Bettertons." [*]

---

[*]   The intersystemic monetary system of exchange was established early in the second century of space exploration

"That's a stiff price, Smith—two hundred and sixty thousand Vanguards."

"Our costs are very high. The charge is not negotiable."

"I didn't suppose it would be. Well, I have to think about raising money. We don't have even a single Betterton among us now."

"Your driveship has been evaluated at one-and-a-half Demetrious," Smith said. "We will make all arrangements."

"*Renegade* isn't for sale. What good will it do me to know the way back to Gilead if I don't have a ship to take me there?"

"The objection is reasonable. Have you no other resources?"

"No."

"Is this information important to you?"

"Of course it is!" I said angrily. "Do you think I'd come all the way to Watson and put up with all these stupid questions if the information wasn't vital to me?"

---

on the planet Gobseck (PC 17/22 112; GSC 12/8/2199.) After much deliberation, and over the strenuous objections of the Karrapada, a seven-fingered race who looked upon a ten-unit base as nonsensical, the Old Earth decimal system was adopted as a universal currency base.

Currency was printed in seven major denominations, a concession to the injured feelings of the Karrapada. Each denomination was named for an early space explorer, financier, or spacecraft. The basic unit was the Vanguard, familiarly known as the "Sput."

$$10 \text{ Vanguards} = 1 \text{ Staviarski}$$
$$10 \text{ Staviarskis} = 1 \text{ Gargarin}$$
$$10 \text{ Gagarins} = 1 \text{ Armstrong}$$
$$10 \text{ Armstrongs} = 1 \text{ Betterton}$$
$$10 \text{ Bettertons} = 1 \text{ Patchik}$$
$$10 \text{ Patchiks} = 1 \text{ Demetriou}$$

"Please remain calm. It is possible that an arrangement might be reached with our Special Operations Section whereby you will be permitted to exchange services for information. Is this agreeable to you?"

"It depends. What kind of services do you want?"

"That can only be discussed by an authorized representative of Special Operations. Do you wish me to arrange a meeting?"

I thought it over for a minute, and decided that I had nothing to lose. I couldn't sell the *Renegade*. I had to make the money somehow or give up the information. "Go ahead," I said.

Smith resumed his tapping at the keys, much more briefly this time, and the response was almost immediate. I got the impression that they were expecting my affirmative answer. "You are to report to Special Operations, Division VI, Section Blue. Here is an identification disc. Report at once, please."

"Where is this place?"

"You will be conducted. Good functioning, Mr. Whitby."

8. Second dealings with the Watsonians; I am offered an interesting proposition.

As Smith said, I was conducted. A white-masked attendant was waiting outside the door. He set off without a word, and I followed him through corridors lined with booths, down endless ramps, across a great translucent bridge joining two massive buildings, each the size of a mountain, through more corridors, and finally to a booth considerably larger and better-

outfitted than the one at Inquiries Prelim. Wonder of
wonders: a man and woman were awaiting me, and
neither of them wore a mask. They were uniformed,
Watson style, but above those blue uniforms were faces,
real human faces. The man's was quite distinguished,
but friendly in expression. The woman's was very pretty.
They looked like a reasonably normal father and
daughter and acted glad to see me, as if I were a
welcome guest to their home. I began to feel tentatively
better about Watson.

"Come in, Mr. Whitby, do come in," the man said.
"We've been waiting eagerly for a look at you in
person." He dismissed the attendant, waved me to a
comfortable seat, and went on, "I'm Johnson, SO 43-59,
and this is my mission technical assistant, Shaw SOZ
617. We've been reading some of your background, and
we're very impressed. Oh, my, yes, very impressed
indeed. We think you're just the man we've been hoping
to find for this mission."

"Thank you," I said. "What's the mission?"

"I'll be in full charge of all technical factors," Shaw
said, beaming at me. "You'll be well cared for, Mr.
Whitby."

"Yes, Shaw is an expert in her field. Your body will
probably be functioning at an efficiency factor of 115%
current peak when she returns it to you," Johnson said.

"That's very nice. What's the mission?" I asked again.

"A fairly standard recovery operation, actually. There
are a few complications that throw it into the maximum-
hazard category, but that's all on paper. A man like
you—"

"Does 'maximum-hazard category' mean that whoever undertakes this mission will probably be killed?"
I asked.

"Well, technically, I suppose it does," Johnson said,
carefully avoiding my eyes. "But you must remember,

these categories are established by men sitting at a desk somewhere in Operations. They tend to exaggerate the danger involved."

"Uh-huh," I said, rising and starting for the door.

"Wait a minute, Mr. Whitby!" Johnson said, alarm in his voice. "True, there's an element of risk, but the profile we've constructed from your records shows that your resourcefulness and adaptability—"

"—and courage," Shaw said, taking my arm and guiding me gently chairward.

"—and courage, of course, are such that the risks are reduced to a minimum. It would be a dangerous mission for an ordinary man, but for you . . . ." He smiled in a superior way and waved a graceful hand to dismiss the very thought of danger.

"You're exactly right for us, Del," Shaw said, drawing me down into my seat and perching beside me.

"I am?"

"You'd be on the planet for six days, GSC. A bit over two days, planetary time. Including preparation and debriefing time, the entire mission would take forty-seven days GSC. When it's over, you'd be given your requested information plus one Patchik, three Bettertons. A hundred and thirty thousand Vanguards, Mr. Whitby."

"That's good pay," I said. It occurred to me that I had a chance to return to Gilead a relatively rich man. I liked the idea.

"Minus a few small deductions for expenses, of course," Johnson said hurriedly. "Still, you'd come out of this rather well off."

"Just what is it you want me to do?"

"I can't give you the complete information until we reach a firm agreement, you understand, but I can tell you this much: a Watson investigatory team landed on a quarantined planet eight months ago. We heard nothing

from them, and four months later we sent a recovery
force to bring them back. We've received no word from
the recovery force. Now our plan is to send a Special
Recovery Unit, one man, to study the situation and, if
possible, to rescue the missing men."

"Do you have any idea of what might have .
happened?"

Johnson shook his head. "None whatsoever."

"What were they doing on a quarantined planet,
anyway?"

"Our investigators go everywhere, Mr. Whitby.
Watson is the information center of the galaxy, and if
information doesn't come to us, it has to be sought out."

"I suppose it does, but a quarantined planet . . . ."

Johnson shrugged. "They had their orders, Mr.
Whitby. They obeyed them. Now we owe it to them to
make every effort to bring them back."

"What am I supposed to do? Drop down and wander
around a quarantined planet looking for bodies?"

"Oh, no, Mr. Whitby. We know where our men
landed, and you'll be able to trace them. You'll be able
to do a great many things you can't do now."

"What do you mean?"

Johnson made an evasive gesture and looked at me
with a pained expression. "Again, I can't reveal details,
much as I'd like to. Perhaps Shaw will give you a general
outline of the planned adjustments."

"You'll be totally protected, psychologically and
physically," Shaw began.

"No one can be totally protected against anything.
The quarantined planets are sure death or raving
madness for anyone who sets foot on them," I said.
Certain passages from those old books on the *Phoenix*
were very clear in my mind.

"Believe me, Del, you'll walk around that planet as
securely as you do here. You'll be provided with sensory

amplification to a selective factor as high as five, and your reaction speed will be increased threefold."

"My body won't handle it."

"Your body won't be involved, Del. What we plan—"

"That's enough, Shaw," Johnson interrupted. "What she says is true, Mr. Whitby, and she hasn't told you half. If you undertake the mission, you'll have the defensive capability of a small army, and you'll experience sensations few men have ever known. I guarantee you that. And you'll be well paid, you'll receive the information you came for, and we'll even provide you with transportation when you return. I don't see how you can refuse."

"Neither do I. I'd like to talk to my friends first, though."

"I understand. Will one day be enough?"

I nodded. "That'll be enough."

"Good. We'll see you here tomorrow at this time. If you agree, we can start processing you at once."

"You'll work with us, won't you, Del?" Shaw asked.

"I'll tell you that tomorrow."

9. *Grax and Scaevius in danger.*

When I rejoined Grax and Scaevius, their greeting was unusual. Before I could say a word, they both loudly announced that they had left something important aboard the ship and insisted that we go there at once. Safely inside the *Renegade,* Grax turned on a noisy ventilator and we drew into a tight group.

"We don't want anyone to hear. We're in trouble, Del," he said.

"What did you do?"

"We went down to the Infomart after you left us, to see if we could pick up some money to help you out. We heard how expensive information services are here, and we thought you might need more than we've got. They pay travelers a good price for information here, you know, and I thought I might get something for a statement on the *Antap*, or *Phoenix XXVII*, or the doings on Skorat. Scaevius has some stuff to sell, too. We looked around to see what was wanted, and we found a request out for both of us."

Scaevius looked around nervously. "It was awful. I have to get off this planet, Del, and fast."

"Why didn't you tell us you were in trouble?" I asked.

"I didn't know I was! I swear that, Del. I had a casual affair with the Universal Protector's youngest daughter, and now he wants me to be brought back to Trulba to pay the penalty for ruining the virtue of a royal princess."

"What's the penalty?"

"I don't even want to think about it. He's had people boiled to death for omitting one of his titles when they addressed him. I get nauseous when I think of what he'd do to someone . . . ." He shuddered and closed his eyes.

"What about you, Grax?"

"I knew I was in trouble, but I didn't think they were looking this hard."

"Is it bad?"

"Depends on how you look at it, Del. I'd do it again."

"What did you do?"

"Shot a few people who had a hand in killing my folks. We had a problem over boundaries back home. The other fellow thought he'd settle it by coming over one night with his friends and wiping us out. He nearly did, too. Got everyone but me. I was only a kid, and I lit out and hid. It took me nine years, but I found every one

of them. By the time I got to the last one, my old
neighbor who started it all, he was Governor-Marshal of
the territory, so I had to leave after I settled with him."

Scaevius broke out of his reverie, raised his hands in
appeal, and said, "Why did I ever get mixed up with
her? She was so *ugly!*" He turned to us, desperate. "I
thought it was expected of the guests!"

"Stop complaining. Nobody's going to turn us in.
We're getting out of here right now," Grax said. "All
right with you, Del?"

It was my turn to explain, and I told them the whole
story. Grax was sympathetic.

"I guess you just have to take on the mission,
whatever it is," he said. "I don't see how we can hole up
on Watson for forty-seven days without being spotted,
but we'll try."

"Let's leave now. We can all work to raise the money,
and you can come back here alone, Del," Scaevius said.

Grax vetoed that. "He can't leave. We'll just have to
stay on the *Renegade* and take turns keeping watch."

"No, you won't," I said. "You leave now, and I'll
meet you when I'm finished here."

"Where we going to hide out for forty-seven days?"
Grax asked.

"Barbary! We can go to Barbary!" Scaevius cried,
ecstatic with relief. "I have friends there. They'll take
care of us."

"Suits me. I always wanted to see Barbary. How will
you get there, Del?"

"No problem at all. They give me transportation
when it's all over. Part of the deal."

"That's good enough for me. Let's get started. We're
leaving tonight," Grax said.

Four hours later, Grax and Scaevius lifted off, on their
way to Barbary and safety. I was alone on Watson. But
at least my friends were safe. I went back to my quarters

and slept soundly, unaware that I would not be doing so for a long time to come.

10. *Third dealings with the Watsonians.*

The next morning, an attendant came to conduct me to my meeting with Special Operations, Division VI, Section Blue. Johnson received me alone, and after I had signed all the necessary agreements, waivers, releases, and pledges, we went together to a laboratory where Shaw and a staff of a dozen orderlies awaited us. I was put through a detailed examination, and when everyone had taken a good, close look at me inside and out, we all proceeded to another, larger room that stood behind three sets of heavily guarded doors. The room was lined with equipment totally unfamiliar to me, and in the center, side by side, stood two white, ellipsoidal objects of unequal dimensions. One was slightly larger than human size; it could have contained a man quite comfortably, as long as he didn't thrash around. The other was more than twice as large.

Shaw pointed to the smaller of the two and said, "This is where your body will be for the entire mission, Del. Your intellectual and sensory functions will be channeled through the occupant of the other casing to an identical carrier we've placed in orbit around the planet."

"That seems like a complicated way of doing it."

"It's by far the simplest. We've found it much faster and safer than physical transportation."

"What does my carrier look like?" I asked.

"Rather unattractive, I'm afraid," Johnson replied. "It's the body of a Crevnite. We've used them as carriers for quite some time now, and they're very satisfactory."

"Co-operative, too, I hope."

"Of course. The Crevnites are a heavy-planet race, exceptionally strong, with a highly developed sensory apparatus. Enormous brain capacity, but very little of it is actually used. They function at a conceptual level of about eight years, human. A mature intelligence can dominate them completely and utilize their unique sensory abilities to great advantage. You'll be in full control at all times, Del."

"I hope you're right. You sound pretty confident, but I'm the one who's taking the trip."

"We've done this hundreds of times. There's no danger at all," Shaw said.

"Except when I'm on the planet. What happens if I don't come back?"

"You *will* come back, Del. A Crevnite body can withstand any known hand weapon, even in direct frontal contact. You'll be almost indestructible."

I shook my head. "That's not what bothers me. The real danger on a quarantined planet isn't physical. People don't die as often as lose their minds."

"You'll be protected by a Mind Lock, Del. In case of any psychological overload, you'll automatically dis-engage from the carrier and return to the counterpart here."

"Why not to my own body?"

"A Mind Lock can't be installed in a human," Shaw said. She took my hand in hers and said, "Trust us, Del. Trust me. I don't want to lose you. I want you to come back."

"I intend to. But I'd still like to know what happens to my body if I don't."

Johnson answered that. "Actually, you achieve a kind of physical immortality. Your body is retained for possible future use in a similar mission."

I didn't like the sound of that at all. "You mean there might someday be another person walking around in my body?"

"Not at all," Johnson said. "It would be his body, just as the Crevnite body will be yours as long as you inhabit it. But you shouldn't even be thinking of that, Del. You'll be back. We've provided you with every protection, and we have great confidence in you."

"Let's get to it, then. You take good care of me while I'm gone," I said to Shaw.

"I'll see that she does. Good functioning, Del," Johnson said, clasping my hand and steering me toward the waiting apparatus.

The orderlies swung open the smaller casing. I stripped and climbed in, settling my weight on a soft web that was to support me until the casing was filled with fluids. Tubes were inserted in every available orifice, and electrodes affixed to my temples, my spine, and elsewhere about my body until I was completely betubed and wired. Last of all came a close-fitting cone over my mouth and nose. I breathed deeply, as Shaw had instructed me to do, and felt myself disengaging slowly. The last things I remember are the floating sensation as the fluid filled my casing and lifted me gently from the webbing, the darkness of the closed, womblike casing, and the soothing warmth that caressed me and enveloped me in sweet oblivion.

11. *The mission of Special Recovery Unit Renegade Blue Q3.*

What happened on the quarantine planet mission is hard to put into words. I'm going to try, but there just

are no words for some of the things that happened, and I
can't even say they happened to me. I can't speak of the
main participant, that Crevnite-Malellan-possibly-Old-
Earth hybrid, as "I", because it wasn't. It wasn't Del
Whitby, and it wasn't a Crevnite. Johnson called it
"Special Recovery Unit Renegade Blue Q3," a clumsy
name, but as good as anything I might have dreamed
up. So what I'm going to try to tell now is the story of
Special Recovery Unit Renegade Blue Q3's mission on
the planet of the screens. For convenience, I'll call him
Q3.

∘ ∘ ∘ ∘ ∘ ∘

Awakening in a brand-new, unfamiliar body was not
at all the shock Q3 had expected it to be. He felt quite at
home in the chunky Crevnite frame, and even the extra
set of arms and legs presented no problem as long as he
didn't think about them, but let them work instinctively.

He took the pilot craft down to the planet's surface
and made a quick survey. It was an ordinary planet,
Watson Category 6SA4-III: slightly more than half
water with three major land masses and seven large
islands, polar ice caps, four major mountain ranges, and
abundant plant life. The continents held sixteen major
cities and hundreds of smaller settlements. The cities
evidenced a high degree of architectural skill, and the
excellent network of linking roads suggested a
considerable amount of traffic. Q3 actually saw none of
this, since Crevnites have no eyes; but he was totally
aware of it on all operant levels of reception.

He sensated no human or animal life on the planet.
Arriving over the small city where the Watson
expedition had disappeared, he became aware of
residual emanations of intelligence. Focusing tightly, he
was able to distinguish twelve individual sources, six

airly strong and six weak. He evaluated, and
etermined that the weaker transmissions were
pproximately eight months old GSC, and the stronger
bout four months old, thus closely corresponding with
he dates of disappearance of the two expeditions. A
econd survey of the planet, concentrating on the cities,
roduced no further emanations, and Q3 returned to his
riginal destination and came to ground.

He made a rapid circuit of the entire city, perception
ocused on all indicators of the original inhabitants'
ppearance and social structure. They were, he learned,
. race of humanoid size and composition, at an
dvanced cultural level. Here, as elsewhere, he
erceived no evidence of war, plague, or invasion. Food
upplies were adequate, and some mass service ma-
hinery still functioned. He submitted the information
athered to full evaluation on every level of intellection
nd could arrive at no logical explanation for the ab-
ence of the inhabitants.

This completed Q3's first program. He sent his
indings to Watson by means of the Mind Lock, nullified
ll deep-perception structures, and rested.

Q3 began his second program at the site of the
Watson expedition's disappearance, a large, open space
hat had served as a gathering place for the inhabitants
f the city. Here he found two specimens of writing. The
nore recent was obviously the last record of the second
Watson expedition; the older was composed in the
anguage of the city dwellers and was of considerable
ntiquity. Upon analysis, the city-dwellers' language
roved to be cognate with an early Akkitan dialect, and
vas translatable within acceptable standards of
ccuracy. It read as follows:

The screens were here when we awoke. Someone
ad set them in place during the night, silently,

working with great speed and care in the darkness. At
first, when there was no knowledge of their number
and each screen was thought to be unique, the erection
of the screens was considered the work of a small
handful of men carrying out some bizarre prank. Only
when it was learned that a screen had been erected in
every inhabited place on *[name of the planet]*
overnight was it clear that *[a large number]* of hands
were involved in a great undertaking whose very
existence had never been suspected and whose
purpose may remain forever unknown.

They were very simple constructions. On that first
morning, when they towered high over us, flat planes
blazing in the glare of early light, they filled us with
awe. But we soon grew bolder and investigated them
more closely, and we found that they were only thin
sheets of some smooth, white material formed into a
gently curving surface, supported at either end by a
high, narrow tripod of darker beams, slender, but very
strong. The beams of the tripods were no thicker than
[untranslatable], but they could not be bent; when
struck with great force they scarcely vibrated and
showed no trace of the blow; *[untranslatable;
probably names of small destructive implements]* left
no impression on them. They were imbedded in the
ground so firmly that all the power of men and
machines could not shake them, so deeply that even
long digging could not uncover their base. The screens
themselves appeared fragile, but proved impervious to
any assault. After all our strength and every tool and
weapon known to us had been used on them, they
stood as white and unscathed as they had on the first
morning.

When it was clear that the screens could not be
moved or destroyed, our rulers instructed us to ignore
them. We accepted the presence of the screens then,

ind awaited the explanation of their arrival. None was
orthcoming, but there was much speculation.

Some said that the rulers themselves had placed the
screens among us as a test, or for other more subtle
reasons which would be useless to attempt to explain.
Few believed these suggestions, since our leaders,
although they did not openly admit it, appeared to be
as ignorant of the origin and purpose of the screens as
were the people.

Travelers brought us many tales about the
phenomenon. A story spread of one village where the
screen had been thrown down and dismantled; the
village was found completely deserted soon after.
Everything in it remained untouched, but no living
thing was to be seen or heard. Many spoke of this
village, but no one named it or gave its location. Nor
did anyone identify the village in which, it was said,
the screen revealed the secret crimes and desires of all
the villagers.

One young man who had traveled far observed that
never in his travels had he seen or heard of two screens
so placed that both could be seen at once. Others
verified this, but the fact was of little interest to
anyone until the images began to appear, and we
wondered if the same image appeared on all screens
simultaneously. All travelers were closely questioned
after that time, but no conclusions could be reached.
Sometimes their answers seemed to suggest that all the
screens showed the same image at the same time, but
always there could be found some variation in the
description, some point of vagueness impossible to
clarify. We could not be certain whether a real
difference, of whatever magnitude, existed among the
images, or whether we were confronting a matter of
inaccurate observation, imprecise phraseology or
misinterpretation, or perhaps a studied attempt to

deceive us. Our uncertainty could not be resolved.

The nature of the images contributed to th difficulty. They were unlike anything we had eve seen before, shifting, swirling patterns of color an amorphous shapes impossible to describe but intensel evocative and hypnotically fascinating. No one coul ignore them, and none watched them without effec The same image might cause one observer to scream i terror, a second to laugh uproariously, a third to weep and a fourth to *[untranslatable]*. And afterwards n one could communicate his experience, or explain hi reaction, to the others. Any attempt to describe wha one had seen on the screen soon broke down int helpless gesticulation and a fumbling for words.

Sometimes the screens were blank for *[a tim period]* and sometimes the shapes and colors move across them uninterruptedly for *[a time period]* o more. There were those who claimed to hear sound emanating from the screens while the images wer seen, but again no definite description could be given Some heard voices, some music, others a cacophanou uproar that rose and fell erratically in volume. I mysel heard nothing, but I will not dispute the tales o others.

In some places the screens became objects o worship. The cult was particularly widespread in th large cities. Travelers told of crowds numbering in *[a large number]* gathered before one of the screens i our capital city (the cities often had a number o screens, but never within sight of one another), sitting, kneeling, or reclining, their eyes fixed on the screen and expressions of rapt attention on their faces. Such scenes occurred even at times when the screens were blank, and had been so for *[a time period]*. When questioned, worshippers said that from time to time truths incapable of utterance were revealed by the patterns shown them. Not all who were present at

ese moments of revelation could grasp their
gnificance, and the great mass of worshippers were
lways unaware of their appearance; but to certain
depts, they offered a glimpse of *[untranslatable]*,
hich men had been seeking since the dawn of reason.
lany accepted this explanation and prepared to
evote their lives to quiet meditation before the
reen. In some locations these disciples were driven
ff or subjected to persecution, and a number were
ruelly put to death; but it was more common for them
be given food and clothing by the people of the
rea. A few of the contemplatives were treated with
reat veneration and credited with the gift of
rophecy or healing.

The screens soon became a part of our daily life,
ven entering into our common speech in a number of
xpressions. It was difficult for us to remember a time
hen the screen had not been standing in the center of
ie village; indeed, an entire generation had been
orn and entered childhood accepting the screen as
iey accepted the seasons and the stars. It was there,
nd if its purpose was not known, at least it did them
o harm.

This morning we awoke and found the screen gone
ithout a trace, not even a mark in the ground where
iose long, thin, incredibly strong props had
enetrated so firmly. The same thing has happened
lsewhere, and in place of the screen there is now a
mall object, so oddly shaped that I cannot describe it,
xcept to say that it has on it a marking that I believe
be the outline of a door.

None of us dares to enter. We are afraid. But we fear
ven more what may be inside, awaiting its time to
ppear before us.

Here the first communication ended.
The other writing, left by the vanished Watson

explorers, presented considerable difficulties. It wa
much longer, covering 241 pages of thin recordin
material. The first 197 pages contained the expedition'
observations on the planet and its inhabitants an
agreed in all major particulars with the observation
recorded by Q3. Page 198 described the discovery of th
old communication, and pages 199-224 were devoted t
a translation of it, fully annotated. This translation wa
in close agreement with the Q3 translation. Th
remaining pages of the Watson manuscript wer
completely incoherent, with the exception of two shor
passages:

P. 231: "Sanders suggests Rinn origin,° intentio
destructive. Martin denies, agrees with me that objec
is some form of dimension gate, possibly extra-galacti
in origin. For ingress or egress? Cannot determine."
P. 240: "Martin under sedation, still raving. Sanders
Taylor, Milman, and Hope missing. Why here, now
The sound is everywhere. The darkness moves. Po
still open but must resist."

The last page of the manuscript relapsed into tot
incoherence. Q3 nullified all structures but highe
intellection, analyzed, and formed a hypothesis: th
object mentioned in the closing lines of the olde
document was related to the disappearance of th
original inhabitants; upon the arrival of the Watsonian
this object either reappeared or was reactivated, or
similar object appeared and was the cause of, or a majo
factor in, the disappearance of the Watsonians. N

° It has since been definitely established that the screen
were not of Rinn origin. Their true source and purpos
remains unknown.

ypothesis concerning the object's nature, appearance,
origin, or purpose was possible. This completed the
second program. Q3 adjusted to primary perception and
waited. He was to act on his own initiative from this
point.

The object became present and Q3 immediately
turned to total function on all levels. The object had not
arrived at its sensed location from any perceptible
direction; it had simply begun to exist in a place where it
had not existed an instant before. Despite all Q3's
efforts, the object could only be sensed as a presence; it
remained undefinable. Q3 approached for close
investigation. Perceptions became contradictory. The
object registered mutually contradictory sensations
simultaneously. On one surface, or on many, a port
appeared, opening on impenetrable blackness. Q3
approached closer and focused perception on a point
within the blackness. He sensed himself being drawn in,
resisted, and perceived the interior blackness extending
to engulf him. He retreated from the presence of the
object and found himself confronting it once more, or
confronting an object identical to it. Again, the
blackness, overwhelming now, immobilizing. A high,
shrill sound commenced, growing steadily in volume,
quickly becoming unbearable. His perception control
wavered and input was disorderly. Something blazed
hot and bright deep within Q3, a sensation of sundering
wrenched him—

12. *Last dealings with the Watsonians.*

—and I was back on Watson, awake in the dark
sanctuary of my artificial womb. Light burst in as the
hatch swung back, and I was lifted out gently, but with

great urgency. The tubes and electrodes were removed
at once, and I was placed on a flat, comfortable surface
and taken to a dim, quiet room where the air had a sweet
smell. As I sank into sleep, I heard my voice, my own
voice, as if it were a separate entity, severed of all
connection with me, utterly beyond my control. It was
shrieking unintelligible words.

I have vague and confused memories of a time of long
rest and quiet, with white-masked figures talking softly
and my own voice, mine once again and under control,
responding to them in words I did not understand; of
Shaw and Johnson; and then only Johnson, and always
the sweet, heavy air that soothed and relaxed me, erased
amorphous fears that plucked at the edges of my
memory in ever-lessening degrees, and pulled me down
time and again into blissful oblivion. Then came a time
when I awoke fully and sat up, clear-headed and feeling
strong. The surroundings were cramped and the air
smelled familiar. Johnson appeared at once.

"Del, are you all right at last?" he asked with real
concern in his voice.

"Yes. What happened to me?"

"We broke the Mind Lock. You came back at once. It
was quite a shock to your system."

"But why? I remember . . . blackness. It was
reaching . . . . It was all around me. I couldn't—"

He broke in abruptly, "Don't think about it. It's over
and you're safe. We lost the Crevnite, but we saved
you."

"What happened to the Crevnite?"

"We don't know, Del. The file on Mission 1, Special
Recovery Unit Renegade Blue Q3 is officially closed. I'd
advise you to forget what happened. It's for your own
good."

I pressed my temples. "I don't remember much."

"It's better if you remember nothing. You've been

hrough a bad experience. Not many men would have
urvived it."

"How long have I been here?" I asked, looking
around the little chamber. "Where are we, Johnson?"

"In orbit above Watson. When you're ready to travel,
'll turn the ship over to you. The Machine will guide
ner back." He held out two envelopes. "The big one
contains the information you requested. The little one
contains your fee. Anything else?"

"Yes. How long have I been back?"

"Twenty-seven days. You had a long recovery, Del,
out you look and sound fine now. Shaw did everything
she could."

"Where's Shaw? I thought she might . . . well, she
seemed sort of concerned."

"She was transferred, Del," Johnson said.

"But she was supposed to stay with me all the way to
the end of this mission. Come on, Johnson, what
happened?"

He looked around nervously, then motioned me to
follow him. We went to the navigation deck, where
Johnson switched on a noisy, short-range scanner to
cover our conversation. He spoke close to my ear. "She
was concerned, Del. She liked you very much. But your
profile showed extreme un-Watsonian tendencies,
ineradicable, and she was ordered removed from all
contact with you. I'm sorry."

"What are 'un-Watsonian tendencies'?" I demanded.

"Strong ego, excessive initiative, behavior ranging
from simple eccentricity to aggravated individualism.
You're almost an archetypal anti-Watsonian." Johnson
grinned guiltily. "As soon as they saw that you were
close to recovery, the officials demanded that we put
you in orbit, so you couldn't disseminate dangerous
attitudes. You scare the pants off them."

"They were glad enough to use me," I said

contemptuously.

"Oh, certainly. Un-Watsonian characteristics are absolutely essential in Special Operations. We couldn't get along without people like you. But a handful of you would have Watson in a turmoil within days."

"I ought to come back and try it some time. Poor Shaw."

"She had her orders, Del, and I had mine. I'm glad we got you back."

"Tell her I'm sorry I couldn't see her."

"I will, Del. One more thing," Johnson said, looking around furtively, turning up the scanner, and lowering his voice to a whisper. "Your friends are safe. I misdirected the intercept mission."

"Intercep—" I began, in a rage, and he silenced me with a horrified gesture.

"I'll be adjusted if they find out! Don't say a word. They were identified at the Infomart. A Hygienic Squad was sent for them that night, but they had left Watson. I learned of the plan to intercept them and had the orders changed." He looked at me anxiously. "I've never done anything like that before, but it just didn't seem right to do that to your friends while you were risking your life."

"It wasn't right. Thanks, Johnson. I won't tell anyone."

"I'd better go now. Good functioning, Del."

13. *I learn something of Commander Corey.*

Whatever their human shortcomings, the Watsonians were an efficient breed. The charts they provided laid out sixty-eight different routes from Watson to Gilead. Apparently they were not sure how much sightseeing I

vanted to do, so they covered all contingencies by
ncluding every system in one route or another.

The information about Commander Corey was less
atisfying. His early career was given in full detail, and
iis combat record with the First Rinn Expedition made
or exciting reading even in that cold, mechanical,
Vatsonian prose. But the part that interested me, the
letails of his trip from Malella on the *Flanders*, was
antalizingly brief, and the little that was given was
nconclusive.

Corey's wife, the oldest daughter of a Malellan water-
guardian, had indeed given birth to a son en route to
Pendelton's Base—but so had five other Malellan
vomen, all of whom were married to Malellan males. I
till had no clear-cut proof of my parentage, but at least
I was coming closer. The odds were down to five-to-one.

Corey's recorded history continued with an impressive series of accounts of his daring raids on Rinn
tragglers under the banner of the Second Expedition. It
vas difficult to draw any inferences from the impersonal
pages of the report, but as I read on, and the accounts of
atrocities against innocent planets began to turn up
more and more frequently, it became clear to me that
the loosely organized Second Expedition, composed
mainly of men seeking either revenge, plunder, or both,
soon degenerated into a fleet of space pirates. No
outright accusations were leveled against Corey, but a
suspicious reader might have put together a fairly
persuasive case against him.

That made me angry. Corey had risked his life in
space combat for nearly thirty years, and the actions of a
few men in his fleet, most of them not even under his
direct command, were casting shadows on all his
achievements. It seemed like a mean, ungrateful way to
treat a proven hero. The fact that I was almost certain

Corey was my father had nothing to do with my feelings
either.

The record of Commander Corey's space career
ended with a terse, provocative statement:

"6/4/2623: Second Rinn Expedition Command
officially decommissioned all driveships of the Second
Expedition and declared a cessation of combat
activities.

"10/8/2623: Message received at Headquarters
Second Rinn Expedition Command reading as follows:
'Decommission and be damned to you. While Rinn
survive, I remain on combat status—Corey.'

"No further information on subject has been
received."

Report complete: END

So that was all they had on Corey. Maybe he was still
alive, out in space somewhere in a scarred old driveship
just Corey and a few tough veterans, hunting down the
Rinn one by one. Or maybe he was a mote of dust in
some far galactic stranger's eye, blasted into oblivion by
some unimaginable weapon out of the Rinn armory; or
sucked into nothingness through one of those infernal
objects like the thing Q3 confronted on the quarantined
planet that I would never forget, despite all Johnson's
admonitions.

I had a lot to think about on my way to Barbary. Not
the least of the things on my mind was the discovery that
the smaller envelope held a little over five Armstrongs,
all in singles to make it bulky. Fifty-two hundred
Vanguards, to be precise. I knew now what Johnson
meant by "less expenses, of course."

14. *Grax meets an old friend, and we all acquire a new one.*

Barbary was a grim little chunk of rock with no natural resources and the ugliest topography and worst climate I've ever encountered on an inhabited planet but a thriving piece of real estate nevertheless. Barbary was in the pleasure business. Whatever you might enjoy doing, you could find someone to do it with—or to, or on, or in front of—on Barbary, provided you could pay the price, which was usually exorbitant. But the Barbary entrepreneurs could have doubled their prices—in fact, several times in their history they had done just that—and still be running full blast and booked solid around the clock. Which they were. Somewhere in those great, domed cities an interested client could find a place to indulge his desires to his heart's content and his body's limits of endurance, and when he was too worn out to continue, he could, if he cared to, watch someone else do their specialty, for a price. It was quite a place. A long way from Gilead, whatever the star charts said.

I pushed my way through the crowd of hawkers at the port and went to the place where we had arranged to meet. Alladale, who was doing a thriving business in extemporaneous indecent ballads, had no time to spare for hosting, so Grax was my guide. Our first stop was a sleazy little den where they sold *hiski*, a powerful stimulant purportedly based on an ancient druidic formula from Old Earth. The bartender said it was made out of grain. Maybe it was, but it tasted to me like what you'd drain out of a drive coil after a cross-galactic hop. Grax informed me that it was a favorite beverage of the greatest Old Earth heroes—Wild Bill Bonney, Buffalo Jack, Jimmy the Kid, and even the

Great White Earp. His Uncle George had told him so.
Grax's obvious enthusiasm stimulated my thirst, and as
I talked on at great length about my adventures on
Watson and the quarantined planet, we both drank
freely. We finished most of a bottle of *hiski* between us,
and then, properly stimulated, headed off to see what
the Barbary night offered.

Grax paid no attention to where he was going, and I
knew nothing of Barbary, so we were soon wandering
aimlessly through a dimly lit and dirty part of town near
the dome perimeter, where all the human and humanoid
galactic flotsam attracted to Barbary by visions of fast
and easy wealth holed up to lay their plans or regain
their health. It wasn't the sort of district a sensible man
would choose to walk through without a heavy guard;
but Grax and I were both armed, with the effects of the
hiski as much as with our sidearms, and we strode down
the dingy streets without a backward glance.

We had been walking for some time, and our heads
were clearing slightly, when we stopped short at the
unmistakable sounds of informal battle. They came from
a cul-de-sac. The light was too dim for me to make out
anything, but Grax took one fast look, grabbed my arm,
and said, "I know this guy. Come on. He needs help."

We trotted toward a husky, bullet-headed giant of a
man backed into a corner and quarter-circled by four
Lixians waving their flaying knives. I had heard tales of
some of the Lixians' pastimes, ° heartily disapproved,
and welcomed this chance to make my opinions felt. The
big guy was holding his assailants off, just barely, with a

° Del later recounted to me the tales he had heard of Lixian
cruelty. They were much exaggerated. In this particular
instance, on which I cannot reflect without shame, I was
under the orders of my Emperor and his chief land-warder
and could not freely challenge my opponent to single combat

huge Bowie knife. His other hand was wrapped in his coat, and he used it to catch and deflect the others' blades. An unimaginative fighting style, I thought, hardly the thing for the arena, but effective in these circumstances.

We didn't come skulking up quietly. Our arrival on the scene was heralded by loud footsteps and some noisy stumbling, but the Lixians didn't even turn around. Such singlemindedness perplexed me, and only when someone landed heavily on my back did I understand why the Lixians could be so intent on the job at hand. They had a solid rear guard.

Things grew very lively in that narrow passage, and in the space of a few minutes I had a dozen occasions to be grateful for the Malellan agility I had inherited from my mother. The air was full of the ugly hiss of flaying knives and did not grow quiet until I had laid out four of the knife-wielders with applications of my fist, knee, boot, and pistol butt. Grax finished up just as I flattened my fourth Lixian, and we turned our attention to the big man.

He had halved the odds against him while we were occupied, but his left arm was bloody from shoulder to elbow and the two remaining Lixians were closing in. They nearly had him, but one of them got overconfident and came too close. That made it one-to-one. Grax and I settled down to watch the outcome, seeing no need to interfere in what was now a fair fight. Frankly, I was curious to see how a Lixian handled himself when the odds were not in his favor; given three-to-one, they could reduce a man to an unsightly stain on the ground within seconds, and three-to-one, or more, was the way they usually fought.

The two opponents slashed and thrust, bobbed and feinted, circling slowly each toward the other's left, looking for that one decisive opening. Then, in an instant, the odds changed. When the big man's back was turned, one of the fallen Lixians dragged himself to his feet and aimed a thrust at the broad back. Without time to shout, I moved instinctively and snapped off a shot, hoping to scare him, and was more astonished than he was when I shot the blade clean out of his hand. That was enough for him. He shot past us, out of the cul-de-sac, and vanished. The remaining Lixian, the biggest one of all, stood poised to fight and was taken completely off his guard by a roundhouse left. He went down like a sack of *bleem*. Certain that the other one had gone to round up a few dozen friends, we cleared out.

The big man's name was Bull. He shrugged off the gash in his arm and began chatting away as coolly and sociably as if we'd come across him in a *hiski* shop. He and Grax had been guards on a scientific expedition to the Yokimyshym system some years back. Bull was now a free lance.

"What do you free-lance at, Bull?" I asked.

"Whatever pays best," he said. "I've been working for the Lixian emperor until a few weeks ago."

"I thought you hated Lixians," Grax said.

"I don't hate their money. Somebody kidnapped the emperor's son. He told me to get him back and I could name my price."

"Did you?"

"Sure. And when I named my price he presented me with a handwritten scroll of gratitude. He said that it was far rarer and more valuable than mere trinkets.° I told him I'd prefer the trinkets, if it was all the same to him."

°   To a Lixian, a testimony of honor in the Emperor's own hand, such as Del here refers to, would be a priceless reward. Unfortunately, Bull was not a Lixian.

"Was it?" I asked.

"No. He told me his gratitude would endure until the end of the day. If I was still on his planet after that he'd have me skinned alive."

"He would, too," Grax said.

"I knew he would. So I left. Wasn't much else I could do." Bull grinned at us. "First I blew up his palace, though. That's why this bunch was after me. Would've got me, too, if you hadn't come along. You saved my skin."

"And now I suppose they're after us, too," I said.

"I guess so," Bull replied casually.

"Somebody is," Grax said. "Don't look back. Somebody's been following us."

"How many?" I asked.

"Only one."

"Let's take care of this right away," Bull said.

We turned the next corner and stopped. A few seconds later, a small, frail man dashed around the corner and stopped short, eyes rounded in terror, as Bull placed the point of his enormous knife just under the man's chin.

"You got something to say to us?" he asked gently.

"Yes. Yes, I do, sirs. I am not armed," he chattered, raising his empty hands high. "I want to ask for your help."

"What for?"

"To save my people."

The three of us exchanged glances. Bull sheathed his Bowie knife and said, "You made a mistake, mister. We're not doctors, and we're not holy men. Get going."

"You're fighting men. That's what we need."

"Fighting men don't save people. They kill people."

"Please. I saw how you handled the Lixians. The three of you vanquished eleven of them."

"More," Bull said.

"Of course. I only saw eleven. The others must have run off. The way you use that knife . . . it's amazing!" The little man then turned to me, awed. "And that incredible shot you made! I've never seen anything like it."

"It was fair," I said coolly. Grax looked at me hard, but kept silent.

"Let's not talk business in the streets," Grax said, taking the man's arm. "I know a *hiski* house near here. Very private. Just what we want."

15. *Steban's tale: The War of The Feather and its aftermath.*

Over a bottle of the best available *hiski* (oddly enough, this time it tasted a lot better. I guess I just had to get used to it), the little man told us his story. He lived on Mazat, a small, pleasant, agricultural planet out toward the rim systems. Life there had been peaceful for many centuries, but now, six times in his generation, the planet had been visited by a band of pirates who carried off supplies, leaving the natives just enough to survive until the next growing season. They also took any women who caught their eye—the women of his planet, he assured us, were unusually comely—butchered any males who annoyed them, and raised general hell with life and property. Word had come that the pirates were on their way for another visit, and that they were hungry, mean, and ready for a bit of sport.

"How many of them?" Grax asked.

"About sixty. Their ship can hold no more."

"And how many able-bodied men on your planet?"

The man frowned thoughtfully. "Hard to say, sir. We are spread out in small communities. There is little contact."

"Guess," Grax pressed him.

"Perhaps thirty thousand."

We looked at him, then at one another, then back to him, dumbfounded. Finally Bull said, "Five hundred to one odds, and you need *us* to do your fighting? Buy yourself a shipload of artillery and cut them to pieces when they land."

"But we cannot do that," the little man said. "Since The War of The Feather our people have unlearned the ways of violence."

"What the hell is The War of The Feather?" Bull roared.

"Let's all have another drink while he tells us about it," I suggested, filling my glass and the little guy's and passing the bottle to Grax. "What's your name, anyway?" I asked him.

"Steban," he said.

I introduced my companions, and Steban proceeded with the history of The War of The Feather.

"Forty-seven generations ago," he began, "our planet was crowded and prosperous. We were a race of warriors, with many conquests to our credit. Our driveships visited many planets and collected rich tribute from them. We were ruled by wise and just kings, and for a long time, life went well. Then two of the kings, twin brothers, had a falling out.

"These two kings ruled jointly and contentedly. Neither one wanted more power than he had. But each was surrounded by ambitious men who sought to advance themselves by urging their master to seize all power for himself. One night, at a banquet, the advisers were given their opportunity.

"The King of the West was entertaining the King of the East. After festivities and entertainment suited to a royal banquet, the main dish was brought in. When the steward raised the cover of the serving dish, a single feather of the *sheeli* bird was found floating in the sauce. The steward immediately tried to conceal it, but it was too late. Both kings had seen it and were enraged."

"What's so bad about the feather of a *sheeli* bird?" I asked.

"The *sheeli* is an unattractive bird that lays its eggs in the nests of other birds."

"So what?" Bull asked.

Steban lowered his eyes modestly. "On our planet, the feather of a *sheeli* bird is given to a man whose wife finds her pleasure with other men. It is the greatest of insults."

We all nodded, and Steban continued.

"Each of the kings had recently taken a wife, and each felt that the other was making a mockery of him. They proceeded with the feast, but they spoke to each other no more that evening, and their parting was cold and formal. The advisers went to work at once, filling each king's ear with stories of his brother's ambition. Eventually, war broke out. When it was over, the great cities were all leveled to the ground and most of the people were dead."

"What happened to the two kings?" Grax asked.

"They and their advisers were torn to pieces by the survivors."

"Serves them right," Bull said.

"Perhaps, but my people were very troubled. They reflected on what they had done to themselves and swore from that day on never to kill again. For forty-seven generations, despite even the coming of the race of Old Earth, my people have patterned themselves to avoid violence and the infliction of death at all costs. We have succeeded."

"How did you manage to survive?" Bull asked.

"We have had no trouble until the pirates came. When they demanded our food, we offered them all they wanted, and more. When they took our women, we consoled ourselves by saying that the presence of our women among them would soften their ways. But when they killed, we had no answers to give ourselves. We could do nothing. Some of us gathered to seek a way to drive the pirates off, but in forty-seven generations, we have lost the will to fight. We do not have weapons, nor do we know how to make them; nor, if we made or purchased them, do we have the knowledge or the will to use them."

"So you want us to fight for you," Grax said.

Steban nodded. "If you do not, we will be destroyed."

"What do you mean, 'destroyed'? Pirates know a good thing when they see it. You'll be inconvenienced a little, maybe roughed up, but why would they destroy you?" I asked.

"Because we have nothing to give them. My people have sold all their surplus in order to send me for help. The pirates will take everything this time and kill us for daring to disappoint them."

"They sure will," Grax said. He and Bull and I looked at each other for a full minute, saying nothing openly, but communicating clearly and unmistakably. I cleared my throat, took a good gulp of *hiski,* and asked Steban when the pirates were expected.

"Forty-one days, GSC," he said. "About thirty days, Barbary."

"And how long to get to your planet?"

"Twenty-three days, GSC."

I looked at Grax. "We can make it," he said.

"Three of us?" Bull said cautiously.

"Our ship holds a dozen men," I told him. "We can pick up a crew here on Barbary."

"My people will be eternally grateful to you," Steban said.

"How grateful?" Bull asked. "I think we ought to get that straight before we start making plans."

"We will give you anything you ask."

"I just went through that routine. Let's get some figures down," Bull said.

We haggled over a fee for a time and finally settled for what must have seemed a fortune to Steban but was really a bargain for this kind of job. Even though I was practically broke, coming home after all those years in space with less than a Betterton in hard cash, I was willing to come down a bit. Steban was a harmless little guy and his people were in big trouble. Mazat sounded to me a lot like Gilead, and I'd have expected anyone in my position to do the same for Gilead. And it wasn't so far out of my way, really; just a few weeks' travel time, and one of the Watson charts covered the route. And the *hiski* was prodding away at my social conscience.

"Okay," Bull said when the fee was arranged. "Now, what about your people—will they do what we tell them?"

"They cannot kill," Steban said.

"I'm not talking about killing. They're farmers— can they dig ditches? Flood fields? Cut down trees?"

"Oh, yes."

"All right." He turned to us. "What'd you say your ship holds? A dozen?"

"If we squeeze in," Grax said.

"Suppose we don't squeeze."

"Eight," Grax said. Bull looked to me for verification, and I nodded.

"That means we need four more men. Any ideas where we can get them?"

"We don't have time to scour the galaxy. I think we ought to look right here on Barbary," I said.

"What do you say, Grax?" Bull asked.

"I go along with that."

"So do I. We'll go down to the port tomorrow and see who's here. I'll get the word around. Now let's have another bottle of *hiski*."

16. *An encounter with Daltrescans; our first recruit.*

Bull, Grax, and I spent the next three days getting the word around, but we found no takers. There were plenty of men on Barbary who looked hard and talked brave, but they cooled off fast at the mention of sixty pirates with empty bellies and blood in their eyes. To tell the truth, it wasn't hard to see their point of view once the *hiski* stopped flowing. But we had given Steban our word, and we knew we had to deliver. If we didn't find four more men, we'd just have to take on the pirates ourselves. That was not a pleasant prospect.

On our fourth day of searching, we were at the spaceport at nightfall when suddenly things began to grow very quiet and tense. Something was up, but exactly what was not immediately apparent. We settled our bill and slipped unobtrusively out of the victualer's shop where we had been cursing our luck over thick mugs of hot *scoof*. Outside, we looked around for indicators of the cause of the sudden tension. Bull pointed to a furtive gang of stevedores

heading, with many a nervous backward glance,
toward a remote corner of the port. We followed
cautiously, at a safe distance. A squat, dark ship was
just touching down, and everyone seemed to be in a
great hurry to get it under cover.

"Daltrescans," Bull whispered, and pulled us into
the shadows between the two warehouses.

The word alone was enough to make my fingers
itch. Those hulking Daltrescan slaveships were
unwelcome in most systems, and even here on
Barbary, where there was less law than usual, they
were offered little hospitality—although I'd already
heard rumors of certain pleasure houses and grogshops
on Barbary where it was not advisable to go alone and
unarmed unless you wanted to end your life, fairly
soon, in the arenas, mines, or other enterprises whose
manpower depended on the Daltrescans. From what
I'd seen of Barbary so far, that made sense.

"What do you think they're up to?" Grax whispered.

"Refueling, maybe. They might be delivering."

"Or making a pickup," I said.

"We'll know soon enough. They're moving fast,"
Bull said.

I was guessing, and I hoped I was wrong, but the
Daltrescans had indeed landed to pick up cargo. Eight
of them came out of a shed leading three men heavily
chained. The drivers used their prods freely and
expertly and supplemented the prods with kicks and
punches. Two of the chained men scurried along as
best they could on hobbled legs, cowering from the
steady rain of blows, but the third captive, a big,
blond-haired fellow who looked to be little more than
a boy—a husky one—didn't move fast enough for the
drivers. That did not sit well with the Daltrescans,
who favored obedience and submission in their
charges. One of them reached down suddenly, yanked

at the prisoner's leg chain, and toppled him. He and two others then began to administer kicks in the midsection. I recalled my last night on Gilead; their methods had not changed. No matter how much of a hurry they might be in, the Daltrescans always had time to work over their captives.

Behind me, in the darkness, I could hear the grinding of Grax's teeth and a methodical incantation of curses from every planet in the galaxy coming in a strangled whisper from Bull. I nudged Bull.

"We've got to do something, Bull," I said.

"We will. Wait," he said.

He moved off, and I tried to follow his direction, but a sudden flurry of motion caught my eye. The kid who had been getting the beating had been hauled to his feet. He stood unsteadily, and then, in a motion too fast to follow, he looped his wrist chain around the neck of one of his drivers, and the high crack of breaking bone could be heard where we stood. Whipping the chain loose from the body as it fell, he swung it at the driver who came rushing at him, and stretched him flat. Then, as the other fled for help, he headed directly toward the dark passage where Grax and I stood.

"Over here," Grax called to him.

The big kid looked startled, but he didn't stop. Grax pointed to an opening in the wall just behind us, and he ducked in, moving as fast as the chains on his legs permitted. Grax said, "You talk to them, Del. I'll back you," and moved into the shadows.

I had been waiting for a long time to talk to a crew of Daltrescans with something more than a handful of rocks to defend myself. I walked out into the soft light of Barbary's double moons and watched as five of the six still-functioning drivers approached me, striding briskly and slapping the prods rhythmically into their

open palms, men who knew just where they were
heading and what they were going to do when they
arrived. When they came within twenty paces, I
stepped into their path and stood there, my hands
down, ready to move. I didn't want them too close.
Once within throwing range, the Daltrescans were
deadly accurate with those prods they carried. They
stopped walking and spread out.

"Where did the big one go?" one of the drivers
demanded.

"What big one?"

"The escaped prisoner," another Daltrescan said.
"He ran this way, right past here."

"I didn't see any escaped prisoner."

"You're a liar. He came this way," the first one said.

"Come on, let's—" another started, but shut up
when Grax stepped out of the shadows of the opposite
wall.

"I think you made a mistake, mister. I mean *you*,
with the big mouth," he said.

"The prisoner came this way," the Daltrescan said.

"I'm not talking about that. You called my partner a
liar. That was a mistake."

"He said he didn't see our prisoner, and we all know
he ran right—"

"There wasn't any prisoner. It was an escaped
slave," I said.

"He's a killer. He knocked one man's brains out and
broke another man's neck. We have to bring him in,"
the first Daltrescan said. "Now, we don't want any
trouble with you boys, we just want to do our job."

Grax launched a long, expert gob of spittle that
landed in the dust at the speaker's toes. "That big
fellow didn't kill two men, he exterminated two
Daltrescan slavers. He ought to be paid a bounty.
Anyone who gets rid of a few Daltrescans is doing the

galaxy a service."

I sometimes thought that Grax had a tendency to get a little too pushy in a tight spot. I didn't like Daltrescans any more than he did—probably a great deal less, since he had had no firsthand experience of their ways—but I wasn't all that eager to force them to a fight. All I really cared about was the slaves.

There was a brief silence after Grax spoke, and then the biggest of the five drivers took a step forward and said, "We don't have to find the big one. Let's take these two instead. We've got plenty of room in the hold."

"Got room for three?" Bull's voice roared out, and the five slavers looked behind them. Bull had worked his way around the warehouse while we were talking, and I was glad for his arrival on the scene.

The Daltrescans hesitated. None of us moved. I think they were all ready to back down, but at that moment a beam of light fell across the field as the port of the ship opened and a dozen men leaped out. The sixth slaver, who had stayed behind to guard the two remaining slaves, had spotted the trouble and gone to the ship for reinforcements. The Daltrescans on hand, emboldened by the prospect of all that help, rushed us. Bull drew his Bowie knife and went for the biggest one. Grax drew and fired, dropping a charging slaver, and the big blond kid came hobbling out between us, flailing his chain around like a scythe.

"We'll take these. You get the others," Grax shouted to me.

I skirted the melee, dropped to one knee when I had a clear view, and took aim at the foremost of the twelve men racing across the field. When nine of them were lying back or belly down on the ground and all was quiet behind me except for occasional moaning and the clink of chains, the three remaining slavers

stood stock-still before me, their weapons flung aside
and their hands high.

They began babbling away, and I doubt that ever
mortal man heard such tales of innocence led astray as
poured from the three broad-backed, thick-necked,
beady-eyed maulers who stood before me pleading for
my forbearance. All, as they told it, were dead set
against the slave trade, just hard-working men down
on their luck, forced into a dirty business to support an
aging mother, an ailing wife, or a crippled child. They
had never mistreated a prisoner. Not these three. They
had risked their own necks to ease the lot of the poor
unfortunates who fell into the clutches of their
heartless shipmates. It was the others who admini-
stered the beatings, cut the rations, and booted trou-
blemakers out of the atmosphere lock as an example.
But not them. They only followed orders, with great
reluctance, and all the while the spark of galactic
brotherhood glowed within their hairy breasts. I finally told them to shut up before I got sick.

"What about these?" I asked Bull when he came to
check my end of the operation.

"I don't care what you do with them. Let's see if the
kid has any suggestions."

With his chains discarded, the blond kid—not such a
kid after all, I noticed—was inclined to live and let
live.

"Why don't we turn them in?" Grax asked.

"If we get mixed up with the law on Barbary, we're
the ones who'll land in jail. You ought to know that,"
Bull said. He turned to the three slavers. "How many
slaves you got on board?"

"None, sir!" they answered immediately.

"That's right. I heard them talking," the blond one
said.

Bull nodded. "All right. Pick up your friends and

move out of here, fast. And stay off Barbary. If you're smart, you'll find another line of work."

"Yes, sir! Oh, thank you, sir!" they gibbered.

The other two prisoners had been lying on the ground, still as stones, throughout all the excitement. Now they lifted their heads cautiously, rose, and hobbled fearfully toward us. They looked like pretty poor pickings for a slaver, and I doubt that either one would have lasted out a single shift in the sulphur pits or put on a good show in the arena. One was a taciturn farmer from Elgar II who had sold some asteroid holdings and come to Barbary for a long-awaited fling, the other a weapons salesman who had stopped in a grogshop for a nightcap and awakened in chains. Both were effusively grateful.

On the way back to town, the big blond fellow, whose name was Ronin, told us how he had been captured by space pirates while prospecting in a dead star system and brought to Barbary to be turned over to the slavers. All his equipment, including his specially built one-man explorer, was either stolen or destroyed by the pirates.

"Those pirates sure did you dirty," Bull said, shaking his big, gleaming head.

"I bet you'd love to get a crack at them, eh?" I asked.

"I will. I don't know how, but I'll figure out a way. There's nearly sixty of them, and I'm alone and broke now, but I know where they're heading."

Bull glanced at me. "Where?"

"They're on their way to a farming planet, Mazat. They're going to provision there and rest up for a while. They ought to be arriving in about forty days."

Bull, Grax, and I stared at each other, then began to laugh and poke one another and look at Ronin, shake our heads, and laugh some more. He watched our show, saying nothing, but I'm sure he was wondering what he was into now. When we quieted down, I told him Steban's story. He listened attentively and then held out his hand to each of us in turn.

Now there were four of us.

17. *Grax and I meet a Master.*

The very next day, Grax and I found a recruit, and Bull and Ronin located another. This time, our job was easier.

Grax and I were walking down a main thoroughfare when we saw a crowd gathered at a corner just outside the entrance to a Round-the-Clock Violence Parlor: give it, take it, or observe it, all one price, no waiting, no restrictions. These places were popular on Barbary, but the crowd here was unusually large. Over the noise came the familiar sound of a man giving a pitch. Barbary was full of people selling never-fail luck tokens, absolutely certain aphrodisiacs, and genuine Old Earth artifacts (all of them manufactured on the busy industrial worlds of Iboki I and III), but this pitchman sounded different, and we were curious to hear more. Before I could make out any words, I caught the tone of his voice, and it was so flat, so bored, so don't-give-a-damn that I was fascinated and so was Grax.

"This space is approximately five meters square," he droned, "and I will stand in a one-meter square area in the center while twelve men, using any type of knife or club, try to strike me down. If I am still on my feet when the sand in the glass runs out, I win all bets. If I am knocked off my feet or forced out of the square, the man who moves me wins the bets. I will be completely unarmed and will use only defensive tactics. Who wants to try?"

A couple of bruisers moved in and announced themselves. Three more followed, then others, and soon the pitchman had his dozen opponents. He unbuttoned his tunic, pulled off his boots, and stood in the center of the little area as naked and defenseless as a newborn *frinkl* except for a loincloth and a wide, woven sash tied around his waist and fastened in a curious knot. He was a skinny little guy, smaller than either of us and dwarfed by the least of his twelve adversaries. He had not a spare ounce on him, but he looked to be solid muscle, what there was of him.

"This ought to be good," Grax said, pushing forward through the crowd. "He's a Sixteenth-Level Master."

"Of what?"

"Of Ti-Kama-No, the Science of the Rippling Waves. It's a technique of unarmed defense taught on Iboki VI. They claim it goes all the way back to Japan, on Old Earth."

"Who was Japan?" I asked.

"I think it was a city in the Pacific States. Whatever it was, they used to specialize in defense techniques. They also made cameras."

"Where'd you learn all this?"

"I shipped with a guy who was a Third-Level Master. Sometime I'll have to tell you about him and the seven Daltrescans." He tugged me forward. "Let's watch."

The thirteen men took their positions, the sandglass was overturned, and the match began. All twelve of the challengers struck out at the Master at once and kept swinging, and for a few seconds it looked to me as though we were going to witness a massacre. But then, through the wild tangle of flailing arms and straining legs, I caught a glimpse of him, and that one glimpse was enough to ease my fears for his safety. He was bobbing, weaving, ducking, dodging, crouching, fending off thrusts and blows with deft flicks of his forearms, and all the while retaining his deadpan look of detachment and absolute boredom. When the sand in the glass ran out and the timekeeper shouted "Hold!" the Master wasn't even sweating, but the twelve would-be assailants were puffing and panting like a *plook* on a mountaintop.

They cleared the ring, and he called for twelve more challengers. No response. He offered to take on fourteen, then fifteen. Still no response. He offered to face sixteen men then, with his arms bound, and the crowd began to melt away, muttering and shaking their heads. Still expressionless, he pulled on his boots, donned his tunic, and started to pack away his sandglass and markers. Grax walked over to him, and I followed.

"Got a minute, mister?" Grax asked.

"Show's over," he said.

"That's not what I wanted to talk to you about. I wouldn't tangle with a Sixteenth-Level Master if his hands and feet were tied and he was blindfolded."

The Master looked up from his packing. "Blindfolded? I never thought of that. How do you know I'm a Sixteenth-Level Master?"

"The sash and the knot. I once knew a Third-Level Master. He explained the markings. There aren't many of you around."

"Only four. Soon there won't be any. There's no chance to use the Science any more, unless you put on street shows like this one."

"We might be able to offer you something a little better," Grax said.

"What? A circus?" He looked at us contemptuously.

"No, nothing like that," I said and went on to tell

him about Steban's people and their problem.

He listened to me, saying not a word, showing nothing in his eyes or his expression, and when I had finished, he asked, "Sixty of them?"

"About sixty."

"Maybe more," Grax said.

"Armed?"

"Head to toe," I assured him.

"I'll go. When do we leave?"

"Tomorrow night," I said.

"I'll be at the port at second moonrise. I'll find you."

"Good enough," Grax said. The Master lifted his bag and started off, and Grax called after him, "Hey, what's your name?"

"Call me Slip," he said, without turning.

And that made five.

18. *We fill our ranks unexpectedly.*

We saw Bull and Ronin that night, and a new man was with them, our sixth recruit, a grizzled ex-legionnaire named Carter. He knew Bull from the Rinn Expedition, and as it turned out, he had once served under my probable father, Commander Corey.

When he mentioned the name—which of course wasn't the one I was using—Bull's eyes widened. "You served with Corey? I never knew that."

"It's been a long time, Bull," Carter said. "I was assigned to his ship after our group broke up. Not many like him left, I'll tell you that much." He shook his head and fell silent.

"Where'd you serve, Carter?" I asked.

"Wherever the Rinn were. Corey commanded the Seventh Attack Force, and we lived up to our name. We were always right up front. He used to light into a Rinn formation like a *snargrax* into a flock of *trettles*. He had reason enough to hate them, poor guy. His wife was a Malellan, one of the last alive. Pretty little thing, she was, too. He showed me her picture. Used to carry a little motion painting of her in an amulet." He fell gloomily silent and looked down at the table, then up at us. "I guess you know what the Rinn did to Malella."

We murmured affirmatives. The story of the Rinn's devastation of the Malellan system was familiar to every race in the galaxy, and by now, to me.

"He rounded up the survivors and brought them to Pendelton's Base," Carter went on. "It was a long trip in those days. His wife had a son on the way, and he decided to resign his commission once they reached Pendelton and find a place to settle down. He could've gone anywhere he wanted. A hundred planets would've made him king if he said the word. But the Rinn were right behind them. The day after they landed the Rinn came. He went up to engage them, and when he got back the base was leveled. After that he didn't care about anything but destroying the Rinn."

Here was verification I hadn't expected; from a man, not a machine, a man who had actually known Corey and spoken with him. Gariv had claimed to, but Carter struck me as a lot more trustworthy. I was exploding with curiosity, but I kept still, not wanting to let on anything until I could be sure of a few more facts. I asked Carter what finally became of his commander.

"Couldn't tell you that," he said. "Last I heard, he
was leading a volunteer force on the Second Rinn
Expedition. It was a mopping-up operation. That
must've been about nine, ten years ago. The Second
Expedition fell apart, from what I hear. A lot of the
ships turned outlaw. But I doubt that Corey went that
way. Now, *there's* the man we could use. He could
clean up those pirates on Mazat without breaking a
sweat."

"Do you think—" Ronin began and stopped
abruptly as a tall Lixian glided to our table and
stopped a few feet away, his narrow eyes fixed on Bull.
Bull's hand eased down to his knife, but he made no
other move, and the rest of us remained still.

The Lixian raised his long arms, palms out, and
touched the fingertips to his forehead, crossed his arms
and touched his shoulders, then his knees. Being a
Lixian, he could manage all this without bending. I
recognized the challenge ritual, and so did Bull.

The Lixians were an interesting people. They were
one of the first humanoid races encountered, and once
the pioneers got over their awe at Lixian size—a full-
grown adult often topped three meters—they found
that there was very little essential difference between
men and Lixians. Lixis was a low-gravity planet with a
thin atmosphere, and the Lixians had developed
accordingly: they were tall and spindly, with long,
thin, very strong arms and legs, a gigantic chest that
tapered down to hardly any waist at all, and a tiny
figure-eight of hips and pelvis. Their heads were
proportionately small, wedge-shaped, and as much
animal as human. Those enormous mobile ears, in
particular, though they were well designed for hearing
on Lixis, made Old Earth humans a bit nervous and
kept contact between the races to a minimum.

Lixian voices always got me. With those big, deep chests to echo in and build up volume before issuing out, a Lixian voice always sounded heroic on a normal-atmosphere planet.

The Lixian code was something quite simple in principle, but it was capable of enormous complication which no non-Lixian could hope to unravel. It baffled quite a few Lixians, too, at times. There was one Supreme Ruler on the planet, to whom all Lixians owed allegiance to the death. Under him, in order, were the seven Emperors, a few score kings, and about a hundred land-wardens, all of whose subjects owed allegiance both to them and to the Supreme Ruler and to everyone else on up the chain of command between. Each of these lesser rulers had his own corps of chieftains, clan fathers, and war leaders, who all had their little band of adherents, and the allegiance of these groups worked the same way. After centuries of wars, alliances, treaties, usurpations, revolutions, and compromises, generations of inter-marriage, and the rise of a new religion which intro-duced a complex of loyalties, the allegiance situation had grown so involved that a man might find himself obliged simultaneously to destroy and protect his own sons or even himself.

Lixian honor depended on the exactitude with which one fulfilled these labyrinthine obligations of loyalty and obedience. One of the frequent means of satisfying all the conflicting claims upon him was for an individual to go into exile, in hopes of winning enough glory elsewhere to atone for his transgressions or shortcomings on Lixis. The other main alternative was suicide, Lixian style, a very messy and protracted process involving one's entire family—several thousand people, in some cases, since the Lixians inter-preted relationship very broadly—and lasting for days. The usual choice was exile, and so most of the Lixians one met around the systems were hunting for glory in order to win their right to return home and take up a place of honor among their own people. It made them eager warriors but rather boring conversationalists.°

This big fellow seemed no different from the rest. "I have sought you out that I might cleanse my honor," he boomed forth, directing his words to Bull and then glancing at Grax and me.

Bull studied him, then said, "Aren't you one of the bunch that jumped me the other night?"

"I am."

"Where are your friends? Lixians don't fight alone."

"I do."

"Well, good for you. Now, if it's all the same to you and your exalted emperor, I'd like to drink with my friends."

"I will await your convenience," the Lixian said.

Bull sighed patiently, leaned back, and looked up at his challenger. "Listen, Stretch, I have other things on my mind right now, and I can't spare the time to worry about your problems. Why don't you just go away?"

"When I fled from you, I disgraced myself before you and your comrades," the Lixian said. "You must restore me, or I must slay you all in order to regain my honor."

"Honor?" Bull sneered. "Where do you come off to

°   This brief sketch of the Lixians and their way, though unflattering, is correct in the essential features. I offer only one correction: Del speaks of the Lixian manner of self-termination as "messy," by which he seems to suggest excessive shedding of blood. This is not so. The process is protracted and excruciatingly painful but involves no blood-shed.

be talking about honor? You're a hired cutthroat for a
crooked emperor."

"No longer," the Lixian said imperturbably. I had
heard that Lixians were cool customers, but this one
was glacial. He made Slip look like a friendly drunk.

"What do you mean, no more?"

"When I attacked you, I did so in the belief that you
had foully wronged my emperor, but I was deceived in
that. Now I am free to challenge you for myself alone,
that I might walk my way with honor unblemished or
die attempting to regain it."

"What good is honor if you die getting it?" Grax
asked him.

"Honor is all a Lixian has in this life. To gain honor
in death is to win life beyond life."

"Well, if it means that much to you, I suppose—"
Bull began, rising from his seat.

Ronin restrained him and turned to the Lixian.
"Let's not be hasty. Sit down with us, Stretch. I think
maybe we can find a way for you to win your honor
back."

"Do you challenge me?"

"No, I don't. Come on, sit down."

The Lixian pulled up a low stool and seated himself.
He still towered over us all. Ronin leaned toward him
and said, "You're looking for a chance to regain your
honor, and we're looking for a warrior to join us in
saving a planet from space pirates. There's a lot of
honor in that, isn't there?"

The Lixian agreed.

"So why don't you come along with us?" Ronin
asked.

"But I am in disgrace. I have much honor to regain.
I have served an evil emperor, and I have been
disarmed by my adversaries."

"If you win honor in battle against the space pirates, that would atone for serving a bad emperor, wouldn't it?"

"True, it would satisfy," the Lixian said. "But my dishonor before these men remains."

Ronin looked hard at Bull. It was all up to him now. He could restore the Lixian's honor with a word if he chose to, but I knew how stubborn he was, and how little admiration he had for Lixians. Still, this one had courage, and he could handle himself well. He'd be a help to us.

"Your honor is intact, as far as I'm concerned," Bull said, with considerable effort. Grax and I seconded that.

"Then I will join you," the Lixian said promptly. "I swear to bring honor upon our endeavor, though it cost us our lives."

"If it's not too much to ask, Stretch, I'd rather come back to enjoy the honor," Carter said.

He spoke for all of us. Even Stretch, I think.

19. *We arrive on Mazat and prepare a welcome.*

We spent the next day making the rounds of the victualers, chandlers, and armorers, stocking up for the long trip and the work ahead. We gathered at the spaceport just at second moonrise, and Slip joined us there right on time. An hour later we were on our way to Mazat.

On a twenty-three day haul, I expected to get plenty of time to find out what Carter knew about Commander Corey, but Carter turned out to be one of the true old breed of star-hoppers. A brawler and an outcast when his feet were on solid ground, he was strictly business on the deck of a driveship. When he wasn't eating, sleeping, or checking stores, his eyes were fixed on the instruments. It didn't matter to him that this ship could have been handled capably by any fairly intelligent six year old. I guess the lessons of alertness he learned in the Rinn Expedition were too deeply implanted to be set aside, even when they were no longer necessary. After a few monosyllabic exchanges of conversation, I decided to wait until we landed to make my inquiries. After all this time, a few more weeks couldn't make much difference.

Bull kept himself as busy as Carter, and remained as laconic, and Slip and Stretch didn't say a dozen words between them on the whole trip. They had their own ways of keeping occupied, Slip with his exercises, Stretch with his long meditations. I spent most of the time practicing with my own weapons and familiarizing myself with a set of pistols the weapons salesman had given me for my part in freeing him from the Daltrescans. When I got tired of that, I played *quist* with Grax and Ronin. When Mazat showed up on the viewers on the twenty-third day, I was happy to see it.

The Mazatlans gave us a grand reception. They were a small, slender people, graceful in their movements, with round, wide-set eyes that gave them a look of perpetual astonishment. They were gentle in every way, and I came to like them almost at once. Whatever their failings as warriors, they were the best hosts I had ever encountered. Bull and Carter set up a scanning system, and when all indicators showed clear, we let the Mazatlans throw a festival for us, and they outdid themselves. Everyone joined in. Slip, after a few rounds of the local drink, put on a wild, weaving dance that had everyone goggle-eyed and dizzy. Ronin grabbed a *linlovar* and started thumping out the music to a string of Old Earth songs he had picked up in the mining camps where he had spent his youth, and Bull, Carter, and Grax joined in with some songs of their own. Some of the kids set up a revolving target, and I did some fancy shooting for them. The crowd enjoyed that, and I think it reassured them. Up to then, they might have been thinking that Steban had brought home a bunch of carousers from a traveling space show to fight the pirates for them. After I went back to my place and settled down beside a cute little Mazatlan girl—Steban hadn't overrated their comeliness, and they were as friendly as they were cute— Stretch got up, slung two bandoliers of finger knives over his broad shoulders, and proceeded to put on an exhibition of knife-throwing that beat anything I'd ever seen. I sneaked a few side glances at Bull while this was going on, and twice I caught him licking his lips and wiping his skull with his dirty old bandanna. I'm sure he was thinking how different things might have been in that alley on Barbary if Stretch had had room to use his finger knives. When it was all over, he was the first one to shake the big Lixian's hand, and he shook it as if Stretch were his long-lost brother.

Hata, my little Mazatlan, brought me breakfast the next morning, and then I joined the others in the marketplace in the center of the village. All the men were assembled, bearing their tools, and Bull assigned a group to work under each of us. He had a big chart set up in plain view of everyone, showing just where he wanted the pits and trenches dug, the tripwires, chokes, and deadfalls placed, and the bridges and crossings mined. His plan was simple and direct. The pirates always traveled on *haxopods*, six-legged Mazatlan beasts that could run like the wind but

couldn't jump even half their own length.° Bull decided to surround the whole settlement with a moat—
the pirates, suspecting nothing from the natives, would
accept it as an irrigation ditch—and once they were
inside, we'd pull up the bridges and trap them in the
open marketplace. After that, it would be easy.

We allowed ourselves eight days for the whole job,
but we finished in six and were lucky we did. On the
seventh day, all the scanners began to flash at once.
Something was homing in on Mazat and coming on

° The *haxopod* is not exclusive to Mazat. It is found
throughout the galaxy, and the general estimate is that some
form of *haxopod,* adapted to local conditions by a variety of
mutations, exists on three out of every four inhabited land
planets. None has ever been recorded on a water planet.

The strain here described by Del is peculiar to Mazat,
where it is employed in farm work and short-range travel. A
similar type of *haxopod* is found on most of the agricultural
planets. On sand planets, *haxopods* have developed into
broad-footed desert lopers with the ability to go for long
periods without moisture. The *haxopods* of the cold worlds
have thick shaggy coats and sharp, ridged hoofs that enable
them to grip smooth ice. On the temperate planets, the
haxopod seems to be developing still further, into a four-
legged beast, its two foremost appendages "atrophied in
the bend of supplication" as Alladale Anthem-maker rather
too imaginatively described them in a minor poem.

The origin of the *haxopod* is still unknown, but all who
have studied the question agree that this creature is among
the oldest surviving life forms in the galaxy. It is believed
that the lost race known as the First Travelers brought the
original *haxopods* from their home planet and allowed them
to mate freely with similar creatures on the new worlds.
Since these events took place between -2,600,000,000 and
-2,450,000,000 GSC, no recorded evidence exists.

I am indebted to Professor Doctor Portteus for much of
this information.

fast. Before long we could focus for detail, and we had
our first look at the pirate ship. She was a beauty, a
long, sleek, deep-space cruiser that could circle the
galaxy without overheating a coil or touching down for
provisions. No wonder they only raided Mazat every
few years, I thought. With a ship that size, they had to
give a planet time for a few bumper crops before they
could fill their lockers.

"All right, let's get ready for them," Bull said,
turning from the viewplate. Carter was still gazing
fondly at the ship, and Bull yanked him away by the
belt. "In a day or two you can inspect it from inside,
Carter. Right now, there's work to do," he said.

He took his place in front of the chart and we
gathered around him while he posted us for action.
Carter and Ronin took the bridges, with orders to
wreck them when the last pirate had crossed. Stretch
was stationed just over the main bridge, inside the
village, to pick off any loiterers or stragglers who
might become curious at the sound of crashing timber.
Grax and Slip were to cover the pirates' rear, at the far
end of the marketplace, and Bull and I were to act as
the reception committee. It was expected that we
would draw the first attack, and as soon as we did, the
others would close in. In a way, I was proud that Bull,
who had been our leader all along, had chosen me to
stand at his side in the most dangerous spot of all; but I
don't know that I wouldn't have changed places
eagerly with anyone else.

We spread out then. Bull and I took up a position in
front of a low wall pierced with firing ports, the bright
Mazatlan sun over our shoulders where it would shine
in the faces of the pirates. When things got busy, we
could be over the wall in one jump, with a clear field
of fire before us. The *haxopods* couldn't clear a waist-
high barrier, and we'd be firing before a single pirate

could dismount. Getting on or off a *haxopod* was a tricky problem at any time; in the midst of a battle, it would be more than enough to occupy a man's attention. Everything sounded very simple and easy when Bull explained it. A busy day's work, then wash up and head for home, the gratitude of a gentle people ringing in our ears and filling our pockets. Nothing to it. Nevertheless, as we waited for the pirates to appear, I felt the sweat trickling down my back and my ribs. And it wasn't all that warm on Mazat.

A tense and quiet hour passed, and then another. I checked my pistols at least a dozen times. This was an elaborate and time-consuming procedure, since I had armed myself for a seige: besides my short knife, I wore Commander Adamson's pistols in my holsters, the new pistols tucked into my belt, and within quick grasp on the other side of the wall, four more pistols hung on pegs. Bull, on the other hand, was a calm as a man sitting down to dinner with his family. He gave his knives and pistols one fast check, then sat down with his back to the wall, pulled out a plug of *zaff* leaves, stripped one off, and stuffed it in his mouth.

"Want one?" he asked, extending the plug.

"No, thanks, Bull," Given my chance, I would have preferred a thorough drenching in Raphanus' fighting-scent. *Zaff* leaves were a poor substitute. Besides, they tasted awful.

"It'll keep you alert," Bull said, smiling.

"I'm alert."

He laughed. "You sure are. Relax, Del. You fought three-on-one when you were on Tarquin, didn't you? This isn't much different."

"Only about three times as bad."

"I've seen you use those pistols. You don't need to worry."

"I'm not worried. I want things to get started, that's

all. I can't take the waiting."

"It won't be long. Just keep your eye on Stretch. He'll give us the signal."

I followed his pointing finger and saw the lean figure perched on a rooftop at the far end of the village, overlooking the main road. I glanced at Stretch many times during that interminable wait, and finally I saw his long arms waving in a slow arc. Bull waved back, and Stretch disappeared to take up his battle post.

"They'll be here soon. I'll do the talking. You watch them. If anyone goes for a weapon, or looks like they're going for one, start shooting," Bull said. He perched on the low wall and I stood beside him, my eyes fixed on the narrow passage across the marketplace where the bandits would make their entrance.

20. *A parley with space pirates.*

We soon heard the first, faint rumble of the splay-footed *haxopods'* steady trot. It grew louder, swelled to a hollow thundering as they crossed the long bridge into the town, and then the bandits burst into sight, riding fast, pouring into the marketplace like a dirty river in full flood. They were a mixed crew, with nothing in common but evil expressions and filthy clothes. All were armed, each with his own particular special weapon. I picked out Daltrescans with oversized prods thrust into their belts; Skeggjatts bearing their traditional double-edged battle-axes; a Lixian weighed down with bandoliers of finger knives; a few Quespodons, hairless and mottled, wearing small knives but depending on their strength for battle; a half-dozen Quiplids astride a single mount, double-blades in hand; and a variety of humanoid shapes, colors, and forms that I had never before seen or heard of. There were red-eyed, coal-black ogres with biceps the size of my chest, blue giants with stubby-fingered, mace-like hands, and three or four breeds I'd rather not try to describe at all, beyond calling them ugly and threatening. Simply put, they were the dirtiest, meanest-looking collection of spacetrash I had ever seen in one place at one time—and I've seen a lot.

They milled around in the marketplace for a time, hollering and taking shots at windows, announcing their arrival to anyone who might have missed it, then they spotted Bull and me. A group of four of them rode straight for us, pulling up their mounts a short jump away. The others rode up on both sides to encircle us.

I guessed that the first four were the leader, his right-hand man, and their bodyguards. On either end was a massive blue giant. Between them was an Old Earth type wearing a dirty cloak that he tossed back over his shoulders to reveal an immaculate blood-red uniform, trimmed in dead black. He had a short, straight, gray-black beard and wore a pair of black eyeshields that concealed the upper portion of his face. At his side was a thin, almost skeletal man, white as spacelight, with a long mane of fiery-red hair that reached to his waist and the wildest, maddest eyes I've ever seen in a human face. I had heard about Bleachies, the descendants of an early mutant strain caused by a still-unexplained reaction to space radiations, a closely inbred race notorious for their savagery, but this was the first one I'd ever seen. One look from those eyes convinced me that every Bleachie horror story I had ever heard was an understatement.

The one in uniform pointed to Bull. "All right, you. What's going on here? Where are the villagers? We've got business for them."

Bull waited for the laughter to fade, then he rose slowly from his perch on the edge of the wall, looked over the polychrome foursome, and cocked his hands lightly on his hips. "They took the day off," he said casually. "We're here to handle business for them."

The Bleachie let out a peal of laughter that made my skin crawl, but everyone else was silent. The chief looked around and announced, "The dirt-scratchers in this corner of the galaxy are beginning to annoy me. We'll have to teach Mazat the same lesson we taught the others." He turned to Bull, leaned forward, and said, "You and your young friend are going to be busy. We want all the provisions they've got stored here. Do a good fast job of loading them, and we may let you live—if you want to live when we're finished with you."

Bull chewed and spat and shook his head. "If we're busy, it won't be loading provisions. There's nothing here for you. So you'd better take your crew and go."

The chief looked around him. Those eyeshields concealed any expression his face might have had, but his attitude was one of feigned astonishment. Faintly smiling, he looked down on Bull. "I don't think I heard you right. Did you tell me to go?"

Bull nodded. "You heard right."

"And if we don't go, I suppose you'll kill us all?"

"Maybe not all of you. We'll need some to clean up the mess when we're finished."

The chief laughed out loud, and his three companions joined in. The Bleachie's high, lunatic cackles stridulated through the uproar. The chief abruptly signaled for silence. He looked at me, then at Bull, and for just an instant I thought I sensed a flicker

of recognition pass between them, but then he said,
"Two of you, and you're going to take on sixty-six of
us. You're so crazy I love you. I think I'll let you join
up with us. How do you like that?"

Bull scratched his gleaming head—the signal for
readiness—and dropped his hands. "We don't join
anybody. Get moving now, fast."

21. *The battle in the mar-*
ketplace.

The blue giant nearest me moved first. I drew and
got him through the forehead, then turned and picked
off two more beside me before diving over the wall.
Bull hit the ground right after me. Without a word, we
began firing through the ports, pumping a steady
stream into the moiling mass of animals and men
before us. The riderless *haxopods* panicked, rearing
and plunging wildly into those on either side, and the
pirates were thrown into confusion and made easy
targets for our fire. They soon regrouped, wavered,
and then the chief ordered them back, and they swept
around the marketplace. I started reloading, fast,
figuring that they'd head back for us when they ran
into Grax, Stretch, and the others.

"How many'd you get?" Bull asked, reloading
methodically, as cool as ever.

"Seven, I think. You?"

"Six. I hope the others do as well."

It appeared for a time as though the others were
doing very well indeed. I couldn't see Grax or
distinguish his fire in the uproar, but I saw Slip zig-
zagging through the middle of the melee, dodging
blows while he made one deadly swipe after another with a long-handled Skeggjatt battleax. Stretch,

perched on a rooftop, his long arms moving almost too fast to follow, was sending down a rain of those deadly little triangular finger knives the Lixians use so well in open combat. I saw no sign of Ronin or Carter.

My reloading completed, I watched Slip cleave a Daltrescan's skull, sidestep a crushing blow from one of the blue giants and then decapitate him with a backhand stroke, duck under a *haxopod* and disembowel a black ogre who lunged for him, then, suddenly, throw his head back and turn to reveal a red stain on his chest as he sank to his knees and pitched forward. The Bleachie rode right over him.

"They got Slip," I said.

"I saw. He did his share, Del. He knew there were some things even he couldn't dodge. Get ready. They'll be coming back this way."

The firing grew more rapid, and the pirates fell back. There were still about half of them left, desperate now and deadlier than before. Surprise was no longer a factor in our favor, and they had an idea of just how few we were. Moving low and fast from behind one fallen *haxopod* to another, they advanced on us.

"Hold your fire until they're up close," Bull advised me.

"What if they all hit us at once?"

"They can't. They need someone to cover the rear."

"It doesn't sound to me—" I began, breaking off when a Lixian reared up and let fly a swarm of finger knives. I got him before he could reach cover, but three others moved up on us. As we turned our fire on them, six more bolted for a low building off to my left. Bull dropped one of them, but the others crashed through the barricaded door and disappeared inside.

Bull swore. "If they can get up to the rooftops, we're in trouble. Somebody's got to go after them. Can you hold out alone here?"

"I suppose so," I said.

"All right. I'm going after those five."

Bull crawled off and vanished into the building beside us. I concentrated on the bunch in front of me, holding my fire for a clear shot. I saw one of the dead *haxopods* quiver and move toward me, then another. The pirates were pushing them up, spreading out to hit me from two sides when they were close enough.

Two of my pistols were empty, and I could not take time to reload. I tossed them aside, took two fresh ones, jumped to the wall, and emptied them at the exposed portions of the pirates, then dropped back to cover. I heard some loud cursing, but it didn't stop them.

Things grew still on the other side of the marketplace. I hoped that Grax, Ronin, Carter, and Stretch would realize that they were needed over here, and that the pirates wouldn't charge before my friends came to support me. A sudden volley of muffled shots came from the left, where Bull had gone to intercept the pirates, and at the sound, as at a signal, the *haxopod* carcasses lurched forward one last time and a swarm of pirates arose from behind them and closed in on me, shouting, swearing, and waving wicked-looking weapons, three of them firing pistols, but with very poor aim.

I emptied my two pistols into them, dropping the three gunmen, the most dangerous of the lot, but there were still too many left for me to handle. Snatching up the two remaining pistols, I headed for the doorway to my left. Just over the threshold, I stumbled over Bull's body and went sprawling headlong. The two pistols skidded across the floor and vanished into the shadows.

I scrambled to my feet, drew my knife, and waited

beside the door. For one silent, motionless moment I almost believed that no one was coming in, then two Quiplids scooted through the doorway, curved double-blades at the ready. I knew their tricks—they were to hamstring me, so the others could finish me off at their leisure.

The second one saw me and swung at me immediately. I jumped over his blade and came down with one boot right on his broad flat skull. The other came at me and managed to gash my leg just below the knee, but his momentum carried him within reach of my blade. I picked up his body, surprisingly heavy for his size, and flung it in the face of the big Skeggjatt who was already almost upon me, following up with an underhand thrust that put him out of action. The others, hearing no shots, grew bold. As the Skeggjatt fell, they burst in en masse.

In that small space, the floor strewn with bodies and slick with fresh blood, the corners in deep shadows, their numbers worked against them. I dodged and slashed, holding them off for as long as I could, until at last my leg gave way under me, and I fell. The pirates closed in.

"Wait! Let him live!" came in a high-pitched voice from behind them. They stopped pounding and kicking at me and fell back. I saw the Bleachie standing in the shadows, grinning down on me. "We'll use this one to buy our way out."

"He killed my brother. I want him," a Quiplid said.

"Once we're clear of this place, you can do what you want with him. Now drag him to the door," the Bleachie ordered.

They hauled me to my feet and stood me just inside the door. A Daltrescan positioned himself on one side of me, a blue giant on the other, and someone else behind. Each of them had a knife jabbed into me.

"At least let me hamstring him now. He'll be less trouble," the Quiplid whined.

"You'll wait until we're out of this place, do you hear?" the Bleachie said. Stepping out the door, he raised his hands and shouted, "Hold your fire. We're coming out, and we've got your friend."

He slid back in to await the reply. No reply came. The pirates began to argue among themselves about the cause of the silence, and finally the Bleachie resolved the question by stripping a tunic from one of the fallen men, tossing it over my shoulders, and shoving me out to draw fire. No one fired. I fell, raised myself up and looked around, and saw not a single living figure. The marketplace was cluttered with the bodies of men and animals. Blood pooled on the dusty ground. The low, agonized moans of the dying mingled with the *skreek* of the carrion-eaters wheeling down from overhead in slow, cautious circles. All was desolation. I sank to the ground and buried my face on my arm.

The Bleachie kicked me in the side and I rolled over on my back. "It looks as though your friends are all dead," he said. "We don't need you any more. Too bad for you." He turned to the others. "Take care of him. Don't hurry. We have plenty of time."

While the others readied their knives, the Bleachie, now their leader, dragged a stool out of the doorway and seated himself to enjoy my execution. I looked around frantically for a weapon, anything at all, even a stone, but found nothing. I was finished. I closed my eyes and tried to think of Gilead, the home I'd never see.

Suddenly, amid a burst of wild shrieks and howls, Mazatlans were everywhere. A score of them plummeted from the rooftop to bury my captors, and more came in a wave across the marketplace, howling and brandishing makeshift weapons, snatching up the arms of the fallen as they ran. They swarmed over the pirates, literally swarmed over them, hacking and pounding and clawing, and their snarls drowned out the curses and agonized screams of their victims. When at last the Mazatlans drew back, exhausted, and lifted me to my feet, I looked on the unholy mess that covered the ground and passed out cold.

22. *Awards and honors.*

When I awoke, Hata was washing the deep gash on my leg while Steban looked on anxiously. As soon as I opened my eyes, he rushed to my side with a cool drink, and as I drank, he told me of the battle.

"You have freed our planet, Del! The pirates are dead, every one of them. The people are burning the bodies now, outside the wall."

"All dead? A lot of them were only wounded."

Steban lowered his eyes and made a helpless gesture. "They are all dead now, Del. You must understand, my people have suffered much at their hands. They could not be restrained."

I remembered the last sight of the pirates I had had and nodded my head. "What about my friends?" I asked.

"The tall one is wounded. The others are dead," he said simply.

"All of them?"

"All."

I lay back for a moment, speechless. We all knew the risks, were all aware of the odds against us, but the plain facts of life and death still came as a shock. It was hard to think of those men I had spoken with only hours ago, men I had grown to like and come to trust with my life, now lying dead. Perhaps they had been comforted in their last moment by the knowledge that they had given their lives in a good cause, but I doubted that. Good causes were all very fine, but to me, at that time, they were not worth the lives of my friends.

"I saw Slip go down, and I fell over Bull's body. What happened to the others?" I asked Steban.

"The one with the pale hair . . . I do not know his name . . . ."

"Ronin."

"Yes, Ronin. He and Carter were dead before the battle began. The bridge collapsed on them and crushed them."

I gave a low whistle. "So there were only five of us doing the fighting. I'm glad I didn't know that. What happened to Grax?"

"He fought bravely, but they overwhelmed him. With his last bullet he felled their leader, the man in red, and then he used his empty pistols as clubs, but the pirates were too numerous for him."

"Poor Grax. He was my best friend, Steban."

"He gave his life for us. His name will live forever on Mazat, as will the names of the others."

I smiled with some bitterness at that lofty prediction. Their names would live forever, but some of them seemed to be forgotten already. "How do you know all this?" I asked.

"The tall one saw everything. He told us."

"His name is Stretch. Don't call him 'the tall one.' And don't call Ronin 'the one with pale hair.' If you're going to remember their names forever, start using them now."

"We will, Del," he said, taken aback. "Can I do anything for you?"

"More water," I said, thrusting the bowl at him. As

he rushed off, I turned to Hata. "You're a good nurse. It doesn't hurt a bit."

"I used an ointment I know of. It will heal quickly."

"Thanks."

She looked up and blurted, "When they carried you in, I thought you were badly hurt. There was blood all over you. I thought you would die!"

"I expected to. If the people hadn't turned up—how did they come to fight, Hata? I thought they couldn't."

She gestured vaguely and returned her full attention to my leg. Steban returned, handed me the water, and said, "Hata told us we had to help, or you would all die horribly. We came in time to save you and the tall . . . and Stretch."

"So you saved my life, Hata," I said to her.

"It was the men who saved you. I spoke. They fought."

"If you hadn't spoken, they wouldn't have fought, though, would they?"

"No." She looked at me, her wide eyes brimming, and said, "Now you are alive, and we are free, and the Mazatlans know killing once more!" She rushed out, overturning the pot of ointment in her haste.

"I'm grateful for my life, Steban. But maybe you'll find that the price was a bit high."

"No, Del. One battle does not make a warrior."

I thought of Agarix, sprawled dead across a bloody table, but I said nothing of this to Steban. "No more talk for a while. I need rest," I said, turning my head away. He left me, and I slept.

A few nights later, at the celebration, Stretch and I sat side by side on makeshift thrones in the place of honor. My leg was bound up, and his arm was in a splint; a pirate bullet had shattered the elbow. We were the only ones left of the seventy-three men and humanoids who had joined battle in the marketplace.

"You are not happy," Stretch said, as the Mazatlans danced and sang all around us.

"No. I feel rotten."

"Your leg pains you?"

"No, the leg is nothing. I've had worse than that."

"You were the last of our band to fall. You fought to the very end. You have gained much honor."

"I suppose so," I said listlessly.

I didn't feel as though I had gained anything, least of all honor. Resting up for those days before the celebration, thinking of my last sight of the silent marketplace, I had come to think that maybe there wasn't and couldn't be any way of killing people honorably or gloriously or nobly. Killing was just a dirty business—for a business it surely was, the major industry, chief export, and true heritage of blood-soaked Old Earth spread out through the entire galaxy. It didn't make any difference whether it took place in an arena, for money, or in a dirty back alley, for revenge, or in a dusty, sun-baked marketplace, for the liberation of a gentle people. Killing was killing, a curse as old as history and as new as the fresh-spilled blood still soaking into the dirt beneath the dancers' feet. I had had enough of it. When I thought of how a bunch of star-hoppers had come to Mazat and taught these good people how to kill again after all those generations of peace, I felt sick. I wanted no more of this kind of glory.

Hata sat down at my feet, carrying a plate of delicacies which she proceeded to feed to me. She looked prettier than ever, her long, black hair and golden skin glowing in the firelight, her wide, dark eyes looking up at me with a warm light of their own. She laid her head against my uninjured knee and began to sing a soft, sweet, Mazatlan tune.

I reached down to stroke her hair, and the thought

came over me that I was living out the old spacer's dream—to find a peaceful planet where a man could raise a herd of *trettles* and a few *haxopods*, grow his crops and walk in the sun and open air with his feet on solid ground; to marry a beautiful woman and live among a people who looked upon him as their liberator and great hero. Here I was, barely into my twenties, and I had it all. If I said the word, I could be king of Mazat.

But I thought of Cassie, waiting for me, alone and frightened for all these lonely years, and I knew I couldn't stay here. And even as I thought of her, I grew troubled. Here I was, closer to Gilead than I'd been for nearly eight years, ready to return and claim Cassie for my own, and the one thing on my mind was this lovely little girl—Hata really wasn't much more than that—who sat by my side and made me feel better than I'd felt in all those years of wandering.

Once off Tarquin, no longer subjected to that aphrodisiac scent that turned my willpower to wind, I'd been pretty faithful to Cassie. Of course, the opportunities for unfaithfulness were hardly abundant in the places I'd been, but except for a few minor encounters not worth mentioning, I had nothing to hide from her. I wasn't coming home like Gariv, with a small army of abandoned wives and lovers and children scattered across the galaxy behind him. And why did I think of Gariv then?

"You are leaving us," Hata said suddenly, breaking into my uncomfortable reverie.

"Yes. I must go back to Gilead. That's my home, Hata, and I haven't set foot on it since I was a boy."

"This could be your home."

"I've thought of that. Maybe . . . . I must return to Gilead, Hata, but I'll try to come back to Mazat someday."

"Soon?" she asked.

"As soon as I can."

"It will be soon," she said in a very soft voice that radiated absolute confidence. "You will come back to us soon."

On what should have been one of the greatest nights of my life, I felt awful. Absolutely awful. I wanted to get back to Cassie, but I also wanted very much to stay here forever with Hata; and perhaps all I'd end up doing would be to hurt them both.

Hata left me for a time. Seeing we were alone, with no one in earshot, Stretch said, "You are sad because of your brother, Grax."

"He wasn't my brother, Stretch, he was my friend. The best one I ever had."

"You should not be sad for him. He died with great honor, surrounded by a ring of fallen enemies. His was the noblest death of all. He fell like a true warrior, on a day that comes once in a hundred lifetimes. Rejoice for your comrades, Del, for Grax most of all. It was Grax who slew the leader of the pirates, the man in red, with his last bullet and then fought on barehanded. This is a good way to die."

Stretch saw things differently, that was clear. I thought of Grax and all the times he had told me his Uncle George's stories of the great frontier days on Old Earth. I didn't believe a word of them, but Grax took them as absolute truth and spent his life trying to *make* them true. He had come out to search among the stars for a frontier of his own where he could live and fight and die as men did hundreds of years ago, and on Mazat he had found his frontier at last. Given the choice, Grax would probably have picked just this way, this place, and this company for his last battle. So perhaps it wasn't so sad after all."

"Maybe you're right, Stretch," I said, "but still, he's

ead. Maybe I just hate to lose a friend."

"But you have gained many friends. All the people
f Mazat hail you. They wish you to be king."

"You be their king, Stretch. I'm going home."

"I am a war leader, Del, not a king. But you could
e a great king."

"Not in a million years, Stretch."

As things turned out, it didn't require anything like a
million years. The next day the townspeople, along
with representatives of all the towns and villages on
Mazat, assembled to proclaim me King of Mazat and
appoint Stretch First Defender of The Planet. I told
hem I didn't want to be their king; I told them I was
nothing but a spacebum with a brace of pistols who
couldn't act like a king any more than he could turn
himself inside out and fly in circles; I told them I was
leaving for Gilead as soon as my leg healed and might
not return for a long time, maybe never. They listened
respectfully, bowed low, and presented me with the
crown. If I made mistakes, that was all right with
them; if I left them, that was all right, too, because I'd
come back, that they knew. I couldn't dissuade them,
and I hated to disappoint them, so I accepted.

After a week of ceremonies and feasting, during
which I did my best to avoid Hata, I was ready to
return to Gilead. I appointed Stretch as regent during
my absence, and he swore that he would act to bring
great honor upon us both. I knew I could trust him.
Stretch had one favor to ask of me, a formality of some
consequence should he desire to regain his standing on
Lixis. He asked me to certify his actions in the battle
on Mazat so he could offer proof of his honor to his
lords at home. When I wrote out a straightforward
account of his actions in our clash with the space
pirates and signed it with my full battery of names, he
was ecstatic.

"Del I, King of Mazat, born Deliverance-from-the
Void Whitby of Gilead, known as Del Cometfire-by
Dawnstar Deletriculus Quickslash Nimblefoot Swift
thrust Threesmiter, twice Champion of the People o
Tarquin VII, affirms the truth of all things herein writ
ten," he read off, and cried, "What honor is now mine
My attester is a king and a champion of Tarquin!"

"My champion days were a while back, Stretch," I
said.

"True honor never fades. It will augment my name
forever. I thank you, my king."

Stretch really loved formality. I still think he would
have been better at kinging than I could hope to be,
but I couldn't convince him or the Mazatlans of that.

I slipped away quietly to board the *Renegade*. I
wanted no goodbyes, particularly not with Hata. That
would have hurt too much. When I reached the ship,
Steban was waiting there.

"Will you leave us, Del?" he asked.

"I must. You know that, Steban. You knew it when I
came."

"But things are different now. You are King of
Mazat!"

"There isn't much work for a king here. Stretch can
take care of things while I'm gone."

Steban shook his head. "The First Defender is very
brave, but we need someone like you to guide us. You
saw what we became in the battle. After forty-seven
generations we learned to kill again, and there were
many who found it pleasing. Already, I have heard the
young men talking of the great days of the Mazatlan
Empire. Some even speak of making weapons. You
must help us."

"How can I help you? I grew up on bloodshed,
Steban. I'm no different from that pack of space
pirates; I just happened to be on your side, not theirs."

"But you have put aside your old ways. You say you
will kill no more."

"Sure I have, and I mean it. But that's easily said,
Steban. I've stuck to my word for twelve whole days.
Your people did it for forty-seven generations."

"Nevertheless, we need you. Come back to us."

I had a growing feeling that he was right. Conceit
may have played a large part in it, but I don't think
that was all that lay behind my decision. I really did
love the Mazatlans and felt responsible for this grim
new turn in their attitude. I couldn't hedge any longer.

"All right, Steban. I'll come back," I said.

"Hata sends a message. She said to tell you that she
will wait."

I nodded, clapped him on the shoulder, and boarded
the *Renegade*. There was nothing more to say.

23. *I return to Gilead and learn the end of my story.*

I pushed the *Renegade* to its limit and reached
Gilead in twenty-seven days. An hour after touching
down, I was walking along the same forest path I had
walked with Cassie on my last night at home. As I
reached the turn of the path, I came upon a group of
men carrying hatchets, scythes, and pitchforks, and I
greeted them cheerfully. To my surprise, they lowered
their tools ominously and moved to encircle me.

"Is this how the men of Gilead greet a brother
nowadays?" I asked indignantly.

"Space pirates are not our brothers!" a big fellow
growled, and the others murmured in agreement.

"I'm no space pirate. I'm Deliverance-from-the-
Void Whitby. I was carried off from this very spot

nearly eight years ago, on the eve of my time o
decision. I've fought my way across the galaxy to com
home, and you offer me poor welcome."

The men encircling me looked dubiously at on
another and studied me closely. "Such a thing
happened, I remember it," one of them said. "It wa
long ago. Surely more than eight years."

"Thou claimest to be of Gilead, yet thy garb is th
garb of a pirate!" the big one said, waving hi
pitchfork in my direction.

I had an apt answer, one of Zealous' favorite lines
and I delivered it promptly. " 'Men are men, and
garments are garments, and only the fool mistakes th
one for the other.' So says *The Book of The Voyage*.
dress myself as I see fit."

"No space pirate knows *The Book of The Voyage*,'
someone said.

"Indeed not. He is who he claims to be," said
another, lowering the scythe he had been brandishing.

"It may be a trick to place a spy amongst us. Let us
test him," one old fellow said.

I folded my arms. "Very well. I was the foster child
of the Whitbys, given into their care by the Elders. My
father's name is Zealous Endeavor and my mother is
Persistence-in-the-Ways-of-Righteousness.   Their
farmstead is the second to the right at the end of this
road."

"How camest thou first to Gilead?" the older man
demanded.

"In a small lifeship marked 'Pendelton's Base.' It
stands in a locked building at the back of the Whitby
garden."

"He speaks the truth. Come forward, Brother
Whitby. Let me look at thee," he said. I stepped
forward, and he studied my face and hands, walking
around me for a close look. "Thou hast grown

considerable," he said suspiciously. "Young Whitby was a small lad."

"I was the smallest in the settlement, but the quickest. We played the throwing game, and I always won," I said. Several of the younger men smiled and rubbed old forgotten bruises. Recognition burst upon me, and I pointed to my questioner. "Elder Scrooby, you were at my house the very evening I was taken. You spoke with my father about my origin. Do you believe me now?"

"Yes, yes, my son, my poor boy," he said, throwing open his arms and embracing me. The others followed his example, and I was nearly smothered in welcomes. But they were curiously subdued, as though everyone was still holding back.

"Why this welcome?" I asked, hoping to draw them out. "Men never traveled in armed groups on Gilead."

"Space pirates," someone said.

I sighed, and nodded, and waited for the inevitable request to come. By now I was resigned to my destiny as an intersystem gunman, and even here on Gilead, home again at last, that looked to be my role. It had all become almost ritualized: I landed on a planet, engaged someone in conversation, heard a tale of woe, injustice, and oppression, and was told where to aim my guns for just one more good cause. I had hoped that here, of all places, it would not be so; and it turned out that my worries were premature.

"Two months ago, they landed here and demanded food and supplies. We refused them. They said they would wipe out one family each day until their ship was filled, and this is what they did," Scrooby went on solemnly.

"But we burned the food and drove off the animals, and then we hid in the forests," the husky young man said. "They left with their bellies empty."

"True, but not before they did their abominable work." Scrooby placed his hands on my shoulders. "My poor boy, thou hast returned too late. The Whitbys were among their first victims. They slew them both and burned the farmstead to the ground."

I had learned long ago not to cry, but I came very close. I laid my hand on Scrooby's and nodded. "Take me there," I said.

The only true home I had ever known was a pitiful waste of charred rubble. In the garden, by the ruins of the shed that once held my lifeship, two square white stones marked the place where my parents lay. I stood over them for a time, silent, then I turned to Scrooby.

"Are the Hammersmiths safe?"

"The Hammersmiths died years ago, Brother Del."

"Cassie? Castle-of-Perseverance, their daughter—is she dead, too?"

Someone cleared his throat and said, "She is well. She lives elsewhere now."

"I must see her."

"We will take you there," Scrooby said.

"These pirates who killed my mother and father—tell me about them."

"They were many in number. Sixty, I would say."

"More. More than sixty," the others murmured.

"Were they led by a Bleachie and a man in red?" I asked.

Everyone began to talk at once, but Scrooby stilled them. "Hast seen them, Brother Del? Have they returned?"

"I've seen them. They won't be back. They're buried on Mazat, every one of them." I told them the story of our battle with the pirates, and it seemed to ease their minds considerably. Even the men who had decided against bloodshed listened to my account with evident satisfaction. The pirates had made themselves thoroughly hated.

"Then we are safe," Scrooby said. "This is a deliverance indeed, Brother Del, and rightly art thou named. They were wicked men who gloried in their abominable deeds and they have been struck down by a righteous avenger. The one in red, the one they called Corey, laughed when he slew your father."

"Corey?" I asked. I had a sudden feeling of overwhelming horror.

"The white one called him that. They said he was once a noble warrior who fought boldly against the Rinn, but—"

I let out a cry that must have frozen their blood and threw myself on the gravestones, pounding and clawing my fingers bloody, raving and shrieking like a madman. The universe fell inward upon me and buried me under nightmarish visions. I groped my way through corpse-cluttered gulfs of space under a rain of blood that fell eternally throughout the galaxy, that hissed down through the void in an eternal torrent, saturating men and planets and suns and space itself with the sweet reek of death. Everything underwent a hideous metamorphosis into the accoutrements of violence and death; comets flashed like knives in the hands of madmen and every point of light was a gleaming skull, and they were all converging on me, along with all the blood I had spilled, all the corpses I had strewn behind me on my way, all the evil and death and corruption that man had sown among a million million stars, and I could not fight off the avalanche. The rain poured down, and a sea of blood rose around me, churning and foaming in a great maelstrom. Heads and limbs and the faces of dying men rose and fell in the flood, and a growing roar drowned out the moans and screams and curses of the victims who whirled with me in that bloody funnel that sucked us all down into nothingness.

24. *I see Cassie once more, and am reunited with my people.*

I awoke in a room much like the one I remembered from the Whitby's house. A husky man sat at each side of my bed and at the foot, smiling down on me, was Cassie. She had changed greatly, but I knew her at once.

"Art thou well now, Del?" she asked.

"I'm all right, Cassie," I said, though I felt very weak. By now, I was growing accustomed to waking up in a sickbed and being tended by someone who had half expected me not to recover.

"Thy dreams must have been frightful. Thou didst cry out and thrash all about. It Toiler and Steadfast had not held thee, I know not what might have happened."

"Thanks for the help," I said to the two men. I raised a hand to salute them and noticed, for the first time, that my hands were heavily bandaged. One of the men looked vaguely familiar, a puffed-up version of a boy I once knew and did not like very much. As I recalled, he was a rival for Cassie's affections in those days. "Aren't you Toiler-for-Glory Dimbleby?" I asked him.

"I am indeed, Del. I remember thee well. Look, here," he said, pushing back the hair from his forehead to reveal a small white mark. "We played the throwing game once, and once was enough for me."

"I'm sorry for that, Toiler."

"We were boys, Del. It was all in sport."

"Leave us now, and go about thy business," Cassie said, waving them away. "Del will rest easily now, but first I must feed him. He is two days without nourishment."

"Two days?" I was astonished.

"Two days ago we carried thee here from the Whitby farm. Some thought thee possessed by demons," Toiler said.

"Maybe I was. But they're gone now. Thanks for bringing me here."

When they were gone, Cassie sat beside me and fed me from a bowl of hot, thick stew. I ate ravenously, and we exchanged no words until the bowl was empty, then she took my bandaged hand in hers and said, "I share your sorrow, Del. The Whitbys were as close to me as my own parents."

"They *were* my parents. I never knew any others, and I don't want to," I said, keeping my voice steady only with great effort. "That little old man taught me how to live, Cassie, but I never understood it until I came back here and saw how he had taught me how to die. *He* was the real hero, not that vicious . . . not like some of the others," I concluded awkwardly.

Cassie looked at me, puzzled. "What others?"

"No one you know, Cassie. I was just remembering."

She took cold water and wiped my forehead, and for all her tenderness, I could sense the distance that had grown between us over the years. Cassie was not treating me as if I were the lost lover returned to claim his beloved; she was mothering me. She even looked motherly and much older than I, despite the fact that she was a year younger. When she leaned close to me, I could see the white in her yellow hair. I pitied her for the terrible hardships she must have endured; then I recalled that Toiler, too, had looked a good twenty years older than I, although he could have had no more than five years on me, at the most. Elder Scrooby, thin and white-haired, had aged considerably more than I would have expected. In fact, everyone here looked far older than I had pictured them, as if my eight-year-long absence had actually been twice that long, or even longer.

As Cassie poured fresh water, she said, "Del, I thought never to see thee again in this life. No one returns from the slavers."

"I didn't always think I'd make it, Cassie. It took me nearly eight years."

"Eight? Oh, Del, what sayest thou? It is nineteen years since they snatched thee away from me!"

Too many things had happened in too short a time, and I was incapable of shock any more. In fact, my mind was quite clear, my memory efficient, and my logical powers unimpaired. I recalled those old books aboard the *Phoenix* and the passages I had tried to puzzle my way through, only to abandon them when they seemed to collapse into nonsense about the dilation effect and how lightspeed travelers actually aged more slowly than those they left behind. It was impossible gibberish, tricks and lies and clever men's deceptions of the gullible. So I thought. But it was true.

"I waited for thee, Del. They all said I was foolish and willful, and still I waited. But three years after I lost thee, my parents died, and I was alone," Cassie said softly, avoiding my eyes.

I sensed what she was trying to tell me and said it for her. "So you married Toiler Dimbleby."

"He has been kind to me, Del, for all these years. We have six strong children. Our way has been smooth. If I had known, if my parents had lived, I'd have waited forever. Believe me, Del."

"I believe you, Cassie."

She left me then, to allow me to rest, and I was grateful for her departure. Had she stayed, I would have tried to talk to her, and that might have hurt us both too much to bear. I had learned everything I had hoped to learn, and now my voyages were over. All but one.

When I left Gilead, half the people of the settlement walked to the *Renegade* with me. News of my return and my terrifying outburst at the Whitbys' grave had spread quickly. My seizure was attributed to grief, and that made it entirely respectable. On Gilead, lamentation and remorse were extremely popular, and a bit of raving and thrashing at graveside was accepted as proof of sincerity. It was glad to let it go at that.

Other stories had been spreading, too. Some close students of *The Book of The Voyage* had been reading the prophetic chapters and found in them a number of provocative lines. "He who was born among the stars shall be their avenger. He shall come among them silently, by night, and live unknown among them as the smallest and the weakest of their number, and he shall depart from them and be forgotten. But in the hour of despair, when the blood of Gilead is shed by the worshipers of the abomination, his shall be the arm of vengeance though he be far away and long forsaken," was quoted solemnly to me, and while I was quite flattered, I did not take it very seriously as prophecy. Looking to the future, someone recited, "He who is not one of us shall become one of us; born among the stars, reborn on Gilead, he shall come to raise us to the stars in the day of the terror." I made no comment on these, or on the other, more cryptic passages, which were being bruited about. Let them believe what they wanted.

I said goodbye to everyone, and at the port of the *Renegade* I addressed them all. "I'm the King of Mazat now, but Gilead is my first home and I'll never forget it. If ever you need me, come to Mazat. You're welcome there always."

And then I returned to Mazat, where Hata and my people were waiting for their king.

o   o   o   o   o   o

BOOK III: THE LONG VOYAGE

1. Some highlights of recent Mazatlan history.

Twenty-two years have passed since I came back to Mazat to stay, and I have never regretted my decision to return. These have been far happier years than I ever hoped to see. Not exciting in the way my years of wandering were; no, certainly not; but richly rewarding in their own quiet way. My path has been smooth, my life uneventful, though not completely so. I could not have endured that. Hata never asked me about Gilead, and I never told her. We have been very happy together. Hata has been a good wife to me.

Stretch, that taciturn giant who once lived only for honor through victory, has turned out to be a true and valuable friend. He is still inclined to be formal, but he has improved considerably in that respect. It took me six years° to convince him that there was no real need

---

° To be precise, five years, ten months, and one day, GSC.

for us to address one another as "All-Honored and Most Puissant Monarch of Mazat" and "First Defender of the Planet, Paragon of Unswerving Loyalty and Shield of the Kingdom." We're back to "Del" and "Stretch" now, and he rarely slips. Nor do I.

It took Stretch almost all those years to make up his mind about returning to reclaim his honor on Lixis. One night he came to me with a request that he be permitted to marry in accordance with his rank, Lixian style. I gladly gave my permission and was a bit shaken to learn that this entitled him to eleven wives. He's the father of one hundred and seven children now, and good-looking kids they are, too. The Mazatlix, as we've come to call them, seem to combine the best features of both parents. Fatherhood has made Stretch stable. He's here on Mazat to stay. As he told me, very solemnly, when his eighty-fourth child was born, "This is a good place to raise a family."

I soon learned not to underestimate Stretch's abilities. On Lixis and under the Lixian code during his wanderings, Stretch had been so intent on preserving his honor by unswerving loyalty and obedience that he had had small opportunity for thinking. But here on Mazat, free from those constricting imperatives, his mind has flourished. When the Mazatlans insisted on building a Tower of the Seven Liberators to commemorate our battle, Stretch served as chief architect and engineer. On his own initiative, he decided to turn the top level into a ceremonial throne room. I don't use it very often, only to receive visitors who might feel slighted by a less stately reception and to initiate the annual week-long festival on the anniversary of the battle with the space pirates, but when I'm there I feel and act and even talk like a true king. I think Stretch, in his subtle way, has made it impossible for me to do otherwise.

In my years on Mazat, I've done a lot of thinking about my beliefs, and Stretch has been a most interesting speaker on that topic, too. I can't accept the Lixian concept of absorption into the infinite,° but it works for Stretch and has of late become popular with many of the Mazatlans, as well. Hata has tried to help me understand the ancient Mazatlan beliefs, but with very little success. They were not meant to be explained but to be felt, and only a native Mazatlan can feel them truly.

I guess I'm still a Rudstromite in many ways, although some features of that creed trouble me. I still can find no answer to one question: where was the Universal Protector of the Smooth Way when the Malellans were being destroyed? Surely they had not made a unanimous decision to be wiped out, and

---

° Here Del touches upon the single area in which we were never able to communicate effectively. He always believed that I, like Portteus, was attempting to sway him to acceptance of my ways, not realizing that the Lixian way is possible only for a Lixian. The Mazatlans try, but they are unable to grasp it fully.

The Lixians have long known the simple truth that All is One. We come from the infinite, crossing the shadow-lines of time, dimension, and extension, and when we have proven our worth by covering our lives with honor, we are accepted back into the infinite. So it is with the Lixians. Others withdraw from the infinite for other reasons, some of them beyond all comprehension. Some are not destined to return. Other beings, superior to us, remain eternally united to the All. We believe these things and do not seek for reasons because we could not comprehend them. When we have achieved honor and become reunited with the infinite, all will be clear to us. Honor is the means, union with the infinite the end, of all Lixians. Others must find their own way.

surely they were not all servants of the abomination. But they died, just the same. That disturbs me deeply, for I can find no justification.

Portteus—more about him later—has tried to convert me to his way of thinking, but I cannot accept it at all. He is a New Galactic Mechanist, the first one I've ever conversed with, although I've heard of them many times. They were mentioned with a kind of stunned horror on Gilead when I was young.

Portteus tried to explain the fundamental concept of Mechanism to me this way: "Imagine a machine of indescribable complexity made up of a billion components. Each component is in turn composed of a billion sub-components, and each of these is composed of a billion parts. Each part is different from every other in form and function; the sub-components and components are likewise completely different from one another. In fact, each piece of this great machine is so different from all of the others that no one seeing only one part, or even one sub-component, could possibly conceive of its relationship to the others or of the nature of the machine itself or of its purpose."

"I can't even begin—" I said, dazed.

"Let me continue," Portteus said. "Now apply this concept of the infinite machine to galactic life. Assume that all of human life on Old Earth constitutes one tiny part. The histories of the other planets also constitute parts, and our whole galaxy, considered together, is one of the sub-components of the great machine, as are all the other galaxies, known and unknown."

I shook my head helplessly.

"On the other hand," Portteus continued, "our galaxy, perhaps even the entire universe, may be one tiny and insignificant part in a minor sub-component of the great machine, and we are—"

"Stop! Stop it!" I cried, covering my ears.

He looked at me, injured. "You asked."

"Sometimes people don't want an answer, Doc, they just want to ask the question."

"Such people could never be Mechanists."

So I remain a Rudstromite, of sorts. Hata observes the old Mazatlan worship, and Stretch, when his duties permit, meditates on the Lixian way.

Stretch has also been the guiding hand behind the New Chronicles of Mazat. He came to me with the idea about a year after my return, when he learned, to his dismay, that there were accounts of our battle circulating that made us sound like legendary heroes out of some Old Earth romance or a Skeggjatt myth. His Lixian reverence for exactitude was outraged at references to magic swords, gory single combats, beautiful warrior maidens, and the like, and he was horrified to find that the space pirates, in one version, numbered ten thousand and we fought them barehanded. Seeing our deeds thus inflated within a year, we shuddered to think of the stories that would have been told when we were not available to give the facts. I told Stretch to compile an authorized account, and when he had done so, we realized that it was a good place to begin the new history of Mazat. It was at this point that I abandoned all intentions of continuing the journal that fills the preceding pages. What happened after my return to Mazat became part of the chronicles, and I saw no need to keep my own personal record. Not until recently.

Stretch and I both tried to learn as much as we could of the period the Mazatlans call the Silent Time, those forty-seven generations of peace that preceded our arrival, but with little success. There seem to be no written or oral Mazatlan records of that time. Our investigations had one fairly spectacular result, however: we found the remains of the first ship to arrive here from Old Earth. That was five years ago, and we're still studying the materials and trying to discover what happened to the people aboard the ship. There's not a trace of them. It's a fascinating story, but since it's contained in the chronicles, I won't bother with it here. No sense in retelling a story Stretch has already told well and in full detail.

We've had some interesting visitors. Alladale came here during my third year of rule and stayed with us for a year, during which time he earned his keep by composing a very long and often very stirring epic about our battle. He called it "The Song of The Seven," and recited it, beginning to end, at every opportunity. As I said, even though there were fine passages, it was very long, and there were several occasions when I wished he'd controlled his admiration. When he left, he promised to spread our story through the galaxy. Stretch was beside himself at the prospect of so much honor, but I had reservations. I didn't feel like boasting about my role in all that killing, even if the boast was given secondhand. I'm no Skeggjatt. If the story had to be told, I wanted it told truly, just as it was. The chronicle makes it sound very orderly and sane, and Alladale's epic turns it into a pageant of high glory and dramatic speeches. But it wasn't like that at all. It was just a bunch of desperate men in a battle they all might have preferred to avoid, killing one another in a dirty, bloody brawl in a tiny marketplace. Maybe if people heard it that way, they'd stop thinking so highly of bloodshed. And besides my ethical considerations, I had practical objections. It seemed to me that we might, through Alladale, be offering a challenge to every band of space pirates still in operation to drop in on Mazat and try their hand against a pair of aging heroes. I might have ordered Alladale to stay on Mazat—made him my jester, or whatever they used to call the king's musician—but I had no wish to be a tyrant. I did make him promise that he'd reveal nothing about the location of Mazat to anyone. We haven't been bothered.

The most interesting newcomer to Mazat, now a distinguished resident of our growing settlement, is Professor Doctor Portteus. The chronicles are studded with his observations, and his notes would fill my throneroom. I suppose he'd be called a scientist, but he's a philosopher, too, a student of everything, and a great talker. Not much of a listener, perhaps, but a great talker. He wandered across the new bridge one day, accompanied by a nervous assistant and a wagonload of scientific equipment, asked a few enigmatic questions of the people in the marketplace, and moved his possessions into the courtyard of an empty house. The next day, he asked permission to settle here and pursue his studies. Within a year, he had established an academy, and it's now the best one on Mazat.

Stretch finds Portteus fascinating, and he, in turn, is much taken with Stretch, the first Lixian he ever met. They spend hours in one another's company, walking around the walls, through the fields, in the hills, or in one another's homes, loudly discussing the Principle of Controlled Variables, the Law of Discontinuous Surfaces, and other things which I can't even begin to understand, all of this in a continuous, loud, contrapuntal double-monolog that began with their first argument and has no foreseeable end.

I'm well out of this, because I have been forced to admit that I simply don't have a scientific mind. My field is Old Earth history. Hata reads it with me sometimes, but she really prefers the Old Earth poetry (which she considers far superior to Alladale's; so do I, though I don't admit it). The real historian here is my oldest son, Delgrax. He has read and practically memorized everything I have in my library on Old Earth. He's particularly concerned with the writings on law and government, which he considers indispensable studies for a man who will one day be king. I'd like him to develop a bit more interest in travel, but I don't force the issue. He has his interests, I have mine. I hope to see Delgrax go to Gilead, at least. The Dimblebys have a daughter just about his age—I've visited Gilead on trading missions and stayed with them—and I think they'd make a good match. But this is hardly the place to discuss that. I can see that I am wandering from my purpose.

The reason that I've begun this last section of my story—and it is the last—is the arrival of a recent visitor who came to me as the representative of the Third Rinn Expedition. His coming troubles me, and my reaction to it troubles me even more. He summoned up things from the past that I had long buried and tried to forget. They were ugly things, and I reacted in an ugly fashion. For the first time in many years, I wore my pistols again, and Stretch slung those bandoliers of finger knives over his shoulders.

2. *Commander Dzik of the Third Rinn Expedition arrives, and hurriedly departs.*

Our visitor's name was Commander Dzik of Third

Defensive Force Command. He arrived with two aides, three advisors, and a score of bodyguards and requested an immediate conference with the king on a matter of great urgency. I let him wait for a time, and he dispatched a second messenger to warn me that the survival of all civilized life in the galaxy might well depend on my cooperation. That was an impressive statement to make; too big to be a bluff, I thought. I told the messenger I would see Commander Dzik in the throne room in two hours' time. He was to come alone.

I turned to Stretch. "You've seen this fellow Dzik and I haven't. What do you think of him?"

"He reminds me of a *kekket*," Stretch said.

Delgrax, beside me, laughed and voiced his agreement. I had been admitting him to state conferences for the past year and more, not entirely for his own benefit. He made shrewd observations, and I valued his opinion.

"Is this a good description?" I asked him.

"I believe so. The *kekket* looks fierce, but he never fights. He gets his food by snarling and posturing to frighten other creatures away from their kills."

"And you think the Commander is no more than that?"

"It remains to be seen. But he comes here in a warlike guise and utters frightening words to pry an audience from you. This is the true behavior of a *kekket*. In your place, Father, I would treat such a man with great circumspection," Delgrax said.

"What do you think, Stretch?"

"The Prince speaks for me."

"Very well, then. I want both of you there with me, in case this turns out to be important. And I'd like Portteus there, too."

"You sound as though you expect this to be a matter

of some weight," Delgrax said.

"I do. Dzik may be a negligible man, nothing more than a messenger, but an Expedition ship wouldn't come here without a purpose. We have to find out all we can. That's why I want my best advisors there to listen and observe."

We withdrew to the throne room to receive our visitor. He arrived with his aides, his advisors, and a squad of guards and made quite a fuss when he was told that by "alone," I *meant* alone. But after registering a formal protest, he entered the throne room alone. Commander Dzik was a tall, well-formed man about my age, clean-shaven, with short bristling hair of grayish-black. His face was mask-like, expressionless, the face of a man trained to tight control of himself, but the high cheekbones and sharp narrow nose suggested aggressiveness and determination. He wore a green Expedition uniform trimmed in red, which fit him like a second skin. His voice was harsh, but flat and mechanical. I at once perceived a certain resemblance to the bristling, green-skinned *kekket* and glanced at Stretch, but my First Defender was standing with folded arms, staring impassively at Dzik.

"I bring the greetings and respects of the Third Rinn Expedition to the King of Mazat, the royal family, the First Defender, and all royal advisors," Dzik said, bowing low.

"We thank you and return your greetings. Our respects and greetings go to the Third Rinn Expedition. You may be seated, Commander." He took a place before us, and I went on, "We are eager to know the reason why the leaders of the Expedition have chosen to honor us by a visit from a high officer. Will you speak of this?"

"Only too eagerly, Your Majesty. You must know by

ιow that the Rinn are assembling their forces for an
ιttack."

"I have heard this rumor, but I discount it," I said.

"It is no rumor, Your Majesty. We have reason to
ϳelieve that even now, the greatest Rinn battle fleet
ϟver assembled is moving toward this sector."

"What is this reason you speak of?"

"I beg Your Majesty's indulgence. I cannot reveal
ͼhe source of our information."

"I see. Then we must take your word for this Rinn
ιrmada," I said.

"Yes, Your Majesty."

I looked to each of my advisors in turn, stared
ͼhoughtfully upward, and after a time, said, "I find the
situation puzzling, Commander. Some years ago, the
First Expedition went forth to seek out and destroy
forever the power of the Rinn. By all reports I have
heard, the Expedition was a complete success."

Dzik nodded eagerly. "It was a glorious victory,
Your Majesty."

"So we have heard. The Second Rinn Expedition
was a loosely organized continuation of the First,
committed to the extermination of any surviving Rinn
forces. It, too, was a success."

"So it was. Your Majesty is indeed well-informed."

This, of course, was just so much polite noise. The
exploits of the First and Second Rinn Expeditions were
by now common galactic knowledge. I was no more
well-informed than any school child on Mazat.

"We thank you," I said. "But now, with all Rinn
forces destroyed not once, but twice, you come to me
with news of the mightiest Rinn armada ever
assembled. It is confusing."

Dzik hesitated, then replied, "It is difficult to
explain. Nevertheless, it is true."

I put on a naive, puzzled expression. "Then the First

and Second Expeditions were failures. I see."

"Oh, no, Your Majesty, no. They were great victories."

Portteus leaned toward me and said in a whisper loud enough for Dzik to hear, "It might clarify matters if Your Majesty assumes that the terms 'glorious victory' and 'ignominious failure' are synonymous in Expedition terminology."

"It would appear so," I said. "And in that case, there is little point in discussing the matter further. Commander Dzik, we thank you for your warning. You may relay our thanks to the commanders of the Third Rinn Expedition."

As I rose from the throne, Dzik cried, "Your Majesty, a moment! There is much to discuss!"

I hesitated, and then, with a show of reluctance, I resumed my place. "We of Mazat are a simple people, Commander. Here, a word means only one thing, not both that thing and its opposite. If you have more to say, say it plainly," I said to Dzik.

"Your Majesty, I can put my request very simply. The Expedition needs your support. We ask you for four hundred men and sixty Demetrious."

"The Expedition asks us to send away our subjects and empty our treasury to destroy an enemy they have already destroyed, an enemy we have never seen." I shook my head, then looked sharply at Dzik. "Tell me, Commander, have you ever seen a Rinn?"

"You don't have to see them to hate them," Dzik said coldly. For a moment, his impassive mask fell away, and raw hatred glared through to me.

"Certainly not. It's often easier that way, in fact. Do you know of anyone who has seen a Rinn warrior?"

"No, Your Majesty. But all have seen their handiwork. You know of the Malellan system."

"I know of it."

"Then you know what the Rinn can bring about. They must be destroyed, Your Majesty."

"So you have said, repeatedly. But the Mazatlans are not warriors. For forty-seven generations they lived in peace with one another and their neighbors, and they do so still."

"But Your Majesty is a great warrior. It is well known that the King of Mazat and his First Defender led the seven who slew an army of space pirates. The story is told throughout the systems."

Stretch and I glanced at one another. He remained straight-faced, but I had to smile. "The story is often told incorrectly. Besides, that was long ago, Commander. Since then, there has been peace."

"All the more reason to destroy the Rinn now! If they should strike, the Mazatlans would be unprepared." Dzik leaned forward and looked at us all, one by one, then, as if he had decided to admit us to his confidence, he said, "Your Majesty, I am empowered to speak for Expedition Command and offer assurances in their name. If you assist us, I guarantee the security of your people. All Mazatlans will be removed to a place of safety—"

"We are safe here," I broke in.

"Not for long, Your Majesty. We have a plan. When Mazat and all the neighboring systems are cleared of our allies, we will turn the entire sector into a huge death trap. When the Rinn launch their attack, the sector and all systems within it will detonate. We have means of doing this, and thus we will destroy the Rinn menace forever."

"And Mazat as well. I will not consent to the destruction of my planet." Dzik half-rose and opened his mouth to protest. "Be seated, Commander!" I snapped in my most kingly voice, and Dzik hastily sat down again. I went on, "Your proposal is madness, and

I will have no part of it. If this is the Expedition's way
of protecting its allies, I prefer to take my chances
with the Rinn."

Dzik looked horrified. "Your Majesty is jesting with
me!"

I stood and roared, "Do you come to Mazat to call
the King of the Mazatlans a jester?!"

"No, never, Your Majesty! I apologize for my words.
But to hear you speak so of the Rinn . . . I could not
believe my ears."

"Nor could I, when I heard you suggest that I ally
myself with those who would destroy my planet."

"But this is no wild scheme, Your Majesty," Dzik
went on hurriedly. "It was done before, with great
success. We have since perfected our methods and
increased our capability ten-thousandfold."

"When was it used before?"

"In the days before the First Expedition, at the time
of the attack on Pendelton's Base."

"What about Pendelton's Base?" I asked. I had not
heard the name for over twenty years, and though I
still carried the scrap of paper from the lifeship in an
amulet around my neck, I had not given much thought
to my origin since my return to Mazat. At Dzik's
words, I felt a sudden dread, but I kept my outward
feelings under control.

"It was a massive raid. Pendelton's Base was of
great strategic importance, but the main body of
defenders were away on rescue missions. It would
surely have fallen to the Rinn, and its fall would have
endangered the entire campaign. The decision was
made to detonate the planet and with it a major
portion of the Rinn force." Dzik looked at me with
triumph in his expression.

"There were Malellan refugees, women and

:hildren, on Pendelton's Base," I said.

"Very few, Your Majesty."

"You chose to destroy them."

"We had to destroy them to save them from the
?inn!" When I offered no response to this explanation,
Dzik gestured casually, as if to dismiss a detail
)eneath our notice. "As a ruler, Your Majesty knows
hat it is sometimes necessary for the few to be
;acrificed in the interest of the many."

It was that easy gesture, that nonchalant waving off
)f several hundred lives, that served as final
)rovocation. Once again, for just an instant, I seemed
:o see that bloody rain and hear its hissing fall as it
;oaked the stars in death. I rose slowly and started
forward. Dzik paled and stepped back, toppling his
chair. My expression must have been murderous. I felt
the firm pressure of two strong hands on my arms and
realized that Delgrax and Stretch were holding me
back. That brought me back to myself. "I'm all right
now," I said, and they released me, but stayed close to
my sides.

I pointed at Dzik and said, "Leave Mazat by
nightfall. If you or any other Expedition butcher ever
sets foot on this planet again, we'll treat you as we
treated the other pirates. Tell that to your masters."

As Dzik hurried out, I went to the trophy room and
took down Adamson's pistols. "Stretch, take your
knives and come with me. I want to be sure they
leave," I said.

"As you wish," Stretch responded.

We left at once, and rode without stopping to a
hilltop overlooking the landing site. A few minutes
before nightfall, the Expedition cruiser lifted off. We
rode back without speaking.

3. *A conference.*

That night I told the whole story to Hata, Delgrax, Stretch, and Portteus. They listened in absolute silence as I filled in the details of my origin that I had left unsaid all these years, and when I finished, Hata rushed to me and threw her arms around me. She was in tears.

"Oh, Del, my poor Del, my dearest! Why did you suffer alone for all our years together? I should have shared this knowledge with you and lessened your burden," she said, holding me close.

"I haven't been suffering, Hata. I've had your love, and that was all I wanted. I thought all this was behind me, and I felt that I had no right to inflict it on you. Nor on you, son," I said, looking up at Delgrax.

"My mother is right. You should have told us," he said, making no move to me or away from me, merely looking at me like a man studying a stranger.

"Perhaps I should have. I don't know. But I've told you now."

"These have been hard things to say. It took much courage to tell us," Stretch said, clearly approving.

"But why?" Portteus asked, and all eyes turned to him. He repeated, "Why did you feel constrained to confess all this to us, Del? I can understand your wanting to tell your family, but why Stretch and me?"

"Because I respect your judgment. Riding back here, I did some thinking, and I want to know how you feel about what I plan to do. I've decided to give up the throne and turn it all over to Delgrax." My son gave a start, astonished by my words, and I motioned to him peremptorily. "Don't argue. You're ready for it, and you'll be a better king than I was. After the way I treated Dzik today, Mazat will never be able to negotiate with the Expedition again while I'm king,

and we may need them someday. You'll know how to
handle them, son."

"I'll never deal with butchers like Dzik and the
Expedition chiefs! Mazat will make its way alone,"
Delgrax said fiercely.

"You speak like a true king," I said. "Mazat will be
safe in your hands."

"You're the true king," Delgrax said, coming to my
side. "You're the only king of Mazat, as long as you
live. Don't leave us now, Father."

"I must."

"Why do you feel this way?" Portteus asked. Trust
him to seek a logical answer at a time like this.

"If you must know, it's because I consider myself
unfit to remain King of Mazat. Since the battle with
the pirates, I haven't used a weapon, and neither has
anyone else on this planet, until today. I've kept the
peace for twenty years, and I deluded myself that I
could go on doing so. But I haven't changed. I was
ready to kill Dzik on the spot this afternoon. If Stretch
and Delgrax hadn't restrained me, I would have done
it. I've got Old Earth blood in my veins, and it's too
strong," I explained.

"Your blood is in my veins, too," Delgrax said.

"But you're half Mazatlan, son. And you've been
raised *here*, not in the arena. You're not a trained
killer. Your mother's people are civilized, and you take
after them. I'm half savage."

"The race of Old Earth are hardly savages, Del,"
Portteus pointed out.

"Aren't they? All the brutality and evil in this galaxy
was either invented on Old Earth or refined and
perfected by that breed as soon as they learned of it.
The Tarquinians and Skeggjatts brought their idea of
the tournament from Old Earth. The Daltrescans
turned to slavery only after they began intermarrying

with Old Earth pioneers. All the vicious little planetary tyrants model themselves after Hitler, or Dzhugashvili, or Hsaio, or Moran. Even the pirates—"

"But they're not all, Del," Portteus broke in. "It was the men of Old Earth who gave us philosophy, art, science, law, all the trappings of civilization."

"I know the history, too, Doc. A few men tried to make good laws, and the rest broke them. A few men created beauty, and the others destroyed it. A few spent their lives working out a way to protect their brothers from one another, and when they were dead—killed by a mob or a madman, more often than not—others took their life's work and twisted it into an excuse for the murders they committed in the name of love, or justice, or God. Their science was magnificent, I know that, and it makes us look like infants. It'll be centuries before Mazat can duplicate even the simplest devices aboard the *Phoenix*. But they turned even their science into a destructive force. You know about the Bloody Centuries."

"They conquered the stars, Del," Portteus said, almost reverently.

"They conquered them to defile them," I snapped back. "It wasn't six hundred years ago that the first ships left, and already the Old Earth stench of death and corruption is rising from ten thousand stars and poisoning all the space between them. The Expedition is nothing but the Bloody Centuries on a larger battlefield. Instead of killing other Earthmen, they kill Rinn; instead of destroying the innocent nations of Earth, they destroy innocent systems in space. But it's all the same, Doc, and I'm caught up in it. If the Expedition threatened Mazat, I'd be ready to fight it single-handed and wipe it out, if I could. That makes me no different from them, and men like us shouldn't rule."

"You have ruled well for more than twenty years. You have made this planet a good place," Hata said. "Stay. Today was a trial, but you overcame it."

Stretch rose and said solemnly, "Queen Hata is right. Twenty-two years of good rule can not be cancelled out by a moment's anger. You must stay."

"But it wasn't just a moment's anger. Don't you see?" I looked desperately at them in turn, but they did not seem to grasp what I was trying so confusedly to say. "Listen. This man Corey, the pirate, my father. He was considered a great man, a hero. He *was* a hero—he could have been king of a hundred planets, if he chose. So I've been told. He had a wife and a son, and he loved them, probably as much as I love mine. And look what became of him. He ended as the leader of a band of murderous scum. He himself laughed when he cut down a harmless old man. Maybe I've been a good king, but I've been a Corey, too, and I don't know yet which one is really me. I want to leave Mazat before I find out."

"Maybe the real you is Del Whitby, the son of that good man and woman of Gilead," Portteus said.

"I've often wished that."

"Well, it's true." Seeing my move to object, Portteus said quickly, "I know you're not their physical offspring, but you can't be positive that you're Corey's, either. You've believed it for so long that you consider it proven, but it's highly suspect. The evidence is persuasive to someone who wants to believe it, but it's hardly conclusive. Malellans have been known to grow as tall as you and even taller, although it's unusual. Your size alone is no proof of Old Earth Blood. And your features and coloration are pure Malellan. But Del, even if you could be certain that Corey is your father—which I very much doubt—you're ignoring the fact that you were raised by devout Rudstromites, an Old Earth people who have avoided violence since before the Bloody Centuries. Surely their influence counts for something."

"Their influence counts for a great deal. I'm talking about blood heredity."

"You might be pure Malellan."

"I might be, but the Malellans weren't a warlike people."

Portteus smiled and shook his head patiently. "You're generalizing, Del. You yourself told me of a Malellan who fought well enough to win his freedom on Tarquin."

"That's true." He had caught me on that, and I hesitated. "But still . . . . Whoever I am, Doc, I've killed a lot of people, and today I was ready to kill again. Whether I'm of Old Earth stock or not, I'm enough like them to be a danger to my people. I've come to love Mazat, and I don't want to cause it trouble. I'd like to leave this planet—this galaxy, if I could—and try to start over."

Portteus laid a firm hand on my forearm and looked at me steadily. "Then wait, Del. Don't leave us yet. Wait, and trust me."

"Yes, wait, Father," Delgrax advised. "I have some ideas for dealing with the Expedition and the Rinn, but I need your advice."

"Listen to them, Del. Stay with us," Hata said.

Stretch raised his arm in a gesture of affirmation. The vote was unanimous.

4. *Across the last great gulf.*

Three years passed after Dzik's visit, and no Expedition ship came near us, nor did the Rinn. Life was busy on Mazat. Delgrax, Portteus, and I devised a plan for a confederation of the planets in our sector, and thanks to my son's efforts, Mazat is now the headquarters of the Planetary League. We have six members, and the sixth to join us, the Qattandri group, may well be the most important people in the galaxy at this moment. They've been in contact with the Rinn for nearly twenty years, and they assure us that the Rinn are willing to meet with us and try to work out a permanent peace in the galaxy.

Among the League representatives who have taken up residence here are Elder Dimbleby of Gilead and his family. His youngest daughter has made a considerable impression on Delgrax. I have the feeling that once a treaty is reached with the Rinn, and he has time to think of his personal life once again, Delgrax will be talking to me about the future queen of Mazat.

And he'll be king sooner than he suspects. A few weeks ago, Portteus burst in on me, wild with enthusiasm, flourishing a sheaf of papers covered with calculations which I found most impressive, though totally indecipherable. After much questioning, I learned that he has worked out what he believes to be a completely practicable conversion of the original Wroblewski Drive principle that will enable a driveship to make the last great jump and cross the intergalactic gulf.

I bombarded Portteus with every objection I had ever heard, and he had an answer for them all—we don't know, because it's never been tried. But now we can try.

So I began, very quietly, to outfit an expedition for the first long trip between the galaxies. This one is going to be different from all the others I've been on. No killers, no gunmen, no weapons at all, nobody bringing along anything but hope. Hata was a bit overawed at first, then merely apprehensive, and now she's eager to go. Our children will stay on Mazat. They don't need a new galaxy; they've got a future here. This trip is for people who want to try to leave their mistakes behind and start over. The universe is within our grasp now. The galaxies are waiting.

Maybe this time, we can do it right.

✿ ✿ ✿ ✿ ✿ ✿

AFTERWORD

It is now forty years since the intergalactic driveship *Zealous Endeavor* departed from Mazat, bearing our beloved Queen Hata and a band of volunteers from the six planets of the Planetary League, seventy in all, led by King Del I, born Deliverance-from-the-Void Whitby of Gilead, known as Del Cometfire-by-Dawnstar Deletriculus Quickslash Nimblefoot Swiftthrust Threesmiter, twice Champion of the People of Tarquin VII, Liberator and All-Honored and Most Puissant Monarch of Mazat, and First Voyager to the Far Galaxies.

The throne of Mazat is now held by King Del II, grandson of Del I and son of Delgrax, a wise and noble king whose reign was tragically brief. King Del II came to the throne at a tender age. For the first years of his reign, I acted as regent. Now he is a man, and my youngest son, Solandel, stands at his side as First Defender of the Planet. Solandel is a strong and faithful youth. May his days hold great honor.

Much has changed on Mazat since the day that Del and I and our comrades freed the Mazatlans from the menace of the space pirates. The marketplace where we fought is now the main square of our capital city. In its center stands a fountain, surrounded by seven columns. All around the square rise tall buildings. Crowds are everywhere. The activities of the Planetary League and the thriving new driveship industry have brought many people to Mazat, and everyone is busy. The League now numbers twelve planets and is the major link between the Rinn and the rest of the galaxy.

There is much to do on Mazat these days, but I find myself turning more and more of my duties over to my children and devoting myself increasingly to periods of meditation. I have lived beyond the ordinary Lixian life span. My movements are slow now, and on cool nights, my old wound gives me great discomfort. It is to be borne.

The time is coming for me to gather my honors about me and undertake the final meditation that will unite me forever with the infinite. Ten of my wives and sixteen of my children have gone before me; I will not be lonely. My wise and beloved friend Portteus, too, has made his union with the infinite. Since his death, four planetary years ago, I have had no one to dispute with, and my life has grown dull. Mazatlans today are not concerned with ideas. They have become a fact-minded people. My own children are concerned with affairs I do not understand, nor do I wish to understand them. My time is in the past.

I find myself wondering if Del has gone ahead and will greet me after my last meditation. Portteus and I spoke of this often, and his opinion was that Del would not join us for a long time. It was his belief that the time dilation factor would enable those aboard the *Zealous Endeavor* to arrive at their destination scarcely any older than they were at the time of their departure. I am not convinced of this, but I hope it is true.

Del was a brave warrior, a great and honored king, beloved by his people, and a true friend. He was a far better man than he ever believed himself to be. It saddened me much to see him tormented by the belief that his blood-father was a murderer. There is a saying among the Lixians, "Honor creates its own ancestry," and this is truer of King Del I than of any Lixian, any man, or any other creature in the galaxy.

I thank him for this final honor, the privilege of being his chronicler. I have copied all things as Del set them down, even those things most unfavorable to me and my people. Del himself did not change words to his own advantage, and for me to do such a thing would be most dishonorable. Let all things stand, to be understood in the spirit in which they were written. May King Del I, my ruler and my friend, be long remembered with honor. He was the best man I ever knew.

> The Chronicler Royal of Mazat,
> In his own hand,
> 6/2/2693 GSC.

THE END